For Every Love There Is A Reason

A Novel

Kenda Bell

Publishing

Published by
Xpress Yourself Publishing, LLC
P. O. Box 1615
Upper Marlboro, Maryland 20773

All Xpress Yourself Publishing, LLC's titles are available at special quantity discounts for bulk purchases for sales, promotions, premiums, fund-raising, educational or institutional use.

Special book excerpts or customized printings can also be created to fit specific needs. For details, write to Xpress Yourself Publishing, LLC, P.O. Box 1615, Upper Marlboro, MD 20773, Attn: Special Sales Department.

ISBN-10: 0-9722990-9-2
ISBN-13: 0-9722990-9-1

Printed in the United States of America

Cover and Interior Designed by The Writer's Assistant
www.thewritersassistant.com

Dedication

This novel is dedicated to everyone who has ever loved, and had the courage to love again.

Acknowledgements

First I must give thanks to the chief architect of my life, the Heavenly Father who continues to show me that His love never fails and His mercy endureth forever. To my Savior Jesus Christ whose light shines, even when the days seem their darkest.

To my family and friends, I thank you for your support, early morning critiques, and late night talks.

Keegan, my king in training; my solider, your faith, strength and maturity in the face of adversity has kept me inspired. I love you!

To my readers who I have yet to meet, thank you for investing in my dream. I hope we get together soon.

Last but not least, Jessica Tilles. Thank you so much for believing in my work and inviting me into the Xpress Yourself Publishing family. Also, thanks for not reporting me to AOL for cyber-stalking.

For Every Love There Is A Reason

A Novel

Kenda Bell

Chapter 1

"I never really prepared for our winter, because I held onto our summer."
— *Keilah*

When Keilah's mom told her André called, she smiled. She knew André missed her because she missed him too. No matter what, or who, he was doing, she always felt she was his heart. In the back of her mind, she always knew she would forever be a "special one" and never "the one." Her heart reluctantly lagged behind; dragging bags of memories, making getting over him difficult, like one emotional hurdle after the next. She was reluctant to return his call. Time passed and she was able to put her feelings in check, even though she knew, deep down past the apathy, the anger, and the hurt, love still endured. He seemed insistent on seeing her, and she was curious. Did he miss her? Did André finally want to share how he had been a fool all this time and beg her to come back to him? Ha!

As Keilah sat across from André, she heard nothing but the three words he casually slipped into the conversation. The clatter of dishes and the chatter at nearby tables were barely audible. Keilah's concerns about the little pimple, which formed along her right temple, seemed minuscule. Even her weight gain was of no importance at the dropping of those three words.

Breathe, Keilah, breathe.

Keilah learned to hide her emotions. Through the years, it had become something of an art form. She quickly learned how to pull lipstick from her purse when she felt her bottom lip quiver, gliding a fresh coat of paint across a false grin. The stiffening of her jaw line could easily be camouflaged by resting it casually within the palm of her hand, while she averted attention to something else in the room. Yes, awkward moments brought out the actor in her.

Yes, that was what the hell he said. Get it together.

Keilah played repeatedly in her mind, how she'd run her lines, the gestures, the movements . . . this one moment she unwillingly prepared for. The one thing she didn't factor was overwhelming her, the solitary tear. One monumental tear, burning the more she tried to hold it back, was building up in the well of her left eye. There was nothing capable of holding back that type of tear. Unlike actual crying, where each tear has its own specific emotion to attend to, a single tear must do the job of a million tears and contain every emotion within itself. As she sat across from André, absorbing the shocking news, she felt like she was trying to hold back a tsunami. That one salty tear was filled with so many powerful emotions—shock, hurt, anger, surprise, mourning, hate, jealousy, envy, and remorse.

After all those emotions built up that one tear, love ran from the back, thrusting through emotional commotion and desired nothing more than to submerge itself deep within that one solitary tear. Aligning itself on the rim of her left eye, love took hurt and anger by the hand and dove in. Hoping to be overwhelmed by hurt and anger, love rode the wave from the corner of her left eye, sliding quietly down her cheek, only to be caught by a napkin and tucked away for later. Hate laughed because love wanted to drown and die—surprise and shock looked on, wondering what was next. Jealousy and envy joined hate and mocked love. Remorse sat close by and wept. Mourning hugged love tightly and whispered, "You know you can't die." Love pushed through and she hated it. She heard those three words clearly. "I'm getting married."

André had found *her*.

"K, what are you looking for?" The sound of André's voice broke the echo ripping Keilah's heart into a million pieces.

Rubbing the tear into her cheek, Keilah responded lightly. "I thought I heard my phone ringing. This purse is so big I can't even find it. Well, I guess we should be drinking Moët rather than Chardonnay."

André nervously smiled at Keilah, trying to read past the obvious sarcasm. He knew she wasn't happy. "I said I was *thinking* about it. I'm not quite sure just yet. You know I am a different type of dude, so a sister gotta really come with something extra to make me take a second look. She's a little different, K, so it could happen; you know what I mean. She's special."

Breathe, Keilah, breathe.

"Yes, Dré, I'm sure any woman that marries you has to be different—special. Well, Special Ed."

Damn, like that, he's just gonna drop this crap on me? Bang. Boom. Does he want my permission?

"Well, K, it's a little more to it. She's pregnant."

What the hell did he just say?

Keilah transformed from an actor to a mime and gave the most animated Joker grin she could muster up. The last remaining pieces of her heart were now wasting away to hollow beats of invisible screams she tried to drown in a sip from her already empty wine glass.

Keilah's mind raced back to a rainy Friday in June when she let their love get sucked out of her and poured down a drain. The uniqueness that would have "been she and he" was changed forever on that day. The uniqueness of André and Keilah, revealing it day-by-day, year-by-year, step-by-step, was sloshed and twisted into unheard cries and silent tears. Her womb wept, again.

You have a baby on the way, too.

Keilah's womb cried out. *Please give her one more chance. Oh, what a sweet and loving place I'd make for your seed. Please let me nurture your seed once again, one more time. Oh God, please.*

Keilah's eyes lied. "Wow, you're really doing it all in one big swoop—baby, engagement, marriage. I guess you stopped tying knots in your condoms after me."

Her womb began to fill with tears of remorse and regret which had been bottled up for two long years. The cap of repentance holding the tears inside burst, the hope of redemption of a past error were now loose and saturating her like bile. There was no second chance to right the wrong, no turning back.

"You ready for all that, Dré?"

Her womb felt like a tomb, overgrown with thorny branches reaching out. All she could hear was her womb asking, *why didn't that precious seed ever bloom? How sad, a bright crisp day in February would have been such a wonderful time to welcome him into the world. Yes, it would have been a boy, with her pouting lips and his brooding brow across cinnamon skin, and welcoming eyes just like his mommy. What a silly insecure girl you were.*

André grabbed Keilah's hand. "Nothing is set in stone, but it's a good possibility it is going to happen." He knew she was hurting. Why she insisted on going through these emotional facades, he didn't know. He couldn't really blame her; he was famous for doing it himself. He always knew she could read between the crooked lines. As he sat across from her, he searched for something in her eyes. They always told him more than she was willing to say.

Alisha meant the world to André and the whole love thing snuck up on him like a thief in the night. The strange thing was Keilah confirmed it for him. In the back of his mind, he almost wished she would have made a move; maybe things wouldn't be where they were. She knew he was hurt, but instead of loving him the way only she knew he needed, she took a moment to grind him. She stepped from "the one" to "her."

"You remember what went down when I called you on my birthday, K?"

Keilah remembered it as if it were yesterday. At the stroke of midnight, on André's birthday, she had left him a "friendly" birthday message, figuring he would call back later, yet still hoping he would call back sooner. Year after year, she would want to celebrate his birthday, or do something special for him. Year after year, he declined and downplayed anything she ever suggested. Why would he deny an opportunity to celebrate? She found his birthday special because it was the day, in her mind, God allowed him to begin a new journey. She often fancied they were playmates in heaven that made a promise to meet and discover the familiar all over again in their new skin. Once she packed away that romantic notion, along with his t-shirts and ties she never seemed to be able to throw away, she put his "birthday thing" as another one of his peculiar ways.

By eight o'clock, Keilah figured André was out and about. When her phone displayed the only number she really wanted to answer, she smiled. She answered light and casual, trying her damnedest not to reveal the delight she felt hearing his voice.

Damn, I love his voice. I miss him so much. Maybe I can suggest meeting him somewhere tonight. This was the big three-oh. I could even fix him his favorite dish.

As Keilah pulled herself back from the back porch of her mind, she realized André was angry and complaining about some other chick on the front steps.

"K, I am so pissed right about now. You know what I'm saying. She took me to Applebee's! Can you believe that shit? This is the big three-oh, and she come out the box with some okey doke Applebee's. They did the whole corny singing and candle in a piece of dry ass cake. What's up with that? Can you tell me, K? How many times have we eaten at Applebee's? She knows that, damn!"

Keilah catches her breath. *Isn't this some shit,* she thought. *He can't be serious.* "Well, Dré, maybe she didn't have any money right now or she got something bigger and better planned for you." She found it amusing how he expected some new chick to take care of him, on his birthday, as she would. She didn't know if she should be insulted or flattered.

"K, come on now she knew my birthday was coming. She didn't try to set aside. . .be creative. . .you know. . .this is like major ... it's the three-oh!"

I am insulted. I'll be damn; Dré has fucked around and caught feelings for this chick. "Dré, I'm sure her intentions were good, don't be mean like that."

André's voice lowered, almost sweet. "K, you wouldn't have done no whack shit like this would you? Come on now, K, you know me."

Uhmm, no I wouldn't do any dumb shit like that, I love you. Wait just minute! Why in the hell is Dré telling me this shit anyway? Now I am mad. "Yeah Dré, I know you. What's your point? What are you looking for me to say? Where are you anyway?"

You want me to say I still love you. You want me to say come scoop me up and let me show you how special you really are. Hell, naw can't go there . . . won't go there! I cannot believe he is calling me about his new chick.

"Damn, say something, K. Am I wrong? Am I judging this situation wrong? She writes poetry on her down time. She could have written me something special on some fancy paper or even better made me a little CD of her stuff, in her own voice. Anything! It's not about big gifts with me. Come on, K, you know me! I took care of her for her birthday. I went all out for her and she come back at me with this. What's really up with this?"

Yeah, Dré, I know you too well, four years of loving you when birthdays didn't seem to matter much to you. Now you have put in a year or two with a new chick and you are expecting something that would have come naturally from me. Please!

"Check this Dré, she messed up... major... but apparently you feeling this sister. So, either you stick with her or you leave her. Sounds to me like your nose is wide open. Plain and simple. You know what you want to do, so do it! What you want me to say?"

I'm through . . . done. Does he want to torture me? He knows I love him, and he wants the very love I placed at his feet, time after time, from someone that is apparently just digging on him. That type of love he was anticipating from the new chick, he had in me . . . truth

6

. . . he knows it, that's why he's calling me. He's using me as the litmus test, the verifier between truth and fiction. He knows it, that's why he called me. Even still, he wants to experience the truth with her. Damn.

"You know what, K; I wasn't looking for this from you. I called you as a friend. But its cool ... I'm out!"

CLICK!"

When Keilah put the phone back on the charger, she wondered what would be next. She knew André liked interesting women but he seemed blown—frighten to be honest. He sounded like he was in love. She threw it out of her mind because she couldn't take the possibility of that. As she looked across the table at him, she knew it was now a reality and it stank like morning breath.

Keilah smiled and nodded to the server to bring her another glass of wine. "Yeah, Dré, I remember. What's that got to do with the here and now?"

André thought to himself, *Everything, K, everything!"*

Keilah watched André pay the tab, starting at the top and slowly worked downward. One thing she always liked about him was how he always kept the tightest shape-ups. His hair was always cut, mustache neat and trimmed. His goatee had a sexy little peak that she loved to play with when he slept. His brow line strong, hovering over some of the most amazing gray eyes, which made her melt. His pointy nose was a source of jokes for her, but the joke was on her when he nuzzled it gently against her intimate places. Though he was, by most accounts, a redbone, his full lips undeniably were sensual and without question African. His broad shoulders were the perfect canvas for the red sweater he wore.

As André stretched his hand out to Keilah, she wondered how she could want to hate someone so beautiful. Their complicated love affair was over. She had to get over him; most importantly, she had to accept he was over her, too. At all cost she had to reassure herself she was past the "in love with André" hurdle, finished crying over the "always love André" long jump, to now being awkwardly perched on the splinter-filled "I got love for you" bench.

The walk to André's car was quiet. The two of them usually couldn't stop talking but silence joined them together in unspoken dialogue. Sitting in the passenger seat, she wanted so desperately to touch him. All she could do was tap his hand as he shifted the gear. What did she want to say? What should she say? What parting words could she leave with him? Even though she had, on the surface, moved on, Keilah always hoped, even prayed, André would get an epiphany in the middle of his many whirlwinds of indecision and realize she was the one and only one. Sadly, he had that epiphany when he called her on his birthday seven months ago.

Love didn't burst. Hurt and anger blocked its path and held it hostage, with contempt running the show. Unbeknownst to Keilah, when the whirlwind stopped, André landed in the palms of Alisha's waiting hands.

André drove slowly, keeping one eye on the road and the other on Keilah. She hadn't said one word since they left the restaurant. He knew her silence meant she was thinking, the longer the silence, the deeper the thoughts.

Why won't she look at me?

André puts in a CD.

No he is not playing Erykah Badu.

"Dré hit that last track on the CD. I think its number fourteen."

Okay, she's not tripping too bad, she said something.

As the words of the song filled the car, André tried to see if Keilah was speaking to him.

Keilah finally looked at André. "I never really listened to this last track, then one day I listened to it all the way through."

André detoured through the park. "*Green Eyes*, but I haven't really listened to it." As the song continued, he realized Keilah was really talking to him. As the tempo changed, Keilah knew Erykah could say what she couldn't. With each verse, the words seemed to be screaming to André; he didn't want to understand where this was going. "It's deep, K." The tempo changed yet again.

Keilah realized how transparent she was at that moment and she felt ashamed.

All André could say was "Damn" as they turned down her street. Then Keilah realized he had placed his hand on hers.

André parked in front of her apartment building. Shifting sharply in his seat, he turned to Keilah, searching for the hidden message she was trying to send him. "Where you going with this, K?" Just as he took his key out of the ignition, she inhaled and motioned for him to put the keys back.

"You know, Dré, everything has a season. It's September and in a week, it will be fall. The leaves are starting to change. Some are still green but most are starting to turn brown and orange. Nature is giving humanity clues that change is in the air."

André touches Keilah's cheek. "Go on, K, kick it."

Keilah sprung back into actor mode; she had to get the words out. "Cool breezes that once were familiar begin to have a chill. Even though it feels so comfortable, so familiar, you know you have to cover yourself, but you don't want to, but you know you have to. Whether you like it or not, change is coming. You know it's inevitable and you don't look forward to it. Seasons change like people change. It's inevitable. You got to roll with it."

Looking exasperated, André unlocked the doors and walked to the passenger side, opening the door for Keilah. "K, you really losing me. What are you saying?"

As they walked up to her door, Keilah grabbed her keys and turned to André. "As humans, we have to roll with it too, Dré. We have to endure all the seasons whether we like it or not."

André knew when Keilah was camouflaging through metaphoric bull. "Keilah spit it out. Better yet, open this door up and let me dissect this over a cup of tea."

Keilah pulled him close in to her. Wrapping her arms around his back, she tips upward, taking in his scent one last time. Pausing again, she stroked her lips against his right ear, and gently whispered. "I never really prepared for our winter, because I held onto our summer."

Chapter 2

"All you have to lose is what you trying to give away."
— Norelle

Keilah spent the remainder of the night replaying her evening with André. What could she had said or not said played like a bad movie, repeatedly in her mind. Reordering the scene or changing the dialogue could not have changed anything, not even inviting him inside.

Leaving André on the other side of the door wasn't what she had planned. Keilah had the silk sheets, she and André used to enjoy sliding across on the bed, sprinkled lightly with the scent he used to love. The incense and candles were in place, waiting to be lit. Jill Scott and Anthony Hamilton were in place, ready to serenade them to a familiar place of love.

By the time Keilah fell asleep, it was four in the morning, and the birds seemed to have a mocking tone to their chirping. Waking up alone, to a wet pillow and a swollen face from a night to tears, forced her to comprehend what happened. She almost laughed at how stupid she felt in André's favorite Vicky's, laying alone. Thank God, it was Saturday and she didn't have to face the world for two more days.

As she rose out of bed, Keilah glanced at herself in the mirror. She thought she didn't look bad for thirty. Yeah she had morphed from a size seven/eight to an eleven/twelve, but she still looked good. A couple light lunches and fruit for breakfast could bring her down to a nine/ten in no time. Her reddish-brown skin was still smooth, with only a zit or two, but with no signs of wrinkle or ash. Her breast had a slight dip, but they were never her best assets. Her stomach was a little pudgy, but nothing that caused much distraction. The stretch marks across her hip were a small price to pay for sexier curves and a few more inches on her booty. Her legs were long, smooth, and almost flawless.

"Not bad, girl, for thirty, not bad at all," Keilah whispered to herself. "His loss, dumb ass!" Keilah screamed.

"What the hell happened to absence makes the heart grow fonder? What about that bull about if you love something set it free and it will come back to you. Yeah, that something will come back to you smiling with an engagement ring in his back pocket for some other chick and a baby on the way. Damn, now I am mad as hell. Forget being hurt, I am mad as hell. Why did he feel the need to tell me? Did he want to see hurt on my face? Did he want my approval or something? What the hell? I am so stupid." The hurt quickly replaced by anger.

As Keilah realized she was talking aloud to herself, she heard the crazy banging on the door. Opening the door, a neurotic Norelle greeted her.

"Keilah, where is my truck? I don't see the truck outside. Where is the truck?"

Keilah motioned Norelle toward the sofa, but she paced instead.

"You left your truck over here last night? I wasn't even home last night. What time? Wait . . .why did you leave your truck over here? You told me you were going to quit with that. See, I knew that mess you're doing was gonna catch up with you. Damn, let me put some clothes on and see if my neighbors saw anything. Wait, what time is it?"

Norelle continued pacing back and forth, wearing an imaginary hole in the carpet.

"It has an alarm on it. You don't think anybody stole it. Oh, God...Raymond is going to kill me if that truck was stolen. You didn't hear the alarm, K? Good looking out, you suppose to be my girl regardless. As loud as that alarm is, how could you have slept through it? You probably want some craziness to happen so you can say I told you so."

Keilah stopped getting dressed and stormed toward the living room, mad as hell.

"First of all, you didn't tell me you were leaving your truck over here. Secondly, I told you I went out and, most importantly, you told me you were going to stop stepping out. You are raggedy and dead wrong. I had one hell of a night and really don't need your added bullshit. Now, aside from me being your girl, I am going outside to knock on people's door at nine o'clock on a Saturday morning to help you clean up the mess *you* brought to *my* doorstep. So get your story together to make a police report while I go outside."

Keilah was looking for her keys when Norelle's cell phone rung.

"Oh, girl it's Raymond. Should I answer it? What am I going to tell him?"

Keilah grabbed the phone, pushed talk and handed it to Norelle.

"Ummm, hey baby. I'm sorry I didn't come home last night. K and I hung out late. We were real tipsy and I crashed on the sofa, but I have to tell you..."

Raymond cut her off. "Tell me what? You weren't tipsy--you were drunk! I knew that when I came through this morning and got the truck to get it detailed. I can't believe the two of you slept through that alarm, especially you. I knocked and everything. Any way, I left the Lex out front for you. You're really hitting it hard with Keilah. I told you about hanging with your single friends. I like my woman at home sometimes. I know you and Keilah are tight, but we are married now. Don't she have a man of her own? She better not be getting you in trouble. LT's already up and is getting ready for his football game. You know he has a game at two today. It's after nine now. You sober up and get home. Love you."

Norelle blew a kiss and smiled as she ended the call. Keilah hung her keys back on the hook and moved toward the

13

kitchen to brew tea. By the smirk on Norelle's face, Keilah knew she had gotten away with murder, yet again.

"Well, Nori. How did you get out of this one?"

Looking pleased with herself, Norelle adjusted her ample bosom and kicked off her shoes. She hated to do Raymond like this but it was something about Tariq that made her want to taste him one more time. She and Tariq had been together since junior high. Tariq was her first kiss, her first love, her first orgasm, her first heartbreak . . . her first everything. She really thought when she married Raymond; Tariq would be in the past. He had been in and out of her and LT's life. Even though LT, Norelle's son, was his namesake and image, Tariq never was much of a father. Tariq could never be counted on for anything except a good lay. When Tariq stopped returning her phone calls and moved out of state, she decided to move on. When she met Raymond, all she wanted to do was get over Tariq. She never really planned to get serious with Raymond; she knew Tariq would be back. Once she got a hold of Raymond's paycheck stub, she got tired of waiting and took a second look at Raymond's blue collar and black Navigator. She had a ten-year-old son, no baby daddy and a dead end government job. Times were too hard to wait on love. Tariq was never Mr. Right and Raymond fit perfectly into her right then and there.

When Raymond asked her to marry him, she called Tariq to gloat, only to find his number had been disconnected. A few months after she and Raymond were married, he asked if he could adopt LT. That was when Norelle knew he not only loved her, but he loved her son as well. It wasn't until Tariq's mother saw the announcement in the local newspaper that she *suddenly* knew how to contact her son. Tariq came back to town and halted the whole thing. From that day, Tariq wormed his way back into her world. Crazy as it was, Norelle didn't feel guilty. She was confirmed in her love for Raymond and her attraction to Tariq.

"Norelle! I am waiting! Tell me before I throw this tea on your ass."

Norelle took the cup from Keilah and sipped slowly. How Keilah looked at her suddenly made her feel a tinge of guilt. She wished Keilah understood.

"Well, K, it seems as though Ray came pass to pick up the truck this morning to get it detailed. When I didn't see the truck, I didn't notice the Lexus was outside. I wonder what time he came through. He said he knocked. You didn't hear anything? What did you do last night? You and Keith made up?"

Keilah hadn't even thought of Keith in the past forty-eight hours. Damn, that was her boyfriend at last check. As she looked at her phone, she noticed Keith hadn't even called.

"Anyway, don't worry about Keith and me. I thought you were going to stop seeing Tariq. What's up with *that*? Nori, you know you're wrong. He isn't worth it. You got a good man in Raymond; don't screw it up for Tariq. He had his time. Is he still sleeping in his momma's basement? Has Tariq started paying back child support he owes you? Better yet, does he have a job yet? You probably don't even know because you're too busy letting him lay in between your legs."

Norelle sat her cup down and was, by all appearances, pissed. "Look, I don't know what crawled up your butt this morning but you don't have the right to judge me, okay? Don't do that!"

Keilah jumped up, grabbed the empty teacup from Norelle, and walked briskly to the kitchen. Fuming, Keilah couldn't hold it in anymore. "You know, Nori, you are correct, I can't judge you! However, as your friend, as your sister girl, I can check your ass. You are using my house as an alibi. You're bringing drama to my damn doorstep. You think Raymond isn't going to catch on. Then what? Yeah, you got it. He will automatically think I am encouraging this mess and blame me—the single friend, the jealous girlfriend, and marriage hater number one. You are wrong. You have a good man who loves you and your son. Let your summer go Nori. Let that shit go. It's over. Tariq snuck out during the fall and slept through the winter. Enjoy your spring with your new man. Damn girl, you're stupid as hell!"

As Norelle tried to figure out what spring and summer had to do with Tariq and Raymond, she noticed Keilah had dropped the teacup and was kneeling on the kitchen floor bawling her eyes out.

Helping Keilah to the couch, Norelle realized something hadn't gotten up her butt so much as it did into her heart.

"André's getting married, Nori." Loud silence took over the room.

For twenty minutes, Norelle sat quietly and soaked in a little of Keilah's pain. Turning her attention to the broken pieces the teacup left behind, she swept them into a pile. Looking at the shattered pieces, she pondered if some how she could pick the tiny fragments up and glue them back together. As she glanced back at Keilah, the teacup seemed like a less daunting task.

"So K, what's the heifer's name?"

Keilah was able to muster a laugh. Pulling out a cigarette, Norelle handed it to Keilah and sat back down.

"No, seriously who is she? Where did she come from? Better yet, I don't believe it. André ain't getting married. He's trying to mess with your head. What, he got her knocked up or something?"

Keilah's eyes gave confirmation. "Yes, Nori, the girl is pregnant. He called over to my mom's and got my new number. We spoke and he just had to see me. So, my stupid ass thought he wanted me back. Keith was acting up so I said what the hell. I'm thinking I can play hard to get, flirt. We can pick up where we left off, you know. We had small talk most of the evening before he dropped the bomb, square in my lap. He's thinking of getting married. Yeah, Nori…married."

Norelle takes a long drag from her cigarette.

"Wait, I thought you said *he was getting married.* What's this thinking stuff? Did he ask her yet? You got to get me clear on this so I can get the correct address to send the kick up the ass Dré needs, if I understand you correctly."

Keilah finally lit her cigarette. "Girl, Dré told me he ways thinking about asking her. Thinking… already asked. What difference does it make?"

Norelle slapped Keilah on the head. "What difference does it make? A whole lot, dag, girl . . . think!"

Keilah jumped off the sofa and walked toward the window, hoping to find the right words. "Nori, it's like this. We dated for damn near four years; he never even mentioned any words that remotely seemed like they might mean a commitment let alone marriage, so the whole idea of him marrying someone else isn't exactly shocking. I wanted it to be me someday but in reality, I knew it wouldn't be. I'm not mad, honestly. We haven't been together for almost two years now, so it was bound to happen. The thing that really burns is that I always saw me telling Dré, rather than the other way around. Don't get me wrong, I am not happy either, but maybe I can really let go of him for real. Anyway, maybe when I tell Keith, he and I can really move things along."

Norelle looked at Keilah and released a sarcastic laugh.

"Keilah Fort! You and I have been friends since sixth grade. Please don't try to play me. First, you and Keith; that right there is a joke, a sick one. Keith wore your single behind down. I can't even see that, actually I don't want to see it. Yuck! You got a case of Not HAM syndrome."

Keilah looked puzzled. "Not HAM? What is that? I stopped eating pork five years ago. What does that have to do with Keith and me?"

Walking to the refrigerator, Norelle chuckled. "It's an acronym for a state of temporary insanity that woman over thirty go through—Not Having A Man. See, you and André had a bad break up. You attracted some losers and turned away some winners, hoping André would come back. You got tired and when you looked around, fat daddy started looking good to you. Don't get me wrong; Keith is probably a nice dude, just not for you. You need to let that old lady have him back. He hasn't called you all weekend. He's probably with her ass now, trying to find an oasis in old girl's Sahara. Don't he have a missing tooth? And those beady eyes, girl I don't know how you do it. That nice guy role ain't fooling me . . . game know game. He may want to be right, but he isn't. I'm telling you, he's running game.

17

I'm taking you're last bit of orange juice. I'll bring you some more tomorrow after church. But anyway ..."

Keilah was embarrassed. In the back of her mind, she knew she was settling. Was it that obvious?

"Wait, Nori. You're not being fair. I know Keith ain't nobody's Tyrese and sure, he isn't smooth like Terrence Howard, but he's got a sweetness about him. He wants to love me and I want to love him. It's not like Keith is a bad guy. Sure, he's not packaged the way I exactly want, but he has some qualities any woman could work with. Keith has a nice sense of style and his chunky body isn't that much of a hurdle once you get into his personality…for a big boy Keith can move. Anyway, Nori, I'm not getting any younger and I have marriage on my mind, even a baby. My job at the phone company is secure and Keith works for the gas company so we could put our bank together and do something. Keith is already buying a house in Columbia Heights. Seemed like a plan. Plus, we have a comfortable place of friendship, so we decided to merge the bridge. Keith was always complaining about his relationship with Constance, day and night, toying with the idea of me saving him from her. So, one day I decided to take Keith up on the offer. Why not? I was free and clear of André, who made it clear he wasn't ready to be my Mr. Right, and Keith was eager to be Mr. Right Now. What's wrong with that? Isn't that what you did with Raymond? Can I get a wedding in the Caribbean, too?"

Norelle almost chocked on her juice.

"Why are you trying to jab back at me on the DL? First of all, Raymond and Keith are cut from two different cloths. Raymond is sweet and sexy as hell. Yeah, I looked at the benefits of the situation but Raymond isn't Keith and Tariq isn't André. Sure, I have been slipping with Tariq but I would never leave Raymond for Tariq's sorry ass. I know that more than ever now. What I have been doing is closure. Like that season stuff, you tried to kick a minute ago. The more I spend time with Tariq, the more I realize he is still the same thirteen-year-old boy I met at the corner store. I am no longer the fast tail girl that let him squeeze her big ole bubble butt behind her momma's house. I am a grown ass woman with needs that go beyond my crouch. He never looked past my fat ass to see my heart or my mind. Now sex with Tariq is the bomb, but what happens when you climb from under the sheets is what really makes you feel in love. I will always love Tariq, but I am in love with Raymond and I am committed to him. I said all that to say, you may want to love Keith because you feel like you should but you won't. It has to exist before it comes to realization. You're trying too hard, boo. Now you and André were real, but you two were too busy playing games to accept it. So what are you going to do girl?"

Keilah thought to herself, *what am I going to do? What could I do?* "Nothing. . ."

Norelle looked at the clock and began to put her shoes on. "Nothing? You are going to let Dré ride off into the sunset with another woman. What's wrong with you? He is the only man you really loved. He came back to you. He wants you to stop him. I am telling you. Why did he tell you he was *thinking about it?* You sleeping on this one, I am telling you. Why is André checking on you? Well, he could be trying to hit it one more time. Did you give him some? Wait, I don't smell that funky incense y'all use to like to burn, so I guess not. Anyway, I have to go home but you need to investigate this situation. Don't get funky acting on him. I told you when he called you on his birthday, that was your queue but no you had buck bad and kick the door shut. Be a little vulnerable, just this once. André knows you're wussy anyway. All you have to lose is what you're trying to give away. A man gets tired of being pushed away. Pull him close. Dré got his mess with him, but you know where your heart is, don't you?"

Keilah hugged Norelle as she walked to the door. Norelle got on Keilah's nerves, but she was her girl.

"André wants you to talk him out of it, I'm telling you. Don't mess it up. Once he walks down that aisle, game over."

By one o'clock, Keilah was sorting laundry and thinking. As she rose to light her cigarette, she began to wonder who this mystery woman was. Where did he meet *her*? Was it at Starbuck's during a morning dash to work? Did the foam on top of her caramel latté catch his attention? Better yet, was it at Borders where he noticed the music she chose and became intrigued? Did he see her pumping gas at the Amoco and decided to ask her name? Or, did André simply see her across a crowded room, recognizing her from a playtime a long time ago, apparently while Keilah was taking a nap amongst the clouds.

Keilah tuned into her inner spirit, trying to make logical sense of it all. They must have skipped away while she went to find the newest rainbow to show André, and he must have enjoyed the sunrays with *her*. He never seemed quite as impressed when she returned. He was happy to see her nonetheless and marveled at how mere drops of water could merge to create the ribbon of colors, still desiring to touch the warmth of the sunray with *her*. Her spirit reminded her that while she and André loved to explore and share together, they sought the understanding of the experiences differently. His spirit sought not only to see, but also to touch. He wanted to encounter the senses from the outside in while she gravitated more from the inside out.

When André left suddenly, without notice, she missed him so much that she left the next month to catch him. *Maybe he slid down this rainbow*, Keilah giggled to herself as she tumbled down.

André landed in Philadelphia to experience life through touch and smell in an unseasonably warm February. Keilah's aim was too far south and she landed in Maryland to swim through emotional extensions of her senses on the first day of spring. It appeared his other playmate had watched from a far, was less anxious than Keilah, waiting a while longer and took copious notes. She floated down, as light as a feather, confident he would recognize her as soon as Keilah fell asleep, again.

Keilah's spirit brought back to her a former familiar that made perfect sense in this new present. The connection between André and Keilah, the constant back and forth, and his decision to be indecisive . . . he had to wait until he met "her" again, then he'd know for sure. This physical journey was too complicated to do without his soul mate. He was waiting on "her" while Keilah was content she had found him, resting on the idea that everything would fall into place. She fell asleep once more. Timing was everything.

Oh, Keilah please get your head out of these metaphorical clouds...get real.

By the time Keilah put her last load in the washer, the spin of the cycle sent her mind into another maze. Was she short and petite? Was she tall and leggy? Was her ass larger? Were her breasts slightly firmer? Was her skin softer? Did she have curly hair? Did she wear locs that smelled of patchouli musk? Or, was she a slick corporate chick with a silky weave down her back? Did she strut in stilettos and St John's suits, with Vicky panties to match? Did she carry Mac in her Micheal Kors or did she keep it simple with lip glass and a hobo bag. Did she work in the legal field like André or was she a true poet living off her art while she worked in some artsy coffee shop? Was she some cute Afro centric Pollyanna André often found so attractive? Had she found the special way he liked to be kissed—tender yet firm, with the perfect balance of just enough tongue to let him know there was an even better kiss waiting? Had she perfected a twirl with a twist that made him forget about Keilah's dip and swirl? Who was this mystery woman who captured him?

André was up working on briefs by six in the morning. Alisha brought breakfast over at eight. By nine, she was moving the papers aside and bringing him closer; by eleven, they were in each other's arms. As he looked at her, again he wondered if he could really do it. She was everything he had been looking for. She was beautiful— not too fat, not too skinny, just right. Her pecan skin was the perfect canvas for her dimples. She had the most beautiful hair he had ever seen. She never hesitated to wear it out, the way André liked it, long and straight back. She was feisty at times but never gave him too much struggle. She didn't really pressure him, she gave him his space when he needed it and seemed to know almost instinctively when he wanted her close. She was bold and so sure of herself. That is what attracted him the most to her. Her eyes always seemed to laugh; they were big and playful. She brought to him a freshness that he himself had lost.

Being the eldest, André had to leave childhood games behind at twelve, when his father left. With a ten-year-old sister looking up to him, he had to assume both the role of man of the house and care giver while his mother worked the double shift at the hospital. While most twelve-year-old boys hurried outside to shoot hoops, after they finished their homework, he had to make sure both he and his sister Tracy's did their homework, heat up dinner, take out trash and run baths, along with anything else his mother left on the list. When Alisha suggested a pick up game at the middle school where she taught, as their first date, he couldn't say no. With her, he began to feel and not just think. She was open and direct, never wasting time with extra words and fluff. He never had to look for hidden messages when she spoke. However, her actions caused confusion. She was so playful; sometimes her actions didn't quite match her words. Nevertheless, she was carrying his seed and he couldn't do what his father did; he loved her. He had no excuses. He finished law school, and even though he wasn't rich, he was comfortable. At thirty, what excuses could he think of? When you love someone, you do what's right by him or her. That was when his mind trailed back to Keilah.

The joy and excitement Alisha had in her eyes when she told André the news was starkly different then look of pain and fear Keilah had in her eyes three years ago.

When André heard Keilah's message on that unusually hot June afternoon, he knew there was something different in her voice. Having spent most of the day studying for the bar exam, he was exhausted and all he could think about was just laying his head in Keilah's lap. She knew how to make him feel at ease; however, the tone in her voice was uneasy and tight. For the first time in the six months they had been together, he wasn't sure if he wanted to go to Keilah.

When André arrived, Norelle greeted him with a quiet awkwardness that confirmed something was up. Norelle broke the silence.

"What's up Dré? You look tired. Have you been getting any sleep?"

"Yeah, Norelle, a lot actually. All this studying I have been doing for the bar has finally caught up with me I guess? Where is K? I thought she was home?"

Norelle looked at him slyly. "K's in the back. She came home early from work; she got sick. She's been in the bathroom all day. Did she tell you?"

At that moment, Keilah emerged. "No! I didn't tell him. He had things to do. I thought you were headed out."

Norelle looked at Keilah then at André and laughed nervously. "Yeah, I'm heading out."

André knew something was up but he really didn't want to deal with what was going through his head.

As Norelle reached for her purse, she smirked and ignored the urgency in Keilah's eyes for her to leave.

"What did the doctor say, Keilah?"

Oh, shit silently echoed throughout the apartment.

As Norelle closed the door, André noticed it. Keilah looked different.

As André sat on the sofa, he surveyed Keilah. Almost suddenly, he noticed how Keilah's breast looked bigger, not enormously larger but slightly perkier. As she walked to the kitchen, her sweatpants seemed to hug her butt a little tighter. When she handed him a glass of soda, he noticed her face. Her high cheekbones looked a little lower and fuller, and her skin had a glow. Then, he noticed her eyes. After indulging her small talk about everything but the obvious, he had to ask.

"So why didn't you tell me you were so sick that you had to go to the doctors?"

Keilah jumped up and began fussing with the curtains. "It was nothing. She said I just ate something bad. I'm fine. It probably was that Chinese food we had last night. Plus they say there is a stomach virus going around."

As André reached for Keilah's cigarettes, he took one and returned the pack to Keilah. "Who are they? I haven't heard about any stomach virus. What's really going on? You know I got a lot on my mind, so what's up?" They both knew what was up, but neither wanted to say.

As Keilah walked toward the kitchen, André went to light Keilah's cigarette and noticed her hesitation.

"You don't want me to light it for you?

"Damn, I can not smoke every five minutes. When did you start smoking?"

André stood up from the sofa and walked to the kitchen. "You know I smoke when I drink. You still got that Absolute in the cabinet or did Norelle kill it?"

Keilah nodded and reached for it. As he reached across Keilah for a glass, he realized she hadn't kissed or hugged him. She sensed his pause and quickly kissed him, almost on queue and walked back to the sofa. He knew something was up and he was going to get an answer.

Sipping from his glass, he noticed the glass he placed in front of her had gone untouched. Not typical of her, Absolute and cranberry was her drink.

"Why haven't you touched your drink? What's up?"

Keilah looked at the glass, picked it up and took a teeny sip before sitting it back down. "There you go; I drank some, you happy. What's up with you? I told you I had an upset stomach. You're tripping!"

André took a gulp and poured another glass.

"Okay, K what's going on? Did Norelle tell you she saw me at Club Deuce last weekend? You mad because I didn't tell you. I told

24

you I had some drinks with Chris and Linc. I just didn't tell you where. Some chicks were on me but I came straight here afterwards. You're not about to start locking me down, are you? We're better than that, aren't we? We both got things to do. I'm trying to pass this bar exam in two weeks and you're trying to jump-start that art of yours so we don't need unnecessary drama."

Keilah hated when André brought up an argument to get to an answer. Had he been patient, he would have gotten the answer he wanted; instead, all he had was his foot in his mouth and a camouflaged response from her that begot another argument.

"Whatever, Dré! I didn't know Norelle saw your ass at Club Deuce and frankly I don't care about them half drunk chicken heads that give you numbers, I throw the pieces of paper away every chance I get."

André finished his second glass and welcomed his third.

"Oh, you're going through my stuff now. That's what's up? Let me guess, you are so upset that it's making you sick, right. You're a real sistah, come one K. Please don't run them games like Norelle. You know I got mad love for you. I'd do anything for you, just don't start this ghetto soap opera shit with me. You know I couldn't really play until I left home. I have to play catch up. No stress, let's just be. Come on baby, drink your drink and let me fix you something. What do you want to eat?"

Keilah knew what she had to do. She picked the glass up and took a long gulp, almost emptying the glass. Reaching for a cigarette, she gave a slight grin. "Yeah Dré, you're right, no stress. I'll let you play. I got love for you too. I never want to restrict you or hold you back, never. And yes, I'd do anything for you."

Keilah waited a week after he took the bar and then told him. In the back of his mind, he knew she was pregnant, but he didn't want to deal with it at that time. All he could think about was passing the bar and getting out of that paralegal job. Things were tight for him and he was trying to move out of his studio apartment. She was temping at a different office every other month so it was obvious what had to be done. She was almost business like when she told him. For one of the first times in their relationship, she was direct and to the point.

"Dré, I am pregnant. I know you basically raised your sister and you really don't want kids so I made some phone calls and got some prices."

Just like that, Keilah dropped the news as if it was nothing. After ten minutes of silence, it registered in André's head.

"I thought you were getting that shot? Wait; wait a minute, why are you just telling me now? I mean its mine right? I know how we been hitting it, ain't no question right?"

With a disgusted look, Keilah lit a cigarette. "Don't insult me. You know what's up, don't play; I knew passing the bar was all that mattered to you."

Suddenly André went from shock to hurt and anger. "Norelle knew didn't she? How could you tell her before you told me? Damn K, that's my seed in you. She knew about a change in my life before I did. What's up with that?"

Keilah lit yet another cigarette and grabbed a fresh bottle of Jack Daniels from a bag next to the door. "Look, I didn't tell her, she just knew. Norelle has been pregnant; she figured it out before I did actually. It's no grand conspiracy to hide anything from André. I knew it wasn't the right time for you so I kept it until I felt you could handle it. I knew you'd want a drink so I picked up this bottle after work."

Surprise had struck André dumbfounded. He could not believe what he was seeing. Keilah acted as if it were another day. *What the hell was wrong with her*, André wondered. As she handed him the glass, he realized he hadn't sat down and really didn't want to.

"You want some food? I have some salmon in the fridge; I can put it in the oven. Damn Dré, we are cool. Its Okay, we cool, I'm cool. Sit down, take your shoes off please, you know Norelle will trip if she sees you strolling up in here with your shoes on."

As Keilah cooked, André looked through the brochures she

had on the table. Each of them said little to nothing. While she pulled the plates from the cabinet, he felt the need to leave. By the time she pulled the salmon out off the oven, he had put his shoes back on and left, without saying a word.

By two in the morning, André was knocking on the door. Sleeping on the sofa, Keilah immediately opened up the door, knowing who it was. Not saying a word, they laid on the sofa and held each other all night.

By five the next morning, André was already up. He had to admit it; he was scared. How could he be a father now? He had practically raised his sister and he wanted to live a little before he even seriously thought about a kid; now that was about to come to a halt. He knew without a doubt he had to pass that bar exam. Looking at Keilah, he knew she'd never intentionally try to trap him with a baby. He wasn't happy about it but they'd work it out. If he didn't pass the bar, he'd pull some dollars together and take it again. He needed some time. He'd be all right; they'd be all right, all three of them.

When Keilah woke up, André greeted her with breakfast. She smiled and walked toward the bathroom. When she returned, he jumped up, kissed her and gave her a glass of orange juice.

"K, I am going to have to give you a bib, you know you slobber when you sleep, it's cute though."

Keilah sipped the orange juice and played with her eggs. "Well, at least I don't snore like a bear. We better hurry up before Norelle bust in here and eat our food up."

André smiled to himself and thought they were going to be ok. "We cool K, for real we cool right?" Just as he finished his last piece of toast, he noticed Keilah's light mood had changed.

"So, Dré I figured we can go to Planned Parenthood on Friday. We both are paid on Thursday, we can split the cost; it should be about one hundred and fifty each. I can call out sick Friday and Monday, which would give me four days off my feet. It should fly with my boss because I'll have a doctor's slip."

As Keilah scooped up the remaining of her bacon, André nodded yes. He guessed it was the right thing to do. He would be able to move out of that studio after all. He felt relief. They didn't know what the future held. What if Keilah's artwork never jumped off, would she go ahead and get a real job. They probably would not even be together by the end of that year. At that split second, he was confidant she loved him, she was willing to make a sacrifice for him, without a blink. For the first time since age twelve, he didn't have to make a sacrifice; some else did it for him...Keilah.

Mourning didn't hit him until he found that slip of paper in Keilah's trashcan that read estimated due date was February twentieth, his birthday. He held back mourning with a weak and quiet groan.

As André sat in his condominium looking at the baby books Alisha left behind, hurt and anger revisited. After almost three years, he had not really thought about it. It wasn't that he didn't love Keilah; it was a question of whether he knew he loved her. *No, no that isn't even an issue, especially now*, he thought to himself. As he began to go over the last four years of his life, he could not honestly say how he felt about Keilah. Loving her was never a concern for him, until now. Picking up his keys, he decided he needed a drive. The briefs could wait; too much was coming back all at once.

After Keilah and André left broken pieces of themselves at Planned Parenthood, they each got back on track. Keilah's temp position at the phone company became permanent and she began working overtime as much as she could. She decided to focus on moving up within the company and began to take having a career seriously. André passed the bar and ran the fast track at a feverish pace. He took a job with the public defender's office and worked pro bono at night, just to get the experience underneath his belt. He made sure he was at every lawyer function, dropping cards, networking most time, with Keilah by his side. They always had fun together, no matter if it was a stuffy black tie affair or hanging out with Chris and Linc.

André liked to watch Keilah work a room; she had the gift of gab and could charm anyone, even stuffy old Jewish men; that was how he got his interview with the law firm of Rosenberg, Klein & Rouse. He could not believe he had been their four years and was almost a junior partner. Back then, Keilah made sure he never over slept in the morning and went to bed at night. However, between receiving cases that were more difficult and Keilah's promotion, things between them quietly shifted further apart.

When they did spend time together, it was at André's place, due to his schedule. As the months passed, he worked later and later and Keilah brought work home. Every other day, turned into every weekend, which became every other weekend. When he did find time to come over to Keilah's, he would be tired and grumpy, sometimes down right evil. Even Keilah's cooking and lovemaking wouldn't soothe his mind or body. Before he knew it, they would fall into bed, grunt, and he would fall fast asleep. Moreover, instead of tea and croissants greeting Keilah in the morning, all she heard was keystrokes and sighs.

As André merged onto Interstate 95, he didn't know where he was going, only where he wanted to go, to see Keilah.

André had to deal with this. What was he going to say to her after all this time? How could he ask Keilah why she didn't trust him, when back then he didn't even trust himself? He knew he didn't put up a fight but she didn't exactly put one up either. They never really talked about it. As he thought about it, she didn't even ask him, she kind of decided for the both of them, and passed it off as their decision. He wasn't even sure anymore. Strangely, he felt he was in the same damn situation again with Alisha. As he drove faster, he came to a realization that had him even more perplexed as he began to recognize the similar variants of two different circumstances that some how were equated.

Chapter 3

"You can't switch up on me like that."
—Norelle

Mornings in the Armstrong house were always crazy. Norelle always took too long in the bathroom, no matter how early she rose in the mornings. Raymond was always in and out, starting breakfast before Norelle even finished fixing her hair. By the time she made her way to the kitchen, LT was finishing his breakfast and Raymond grabbing a kiss goodbye, but this morning things were slightly off.

When Norelle exited out of the bathroom, she noticed the bed had been made and the only thing she smelled from the kitchen was coffee. *Where was the bacon and burnt toast,* Norelle wondered. By the time she descended downstairs, an empty kitchen and a pot of coffee greeted her. She was about to call out for Raymond and LT, but she looked out the window and noticed that only the Lexus was left in the driveway. She wondered what was going on as she picked the phone up to call Raymond. When Raymond answered, he sounded upbeat yet at the same time distracted.

"Hey, baby. I wanted to get to work a little early this morning and LT was ready to go so I picked up some Mickey D's and dropped him off at school. You never really eat in the morning anyway so I just left you some coffee. I told LT to tell you we were leaving but I guess you didn't hear him because of the shower."

Norelle laughed to herself and wondered why she got so upset.

"Okay, you can't throw me off like that. I know you like clockwork. You can't switch up on me like that."

Raymond responded with a slight chuckle. "Yeah, I know. Listen let me go this traffic is crazy. Oh, you are going to have to pick up LT today, I have to work overtime tonight. All right, I'm gone."

As Norelle hung up the phone, she knew she had to make another phone call. From the clock, there was no time and she would have to make the call from the car.

Pulling out of the driveway, she realized how lucky she was. Owings Mills was a far cry from North Avenue and Longwood Street. Norelle's mother did the best she could do and she never felt like she lived in the hood. It had always been rough around there but not like it was now. Back in the day, you may walk around a drunk or step over a junkie but now crack addicts met you at every corner. Norelle was so glad when her mother decided to sell that house and buy a condo in Towson. The only time she saw the house was when she went to pick up Tariq.

Tariq's family never moved out of the neighborhood. Tariq's mother had Section 8 housing for as long as Norelle could remember. By the time Norelle had LT, Tariq's mother had given birth to her fifth child and finally decided to have her tubes tied. She made sure to let Tariq and Norelle know that she didn't have room for anyone else but the kids she already had. Norelle laughed to herself just thinking about it. Why would Norelle want to live in that congested ghetto central station?

Norelle and Tariq's mother never really liked each other. Norelle thought she was ghetto and his mother thought she was uppity. There was jealousy from both of them. Back then, Norelle liked the chaotic regularity of his house. No matter what the day of the week, there was always something jumping off. If it wasn't one of his newest step dads having a card party, there was surely a fish fry for an uncle who had been released from jail. If you wanted to know the latest gossip, all you had to do was dip quietly in the kitchen when the women down the street came to visit. Who ever needed a French roll or braids; the kitchen was the cheapest beauty shop on the block. It was a far cry from her house.

Norelle's mother kept to herself and liked to keep the neighborhood out of her house.

Norelle lived three blocks over from Tariq in a little tucked away block that didn't even look like it belonged in the area. The street Norelle lived on was comprised largely of retired homeowners.. Everyone had covered porches with nice benches rather than the old beat up kitchen chairs like Tariq's neighborhood. Most of the front yards were filled with pretty flowers, with tomatoes and collard greens planted in the back. Dinner was at six, followed by dishes and a bath. Visitors were restricted to the immediate family and a select group of friends, none of which lived in the neighborhood.

Lucky for Norelle, Keilah made the cut. The only reason she could come over was because she went to Roland Park with Norelle. Her mother felt Keilah came from a respectable working class household like theirs, most importantly both of them had father's that left them. Keilah's father moved in with another woman in Cedonia, while Norelle's father moved on in another way.. Even though it had been over twenty years since Norelle's father left, it still hurt her deeply.

After Norelle parked her car, she walked toward her office building. The sadness blanketed her like a heavy overcoat. Her Mom and Dad looked like the ideal couple. They worked for Bell Atlantic; her mom was an operator and her dad was a technician. Just before he left, they were looking to move to Randallstown. That was when the arguments started between the two of them. Norelle's mother didn't want Norelle to have to transfer out of Roland Park while Norelle's dad felt that Baltimore County schools were better. Then it became an issue of them having to car pool. Norelle's mother demanded they purchase a second car before they even decided on a house because she didn't want to catch the bus when Norelle's father had to work late. Norelle's father assured his wife it wouldn't be a problem because he hardly worked late as a lead tech. Norelle's mother quieted down and went about her routine. Home by five o'clock, with dinner by six, followed by dishes then a bath.

When Norelle's dad was still around, the routine was filled with funny stories about his day and sweet kisses goodnight. The only time the routine was deviated was Thursday nights. That was the night Norelle's mother designated as girl's night out.

On Thursdays, Norelle's mother used to take longer than usual getting ready for work. While she cooked breakfast, she played the radio a little louder and even danced around a bit. Norelle and her dad were always amused by the show. By the time her mother was dressed, she looked like a model. Most Thursday's she'd wear something red or orange. To her mother's slight irritation, Norelle's dad would get a little frisky. Norelle didn't catch it then; nether did her dad.

Since Norelle's mother didn't come straight home on Thursdays, Norelle and her dad made that night their own special date night. Her dad would even take Keilah with them sometimes. They'd go to Ponderosa or Rustlers, on a pay week they might go to Kings Court in Reisterstown Road Plaza. They would talk about everything, even boys. She knew had her dad been around, she probably wouldn't have even looked twice at Tariq.

By the time they returned home, Norelle's mother would have left a message on the answering machine saying she's running late. Norelle's dad would usually shrug, cut the TV on and send her to bed. Sometimes, her mother would come home after eleven o'clock, because the sound of the running water from the bathroom always woke her. It always amazed Norelle that her father never woke up since most of those nights he fell asleep on the sofa.

The next morning Norelle's mother was quiet with the radio low and back on task scrambling eggs while her father sipped his coffee. Norelle always felt the tension the morning after but her parents smiled through it and went about the routine. Things got crazy when Norelle's father bought the second car.

The new car brought on graduating changes to "the routine." Thursday nights got increasingly later. Then late evening runs to the store became more necessary and early Saturday morning errands ran solo. The arguments became more frequent and louder. Her mother worked later and her dad decided to work overtime, then silence. By the time her dad found the new house, things were slowly returned to normal. The Thursday girl's night out became once a month and her dad decided to cook on the Thursdays her mom was home. Things were peacefully aligned again until that one Thursday her mother came home early from her girl's night out.

By eight o'clock, Norelle's mother walked in looking upset. She kissed her father and went straight upstairs. Her father continued to watch television and Norelle finished her homework at the kitchen table. Norelle couldn't remember why she picked the phone up, but when she did, she overheard bits and pieces of a conversation she knew she wasn't suppose to hear. Before Norelle could get a handle on what her mother was talking about, her mother yelled for her to hang the phone up before she got knocked sideways. Catching his attention, Norelle's dad got off the sofa and went upstairs to investigate. All Norelle could remember was her mother being mad about being stood up by her friends.

For the days that followed, Norelle's mother became more and more withdrawn. She had even caught her mother crying when her father wasn't home. The following Thursday, her mother stayed home from work where she spent the entire day in bed. She called in sick that Friday morning saying she had a funeral to go to that Saturday. When her father said he had to work, her mother quickly snapped that he didn't need to go anyway. When he asked who it was, she quietly told him it was an old high school friend.

Her father's eyes got big and watery. "Who was it, Tyrone?"

Turning to walk away, her mother softly said, "Yes."

Norelle sat at her desk reevaluating how angry she was with her mother, her present mess deviously winked at her from a cracked mirror of past hurts.

The day of the funeral was cold and rainy for May. Usually, Norelle slept late on Saturdays but this morning she wanted to watch her mother. Her father left before dawn and by seven in the morning, her mother was in the bathroom. By eight, she was eating a bowl of cereal and watching her mother. Her mother wept quietly to herself then laughed and muttered, pacing back and forth looking for something. When she asked her mother if she needed help, she looked at her blankly and said no. By the third time she asked, her mother grabbed and shook her, screaming "No!".

Bursting into tears, Norelle's mother ran down to the basement and began moving boxes. As Norelle gently crept down the basement stairs, she found her mother sitting in between two boxes surrounded by old clothes, eight track tapes and a yearbook. As she got closer, she noticed her mother was rocking and crying. The creaking of the steps startled her mother, who upon notice of her daughter dropped a tiny ring from her hands. Scared of a beating, she ran up the basement stairs and straight to her room. The next thing she heard was footsteps and the closing of the front door.

It was almost seven by the time Norelle's mother came home. Looking worn out, she walked in the house, like a zombie, and headed straight to the basement. Norelle's dad didn't say a word. When Norelle started toward the basement, her dad grabbed her by the shoulder, kissed her on the forehead, and asked if she thought she could spend the night at Keilah's. As she dialed Keilah's number, a loud knock on the front door broke the silence of the house. The next thing she heard shook the foundation of the house. By the time Norelle's mother came from the basement, pieces were everywhere.

"How could you Lynette? All that I do for you and Norelle, this is what you have been doing? These past twelve years have just been nothing."

Norelle's mother, not uttering a word let the tears stream down her face. As Norelle peeked around the corner from the den, she saw her father holding her mother's neck with one hand, with pieces of papers in the other. When Norelle's mother pulled away, the same ring that Norelle saw earlier that morning fell to the floor along with what looked like a dozen sheets of a paper.

Fearing her parents would notice her; Norelle retreated behind the wall. That was when she heard it, her father sobbing. She had never heard her father cry. Peeking again around the corner, Norelle saw her father kneeling on the floor, looking at the sheets of paper, shaking his head and crying even harder. That was the first and last time Norelle saw her father cry.

Shoving her mother aside, her dad frantically looked for his coat and car keys. Norelle's mother crazily follows behind him, crying and pleading with him not to leave.

"James, please don't leave like this. Please, baby I love you; you know I do. Can we talk about it? James, you don't understand everything. I love you. You're too angry please don't leave out this house tonight like this. Say something to me please, James."

Upon finding his keys, he put his coat on and paused at the door.

"You know what, if Norelle didn't look just like my mother I wouldn't know what to think. You married me because you were pregnant. I always felt that but I put it out of my head. I know it now for sure. What was it Lynette, was I secure? Yeah, that was it. You looked at my ass and said 'That nigger right there got a good job with the phone company, driving a Monte Carlo, shoot I better get with the program.' Yeah, that's how it went down. You got tired of Tyrone's nowhere ass and decided to stick your claws in my green straight from Mississippi ass."

Lynette ran and hugged James, crying whispering, "No." For a minute, James held Lynette close in his arms, looking like he may have a change of heart. Then he saw it … the ring.

Tossing Lynette aside, James cried as he picked up the ring. Turning back again, he picked up the papers too. Norelle noticed that her father's face was red and his breathing erratic as he walked toward her frightened mother.

Lynette tried in vain to grab the sheets of paper. "No Lynette! Let me read these love letters you wrote to Tyrone. His wife was nice enough to drop them off. She said she found them in his work locker.

Deciding to take a seat, James snatched Lynette down in the chair beside him. "Okay, here's one. . . March 20, 1978. Norelle was about to turn two years old and we'd just been married a year...

The first day of spring will always be special to me because that was the first day we met. When I saw you walking across the schoolyard in that red sweater I just knew I had to get your attention. When I passed you that note in Biology I never knew how much I'd be loving you.

Damn Lynette, if I'm not mistaken you told me the same thing on our first wedding anniversary."

Lynette tried to grab the letters, but James flung her hands away.

"Get off me woman, I ain't playing with you. Okay, here were go. . . May 8, 1980, Norelle had just started head start and you decided you didn't mind me working nights.

Tyrone I love you so much and pushing you out of my life was one of the most difficult things I ever had to do. Every time we meet for lunch at Lexington Market, I think about the times we would stop there after school and split a corned beef sandwich from Mary Mervis. When I go back to work, I think about the times we shared and smile. Then I get sad when I think about the time we spend apart . . .the trips we had never taken, the love we never finished making, the peace I felt in your presence. I can't imagine my life without you. We will have to make it work. Having you around is the only way my marriage with James will work, so no matter what Thursday is our special day."

Lynette tried to get up from the table only to be pulled back into the chair by James.

Kenda Bell

"No, no Lynette! You are going to sit right here and listen to how fucked up this sounds. Here's yet another one . . . dated June 19, 1980. . .

I have to admit that I am jealous of Joyce. I know she is your wife but I hate that she gets to sleep with you every night while I only get a few hours to lay with you. Now I know what you must feel when I go home to James. I never knew how one person could love two people, now I understand. Each of you is so different yet I wouldn't be whole without either of you. I could never leave James but I can't ever let you go. James is my head and you are the crazy tail of my coin. You are my air but James is my wind. I know you love Joyce and its ok...she'll never replace me like James will never replace you. Until Thursday, I love you T."

As James read on, Norelle couldn't believe what her young ears were hearing. There were letters that went from the year Norelle was born up to February of 1988, just four months ago.

James balled up the sheets of paper, threw them in Lynette's face and rose up to leave.

"James, we broke it off...honestly. You and I began to argue and fuss, he started getting static on his end. We didn't want Norelle or his kids to suffer so we cut it off right after Valentine's Day. Then he called me last month and told me he had been diagnosed with late stage cancer of the liver, and didn't know how long he had. James, please try to forgive me but I had to see him again … just a few more times. We didn't do anything but meet at a restaurant and talked. The Thursday before last Tyrone got sick during our dinner and left the restaurant early. By Friday morning, they admitted him into St. Agnes hospital. I only got to see him Saturday and then again on Monday. The days after that I called Tyrone's room, but never got an answer so I decided on Thursday to stop in to see him after work. He had already passed two days before."

For a few minutes, Norelle saw compassion on her father's face.

38

James held Lynette tightly in his arms and rubbed her hair. He knew about Tyrone when he first met Lynette. James never knew how deeply Lynette and Tyrone were involved. All he knew about Tyrone was that he was an old high school sweetheart that never wanted to grow up and Lynette was ready to get serious. By the time Norelle was conceived, all that James knew was that Tyrone was an old friend that Lynette ran into sometimes when she went to Lexington Market. James always knew in his heart that it was more to it but Lynette was having his baby and he had to do the right thing by the woman he loved.

James was snapped back to reality when Lynette whispered in his ear.

"We can work through this, baby. I know you loved someone else before me."

Backing away from his wife, James' eyes showed hurt flashing inside anger. "Yeah, Lynette, I did love someone else before you but not after."

Grabbing Lynette by her hands, James kissed her softly then removed the wedding set from her finger. "You know it took me almost a whole year to pay that ring off, Lynette. This ring you kept of Tyrone's isn't even real, look at the tarnish! This right here in the center is what people call cubic zirconia. You can wear this one now. Tyrone's wife was nice enough to take it out of the casket and returned it to you. How could you marry me knowing you were still in love with him? I was just the logical choice."

After roughly placing Tyrone's ring on Lynette's finger, James grabbed his keys and threw them across the room. When the keys landed near Norelle's feet, Lynette broke into tears. James ran to his daughter and hugged her tight.

"Norelle, baby girl, I am so sorry you had to hear all this. Don't cry. I need to leave out. I'll be back, I promise you."

Norelle didn't want to let her daddy go. She felt like he wasn't coming back. As James walked out the door, he looked at Lynette once more with disgust, blew a kiss to Norelle and left. By two in the morning, Norelle heard her father's Seville pull up. Norelle waited to hear the front door open. By two-thirty in the morning, Norelle crept down stairs to see if she missed anything. Lynette was in the vestibule, standing in the dark. Hearing Norelle's feet sliding across the hardwood floor, Lynette without even turning around told Norelle to go back to bed, her father was sleeping in the car.

When Norelle woke up the next morning, she found her mother asleep next to her in the bed. Rising out of the bed, Norelle looked out her window to see that her dad was sitting in the car. Putting on her slippers and robe, Norelle decided to wake him up.

As Norelle walked toward the car, she remembered it was Sunday, when she noticed that their neighbors were headed to church. Norelle figured they wouldn't be going that morning. When Norelle got directly on the car, she noticed her father was slumped over the steering wheel. Norelle tapped on the window with no response. As she pulled on the car door, banging on the window, still getting no response, Norelle knew something was terribly wrong. The neighbors began coming over to investigate. By the time Lynette came outside, two men had bust one of the windows and pulled James out of the car. One of the men performed CPR on James while they waited on the ambulance. No matter how many times Lynette cried out no, before the paramedics confirmed it, Norelle knew her daddy was dead. The official cause of death was a heart attack brought on by high blood pressure and elevated levels of stress.

At the present, as Norelle cried at her desk she knew the real cause of death... a broken heart brought on by a cheating wife and elevated levels of deceit. Norelle was no better than the woman she had grown to hate.

Chapter 4

"It wasn't all him."
— Keilah

As Keilah walked to the subway station, she gave a sigh of relief that another workday was over. Descending the escalator, she pulled her jacket tighter; the air was definitely changing. As Keilah reached into her bag to pull out her sketchbook, she noticed that she had a missed call; it was André. What did he want she wondered; hadn't André said enough last Friday?

Taking out her pencil, Keilah began to etch along the lines she had begun a few days before.

It had been just over a week since André dropped the news on her. Keilah couldn't decide if the idea of André getting married hurt her more than the fact of him having a baby. Logic gave cold comfort in the fact that the two of them had been apart for close to two years so it shouldn't be that hard to accept. Keilah's heart on the other hand twisted and turned the notions repeatedly. Why? Keilah had to acknowledge if to anyone but herself that she had been waiting for André to comeback. No, Keilah thought to herself, that wasn't quite right. Keilah only hoped he would, she never really expected him to.

While Keilah gave more definition to her drawing, the moments from she and André's relationship gained definition as she reflected on her own past. Keilah never saw committed relationships as a reality… least of all marriage. Unlike André's father's quiet, late night exit, Keilah's father left loudly in the broad open daylight. Keilah always knew her father was going to leave them; she just didn't know how or when. It wasn't until she was about 13 years old that she got her first lesson about love and commitment.

Like most women of Keilah's mother era, her mother accepted her husband stepping out here and there. It was never spoken of openly. Keilah's parents quietly negotiated through the three golden rules: The wife took care of the house; the husband took care of the bills and kept his mess out in the street. For the most part, it worked out well, every so often Keilah's father would come home too late and an argument would ensue. Keilah's parents would not speak for a few days then her dad would come home with flowers for her mother and new doll for Keilah and things would fall back into place. As the years went on, Keilah noticed her mother's growing bitterness as her father became colder. By the time Keilah started Roland Park Junior High things had starting getting bad. Keilah's father started staying out all night then whole weekends. Mean glares became harsh words that graduated to abusive ones. Sloppy apologetic smooches turned into rough kisses that were followed by pushing and shoving. Nothing changed except the pushing and shoving when Keilah's mother became pregnant again.

When Keilah overheard the news outside her parents' bedroom, she was excited. Keilah's father however was not.

"Yvonne, I thought you were using that diaphragm thing. How did this happen? We don't need any more kids. You did this on purpose, didn't you?"

Keilah's mother sighed, "Did it on purpose? We are married, what are you saying to me Carl? I am your wife.

"Look Yvonne, all I am saying is that Keilah will be in high school soon. Didn't you say you wanted to take some classes so you could get out of that receptionist job at Rosenberg, Klein & Rouse? How do you expect to do that with a baby on your hip?"

Upon hearing Carl's statement, Yvonne collected her thoughts and responded. "I figured after the baby's about six or seven months I can take a class in the evening. Keilah's not used to taking care of a baby, so you could spend some evenings home. You were so good with Keilah so…"

Carl abruptly interrupted Yvonne. "I ain't babysitting anything. Keilah was planned, this one wasn't. The fire station just started putting us on call anyway so that isn't going to work. You know I am trying to get promoted. I thought when we had Keilah we agreed she would be it. You better figure out something."

Keilah heard soft weeping from her mother.

"I better figure out something! It's not just me in this marriage; it's supposed to be you and me! No, excuse me; it's me, you and Gigi. I sat back and let you do what you wanted to do. I let you dip and dab out there but this right here, hell no. Gigi ain't running nothing in this here house. When you see her raggedy behind before work tonight, you tell her *your wife* is having another baby and she's going to have to step back. I am not taking this off of you anymore, plus Keilah doesn't need to see this!"

For ten minutes, Keilah heard footsteps, followed by the closet door opening then shutting loudly.

"Look Yvonne, you knew who you were marrying. I take good care of you and Keilah. You wanted to get married; we got married. You wanted a baby; we had Keilah. You wanted this house; I worked overtime and made it happen. You really didn't have to work but I let you. All I asked you to do was let me be me. You can't try to change the rules of the game when you already on the field. Now you better think about how you are going to handle that little situation."

As Keilah pressed her ear closer to the wall, she tried to understand what her father was saying...then she heard it.

SLAP!

When Keilah peeked through the cracked door, she saw her father holding his face.

"Yvonne, you're taking full advantage because you know I'm not going to hit you back while you are pregnant. You are not going to control me with that baby in your belly. I can show you better than I can tell you. I'm going to spend a few nights at the station. When I come back home, you better have some information for me."

When Keilah saw her parents' bedroom door open, she ran back to her room and acted as if she was drawing. Her father walked past her room, not even stopping in to kiss her goodnight. As tears hit the picture she was drawing, she heard her mother screaming and crying in a frightening catatonic state.

Carl left Tuesday night, returning Thursday evening. When he arrived, Yvonne had finished cooking dinner and Keilah was in her room doing homework. When she heard her father heading up the stairs she peeked out to greet him. As she smiled at her father, he glanced at her blankly and continued walking past her. She watched her father close the bathroom door behind him and pick up the picture she started a few nights before. Taking the eraser, she frantically erased and reordered the figures she drew Tuesday night. When she heard her bedroom door open, she quickly put the picture underneath her pillow and looked up to see her father.

"Hey, Pumpkin, what are you doing in here? Your mother just finished dinner, let's go eat." Keilah smiled, her daddy was home. He picked her up and carried her downstairs to the kitchen.

Seated at the table, Keilah's father looked pleased while her mother looked uneasy. After grace, they sat quietly eating. The more her father ate, the more he smiled. The more he smiled, the more comfortable her mother would be.

"Dag, Vonnie, this is like Sunday dinner. These greens are good, as I don't know what. My Vonnie knows how to cook a pot of greens."

Yvonne smiled as he rose up to kiss her. Carl talked about the crazy emergency calls he had the night before. Yvonne shared little tidbits about who got fired and who got hired at the law firm. Keilah even proudly shared a ninety-five she got on her history test.

Amidst all the laughter, the phone rang. Carl motioned to his daughter to answer the phone while he ate another piece of roast. Just as Yvonne got up to get more cornbread, Keilah nervously said, "Daddy, the phone is for you."

As Carl munched on his cornbread, he threw his hands up and whispered to tell who ever it was he was busy. After relaying the message, Keilah began shaking. Looking first to her mother and then to her father Keilah softly says, "She says her name is Gigi and it's important."

As soon as the words fell from Keilah's mouth, Carl and Yvonne made a mad dash for the phone. Not knowing who to give the phone to, Keilah dropped the receiver to the floor and ran back to the table.

With a steak knife in one hand, Yvonne froze Carl in mid motion as she placed the phone to her ear.

"You crazy bitch, don't you ever call my house again! Do you understand me! If I don't call your house, you damn sure better not call mine. You better keep on paging him like you have been doing. He's with his family. You better get use to it, because we have another baby on the way so you about to be cut off. Your time is up, Gigi. I gave Carl a free pass for two days to tell you goodbye… so bye, bye bitch."

As Yvonne slammed the phone back on the wall, Carl looked on in shock. He had never seen Yvonne so enraged. He also noticed that she hadn't put the knife down.

As Yvonne collected herself, she smiled crookedly. "Keilah, you look like you are finished eating. Go upstairs and finish your homework."

Keilah quickly obeyed her mother and left the kitchen. Instead of going to her room, Keilah sat at the top of the stairs and listened.

"Now, Carl why in the hell is Gigi calling my house? Our daughter answered the phone. What type of mess is that? What, does Gigi feel like she got it like that? I told you to keep your stuff out in the street now it's gotten out of hand. I know you're going to cut her. I am definitely not dealing with this."

Yvonne continued to mutter to herself as she cleared the table.

Carl finished his cornbread and cautiously handed his empty plate to Yvonne.

Keilah sat at the top of the stairs, waiting to hear what would be next. By the time Keilah realized she had fallen asleep, she looked up from her bed to see her father looking down on her. Before she could speak, her father placed his large hands around her face and kissed her forehead.

"Pumpkin, your daddy loves you. You are my little diamond. All this craziness between your mom and I don't have anything to do with you. I may not be around all the time but know I love you Pumpkin. No matter what, you understand me?"

Keilah nodded and hugged her pillow, as her father covered her with the blanket, before exiting her room. Keilah reached underneath her pillow and ripped into pieces the picture she knew never would have been anyway.

The sun was barely up when Keilah heard the commotion from the next room. Jumping out of her bed, Keilah opened up her door to see her mother on her knees, pleading with her father. Before Keilah shut her bedroom door, she noticed the bags in the hallway. Daddy was leaving.

Carl didn't even notice his daughter peeking threw the slightly shut door as he pried Yvonne off of his ankles.

"Yvonne, don't do this. I told you what to do; you aren't going to do it so there it is."

Yvonne picked herself up and shook her head. "Carl, how can you do this to me? We are married. I am your wife. Don't you love me? Don't you love Keilah? You know you will love this baby too. Let me fix you some breakfast. I'm gonna run downstairs and get a pot of coffee started."

As Yvonne ran past her husband, he grabbed her by the arm sharply and said with a low voice, "Yvonne, it's over. I am leaving. Everything was fine. We had things going good and here you come with another baby. You know how I never really wanted kids anyway but I gave in and gave you Keilah; she should have been enough. You knew but you did it anyway."

Yvonne broke away and ran down to the kitchen. All Keilah could hear were pots and pans. When Keilah saw that her father had gone downstairs, she went to the top of the stairs and listened again.

"It's Gigi isn't it? She got you all supped up to just up and leave your family. What about the promises we made? Don't our vows mean anything to you?"

Keilah could hear a kitchen chair move and her father's keys jingling.

"First thing, Vonnie, when I met you I was dating Gigi and another woman. The other girl hassled me too much so it got down to just you and Gigi. Both of you knew about the other. She tried to out-do you; you tried to out-do her. It all became a game to both of you. You turned a blind eye to Gigi, focused on me and got me hooked. You ain't the jealous type you told me, you'd never try to change me, that's what you said. All of that was just to get Gigi out the picture. You knew I was still seeing her but after you got that ring on your finger, you said, 'Yeah, I got his ass now'. Your mask slowly started slipping with each year. As a matter of fact, it started cracking right after I said I do."

Keilah could hear her mother wailing.

"The way I remember it you weren't so perfect either Yvonne; you dipped a little too. I remember Eddie from the dry cleaners and that mail clerk named Bobby from your job. Hell, some guy named Harold was still trying to come pass your house after we got married. That was one of the reasons why we ended up moving here when we did."

Keilah could hear her mother mumbling something underneath her breath. As Keilah stepped further down the steps, she strained to hear what was next. As she heard the coffee being poured into a cup, all she could hear was sniffling.

"Carl, you want some grits? They are almost ready."

Before Carl could answer, a loud car horn woke up the whole neighborhood. "That's my ride. I left money on the nightstand. I will always take care of Keilah. I'm out."

47

Pulling and shoving ensued yet again between Yvonne and Carl. As Carl opened the front door, his young daughter ran up to him, begging him not to leave. At that moment, Keilah's eyes became fixated on the person getting out of the car her father said he had sold…Gigi.

Keilah's trance was broken when she felt something wet and hot hit her cheek. Before Keilah could figure out what was going on, her mother had knocked her down to the ground and was running out the front door. As Keilah's father reached down to pick her up, she saw the huge pink rollers emerging behind his back. Her mother had her father by the collar with one hand and a silver pot in the other one.

"Keilah, move!"

As Keilah stumbled to her feet, she heard her father give out a scream of pain as the sticky white goo ran down his face like steaming hot lava.

The only thing that saved Gigi from the rest of the grits was the big wig she had worn that morning. Carl didn't press charges when the police came, he told them his wife had slipped with the pot in her hand and the burns weren't that bad. The two officers waited as Carl packed the rest of his things. Taking his house keys off his belt, Carl placed the keys on the coffee table; looked toward his daughter and blew her a kiss. "Keilah, your mother did this, you remember this."

The months that followed saw Yvonne going through periods of depression. Crying spells quietly in the middle of the night after Yvonne thought her daughter was asleep. Then as the baby grew in her stomach, the crying spells turned to fits of rage. When Yvonne couldn't get to her husband, her aim was Keilah. Every blow Yvonne couldn't lay on Carl fell on Keilah. If Keilah broke a dish, she was clumsy like her father, ensued by a shove. If Keilah didn't put her shoes in the right place, she was sloppy like her father, followed by a slap across the face.

Carlita was born on Easter Sunday, looking like her father, and things changed. Carl started coming around again to visit. Each time he came, he bought gifts for Keilah and Carlita. Yvonne acted cold at first but eventually warmed as Carl's visit became more frequent and later into the night with him slipping out early in the morning to go back to Gigi's. Yvonne gave up getting her husband back and accepted having her man around, resigning to become the other woman to her own husband's mistress.

As Keilah exited the subway station, she reflected on how she applied the crazy lessons she learned from her parents in her own relationships. Most importantly one phrase her mother often used: men will only do what you allow them to do.

Unlocking the door to her apartment, Keilah reluctantly unlocked her thoughts. Walking through the living room, giving Sashay a rub of apology for forgetting to feed her that morning, she poured the cat food into Sashay's bowl, and released her one sided view of the relationship she once had with André. It wasn't all him.

Chapter 5

"It was that annoyingly vacant space that
sat between like and love that was not being used."
— Keilah

Having sat in his car for half an hour, André decided not to knock on Keilah's door. It was apparent she didn't want to talk to him. Maybe he was expecting too much from her. He didn't truly know what he was expecting of her he thought to himself as he drove off.

She had the right to be angry, didn't she? *No*, he thought. Keilah didn't have the right to be angry but maybe she had a reason to be hurt but what did she expect after all this time. She was the one that called the relationship off, as André recalled.

After getting in touch with Chris, André turned his cell phone to vibrate and walked into Club Deuce. He was happy when Chris agreed to meet him at their old hang out. When Chris walked in, André was relieved that Keilah would be off his mind for a while. Chris was his boy and they had a lot of catching up to do.

Since André moved to DC, they really hadn't had a chance to hang out as they used to. With Chris being married along with a set of twins and a growing contracting business, they had lost touch.

Noticing the serious look on André's face, Chris decided to bust him. "What's up player? I was surprised to hear you were in Baltimore tonight; old man Rosenberg let you off the plantation?"

André gave him dap, motioned for the bartender and ordered two Hennessy and Cokes. "Yeah man, I had to get a change of scenery for a minute. I didn't realize how much I missed Baltimore. What's good?"

Taking his drink from the bartender, Chris could tell André had something on his mind. "Everything is good. Carla and the boys are fine. Business is steady. What's up with you? You don't just call and breeze through on a Monday night. What's up man?"

André took a heavy gulp of his drink, and paused. "I'm thinking of asking Alisha to marry me."

Chris removed his eyeglasses and laughed "You! Getting married. What, come on man, are you serious?"

André had to laugh too. "Yeah, man. I wanted the name of the jeweler you went to, wasn't it in Annapolis?"

Chris took a sip and looked closer at André. "You sure about this, right? Alisha's the one…you are sure? You know getting married is serious business. How long have you been thinking about it?"

André smiled nervously. "Long enough man, come on. I know what I am doing. While I'm at it, what do you think about being a godfather?"

Chris jumped out of his seat and slapped André on the back. "You're really messing with me now. Alisha is pregnant, damn. You're serious? Was it planned?"

André shook his drink, trying to figure out how to answer the question, as Keilah entered his mind again. "Naw, it just happened. Hell did you plan yours?"

Chris smiled. "Yes, I did. Carla and I were already married two years before the twins came, but hell you old enough, congratulations man."

André continued. "I was down here last weekend; you and Carla must have been out. I saw Keilah. You remember her don't you? She's doing good…"

Cutting André off in mid-sentence, Chris sat his drink down. "Yeah, of course I remember Keilah? You two still talk? Dré, what's up man? What are you doing seeing her? You two still talk?"

On the defense, André responded quickly. "What do you mean, 'What's up man?' Everything is fine between us, I saw her. What's the problem?"

Chris laughed. "What's the problem? Last time I heard, Keilah called your house, Alisha answered your phone and you were picking up the stuff you left at her house off your parking lot at three o'clock in the morning. Didn't you say Keilah told you her mother poured hot grits on her dad?"

André took another sip from his drink. "What ever man. Yeah it was ugly when we broke up but she and I still talked after that. She's good people. I love her man."

Chris finished off his drink and looked around for the bartender. "You love Keilah. That's the first time I heard that out your mouth."

André shrugged Chris off and caught the bartender's attention. "You're gonna give me the number to the jeweler or what?"

Chris pulled out his wallet. "I am going to find this number for you but you better get your business together. No man that is ready to get married looks up his exes. I mean, you might want to hit it one more time but you say you love Keilah, so don't do it. Leave her alone."

After André paid the bartender, Chris handed him the jeweler's card. "Dré, you are my boy, forever, but know what you're doing."

André snatched the card from Chris. "Man, I know what I am doing. It's not even like that with Keilah. She hasn't even called me back since I told her last week."

Shaking his head, Chris removed his eyeglasses and wiped them with bottom of his shirt. "You told her? You are crazy as hell. What do expect, Dré? You told Keilah you are going to marry the woman you cheated on her with. What do you want, her blessing or something?"

André looked down at the card and realized he never had the chance to tell Keilah it was Alisha; truth was André didn't know how to tell her.

Still looking disgusted at André, Chris decided to call it a night. "Man I got to get home. I'm done. Call me if you want me to ride to Annapolis with you."

When André reached his car, Chris yelled to him from two cars over. "You said you love Keilah so leave her alone."

The more André thought about his love for Alisha, the more he thought about Keilah. As he headed toward Interstate 95 South, André resolved that he was in love with Alisha but loved Keilah. When André decided to turn around and head back downtown toward Bolton Hill, he contended with the nagging reality that loving one and being in love with another was a true quandary rather than just a philosophical basket of oranges and apples that he used to be able to pick from at will.

When Keilah heard the knock on her door, she figured it was Norelle on yet another one of her late evening runs. When she looked through the peephole, she was shocked to see who was on the other side of the door. As soon as Keilah opened the door, Keith immediately grabbed her and planted kisses all over her face. Untying her robe, Keith closed the door behind him and moved Keilah toward the bedroom.

Pushing him away, Keilah tied her robe tightly around her waist and gave Keith the once over.

"Come on Keilah. You still not mad about last weekend. I told you my cousin needed me to drive him to New Jersey at the last minute. You know how Sprint is. I was out of range and couldn't call you until I got back in state. Come here." Just as Keith goes to grab Keilah again, she walks away and lights a cigarette.

"Keith what's really going on? I mean really. You think I'm stupid."

Keith walked toward Keilah, has a second thought and decided to sit down on the sofa. "Keilah you are the one. When was the last time we got down? It's been almost a month. What's up with that?"

Keith knew what was up Keilah thought, *Constance.* Keilah chooses not to respond, leaving Keith in the living room while she ran her bathwater. When she returned to the living room, she was disappointed to see Keith had taken off his shoes and turned on the TV.

"Look Keith, I'm tired. Why don't you go home, shower and rest tonight? Maybe Friday, you can come down. I'll fix us something to eat." Dead air, Keilah knew what was next. Keith was so predictable.

"Damn, I just came down here to your house tonight, like I always do. Why don't you ever want to come to my house? I work twelve-hour shifts on my feet and you expect me to come to you all the damn time. You need to start coming out to my house. This is my last night coming to you."

Keilah was relieved to see Keith putting on his shoes. It meant he was pissed and getting ready to leave. She tried to hide her grin as he walked to the door, she wasn't in the mood to hear his whining and complaining; they both knew the real reason why she didn't like coming out to his house.

"Okay, Keith your right. But let me ask you this, has Constance stopped her drive bys? When was the last time you spoke to her, hmm? Is she still calling leaving ten messages a day? Oh, wait maybe she has chilled out some since you spent last weekend with her ass." Dead air again. "Hello? Keith, I didn't hear your answer. What's up with Constance?"

Giving an exhausted breath, Keith turned the doorknob to leave. "Okay, Keilah. I am too tired to deal with this."

Exactly, Keilah thought to herself as she locked the door behind him.

Getting out of the bathtub, Keilah watched the water drain out of the tub, as she rubbed herself down with lotion. She wished her thoughts could be washed away that easy. Pushing André out of her mind, Keilah wondered what she was doing with Keith.

Sure Keith wasn't exactly the type of man she saw herself with but, with time and some extra effort, things could work. She didn't care what Norelle said, he wasn't that funny looking and yes, he could spend more time in the gym and less time at the table, but he was actually cute to Keilah; he was her own chocolate Buddha.

To be fair, Keilah and Keith had a comfy situation. They enjoyed each other but still there was an unfilled space, an annoyingly vacant space between like and love that was not being used. As Keilah tied up her hair, she knew it wasn't as vacant as she'd liked to believe. There was that large elephant that sat defiantly unmovable... Constance. Why did Keith feel the need to hold on to Constance who, by his own admission, was so wrong for him? The same reason she had held onto André, if only in her mind, Keilah reconciled.

As Keilah finished putting on her face cream, she heard a knock at the door. Walking from the bathroom, she grabbed her robe and looked at the clock. It was quarter to eleven. If it was Keith again, she was determined not to answer the door.

Keilah's heart dropped as she looked through the peephole to see André walking away. Should she open the door and let him in? By the time she decided to let him in, André was in his car and driving off.

Keilah called his cell phone, three times in a row. *Now he doesn't want to talk to me* Keilah thought. After the fifth call, she gave up and sent a text message.

As André pulled off of the highway, and turned on to Georgia Avenue, he glanced at the jeweler's card Chris had given him. When he got out of his car, he noticed his phone was still on the back seat. Putting the phone in his back pocket, André hoped Alisha was waiting for him.

When he opened the door, he was happy to see Alisha pop out of the bedroom. Placing his wallet and cell phone on the coffee table, he eagerly joined her in bed.

When Alisha leaned in to kiss him, André stopped her and looked directly into her eyes. "Alisha, do you trust me?"

Alisha smiled softly and nodded, leaning in to kiss him again.

André knew he would be headed to Annapolis the next day and if Keilah wanted to stay in his past, he had no choice but to agree with her.

By four in the morning, André was fast asleep and Alisha was quietly getting ready to go back to her place.

Damn, Alisha thought, as she heard the buzzing again; she had to find that cell phone. Alisha knew André was a heavy sleeper but she didn't want any problems. Things were going along fine and she didn't want anything or anyone to pop up.

By the time she traced the buzzing sound to the living room, she was relieved that it wasn't her phone. However, her relief turned to curiosity . . . Who would be calling André's phone at this hour? Alisha knew she was wrong for looking at André's phone but she wanted to know who was calling him at four o'clock in the morning.

When Alisha saw Keilah's name appear, she got angry. "Where did she come from?" Alisha whispered to herself as she looked toward the bedroom where André was still slumbering quietly. When Alisha saw the text message Keilah left André, she got enraged.

Dré, I am ready to talk now. Please don't get married without talking to me, please. I need to say some things to you first.

Wait, Alisha thought, married. Then she got excited. André wanted to marry her; this was working out better than she had hoped.

Alisha's excitement changed to confusion. "Why did he tell Keilah before he even asked me?" she pondered to herself. She put the question out of her head. She was not going to make Keilah an issue; too much was at stake now. She was not going to throw her own monkey wrench in the plan and she surely wasn't going to let Keilah do it either. As she erased the calls, she knew it would be even easier than it was the first time. She knew she had the Trump card this time as she rubbed her little bump. She decided to send a preemptive strike via text message.

Chapter 6

Keilah always knew everything...
—André

It had been almost a month since Keilah received the text message from André. Even though she went about her day to day, she was broken. She took the love she had held for André and lavished it on Keith.

Keith found the sudden change of affection strange but didn't question it. All he knew was he was getting more sex than he could handle and she was off his back about Constance. Norelle, on the other hand, was not convinced.

"Keilah, I still don't think André sent you that text. That's just not like him."

Keilah picked at her salad wondering why she kept wasting her lunch breaks meeting Norelle.

"I am serious K. I bet you that girl sent you that text. You need to call André."

Looking past Norelle, Keilah called the server over and ordered a hot tea. What could she say now? André had made his choice, and she wasn't it. Why should she embarrass herself even more?

"Hey, this is what I meant to ask you, what hotel did you and Raymond stay in when you went to Atlantic City? Keith and I are supposed to go next weekend."

Norelle pursed her lips and shook her head. "Why, K? You know Keith still keeping time with the old lady. Why are you doing this?"

Keilah glared at Norelle with contempt. "Look, André has moved on so why shouldn't I? I am happy with Keith. As long as I make my presence known at Keith's crib, Constance doesn't have any more room. She'll get tired and give up. There is no such thing as fidelity, only loyalty. Everybody cheats; you know that for yourself."

As the server approached with their order, Norelle decided not to be defensive. "No. Ms Constance is not going to give up. *She* loves him. She believes they love each other, which is why she hasn't gone anywhere. Keith believes it too, that's why he isn't letting her go. Keilah, people who believe in love don't give up like you do. The get crazy…they get extreme…do things they have never done before. You need to see André, at least talk to him."

"You know what Norelle; I really would like to know where you get this fairytale version of André and me from. If you remember, we broke up every four months. You remember why?"

As Norelle examined her sandwich, she searched for the right words. How was she going to get through to her friend? Blunt truth. "Okay, K. André stepped out…but you let him. You agreed to an open relationship. Rather than telling him you wanted more, you would get an attitude; pick a silly argument and breakup with him…playing games. When you and André were together, y'all were together. Shoot y'all were Jada and Will before Jada and Will. André never lied about what he was about, but you, on the other hand, did."

Keilah threw her fork down. She couldn't believe what she was hearing. "Open relationship, no, understanding, yes. I gave André space to be him. He did the same for me. I never fooled Dré anyway, he knew how I felt but he never put up a fight. He took his free pass and left. So what does that say?"

Norelle took a bite of her sandwich and sighed. *Keilah is so in denial*, she thought. "Keilah, things very well may have turned out the way they are right now but sadly you will never know because you never put up the same effort you so desperately wanted from André. How could you expect something from André that you were too scared to give yourself? Yeah, the both of you were flawed and misshapen but your pieces fit together perfectly. You can't deny that."

Keilah knew what Norelle was saying was true and it hurt. When she looked at André, it was almost like looking in a mirror. When she listened to André, it was like a whisper from her own spirit.

Keilah had no idea when she spilled that drink on him so many nights ago that she would be opening a familiar door she had yet to know again...her soul mate.

As Keilah took the hot tea from the server, a crooked grin appeared on her face. *How ironic* Keilah thought. She used to get angry because she could count the number of times André said I love you. Yet she realized she may have said it verbally the same amount of times. Keilah always looked to André to lead her to that place.

The love Keilah was looking for André to show her was the very love she feared to reveal to him. Deep down, Keilah knew he was in love with her. But, she was so damn afraid that the minute love was recognized for what it was, she'd lose it.

"So what are you going to do now? Make Keith chose you. Then what, get married to Keith and show André something? You don't love Keith and he doesn't love you. The both of you are trying to make sense out of love. Love doesn't make sense. Keith is safe for you because you know you really don't have to invest that much of yourself. Losing him will hurt but not that deep. It will hurt kind of like losing a pair of earrings. You like them, hell, you treasure them but you know you can get another pair when you're ready. Losing André is like losing a leg. You understand how it happened but it's still traumatic. You can get around without it but you walk with a limp. You still feel that missing limb even though you know it's gone."

Keilah started to respond, and then changed her mind. Taking a bite of chicken, she allowed her heart and mind to dialogue.

Keilah knew André was the man she would have grown with and not apart from, forever exchanging the roles of teacher and student between them, finding the beautiful balance of friends and lovers. It was the question of loyalty that was complicated by André's constant searching.

In the beginning of their relationship, Keilah and André rummaged through the world together; investigating and debating all

59

the five senses then quietly things changed…he was more willing to search without her. Strangers seemed more intriguing to him. She felt she was only around to keep him sharp for the one that fit his criteria better. He never directly made her feel that way; it was mainly her own insecurities. She was a struggling artist and temp of all trades when they met. Even after she got a real job with the phone company, she still struggled day to day. He was on course while she strived to walk steady. The more he moved further along with new people; the harder she tried to catch up. As time passed, Keilah felt she could never measure up. Picking at her chicken, she wasn't sure when she actually believed it—before or after the baby.

Keilah knew they were always connected even before the baby but instead of looking forward to something more out of love, she looked backward and expected love the only way she had seen it and it terrified her. She couldn't bear the possibility of André becoming her father. She allowed her past to steal away her future. Rather than taking a chance on love, she surrendered him over to another.

The question remained in Keilah's heart, why compete? Hadn't she proven her love to André? She laid her body down for him. Unlike her mother, Keilah didn't try to force a baby on someone that didn't want it. Didn't that mean anything to him? Didn't he know she did it for him?

Cutting another piece of chicken, Keilah finally responded. "Nori, I am getting too old to wait around for some prince charming to ride in on a white horse. Keith is around when ever I need him. The few things I ask of him he does without question. As long as I take care of business, we will be fine. I am content and that is fine with me."

Norelle took another bite of her sandwich and slowly sipped her soda. She couldn't believe her best friend had given up on love. "So you'd rather compete for a man that you really don't love rather than going after the man you are in love with?"

Motioning to the server for the check, Keilah reached into her purse. "It's over. André sent me a fucking text message telling me that the woman he is having a baby with is Alisha, the same woman he cheated on me with. This is not Brown Sugar, Norelle; this is real life. There is no happily ever after to this. André got his career on point; Alisha apparently fits better into his world than I do. André is having a baby and he is marrying her. That's the woman André wants his children and his life with; not me."

Watching her best friend on the verge of tears, Norelle understood. Taking Keilah's hand in hers, Norelle leaned over and whispered, "It's the baby isn't it? You aren't just hurt that André is getting married, you are more hurt because he didn't want to keep yours."

Upon his return from lunch, André was relieved to see the note that his hearing had been postponed. He could spend the rest of the afternoon catching up on paperwork. Shuffling through his files, several fell behind the bookcase. When he moved the bookcase away from the wall, he noticed something he hadn't seen in almost a year… a photograph of him and Keilah.

Blowing away the dust, he looked at the picture and smiled. Keilah never liked taking pictures and he never understood why. He always thought she could be a model, with eyes like a Siamese cat. Whenever she looked at André, he knew she could see deep into his very core. Keilah always knew him. He never really had to teach her how to do what ever it was she did so well when they were together. Keilah was who she was and she flowed effortlessly with André. Thinking back on the day they met, he felt she would always be around.

André and Chris were hanging out at Club Deuce. Brothers were lined across the wall bumping their head to Jay-Z, trying to pick out a cutie for the night. The place was a smorgasbord of women. Big booty Baltimore girls, with big Baltimore hair filled the place along with a generous helping of New York chicks and Philly girls wearing slicked-back ponytails and dark lined eyes with glossed-out lips. By the scent of strawberries and champagne overpowering the club, every sister that walked by must have caught the sale at Victoria's Secret.

Watching as Chris followed a pair of thongs to the dance floor, André decided to freshen up his drink and check the afro chic at the end of the bar. In the midst of all the strawberries and creams, and cigarette smoke, a sweet and seductive smell of cinnamon found its way to André. Turning around, he saw no one but the scent lingered. Returning to his spot, he noticed the afro chic was gone and another cutie had taken her place. As André made eye contact with the new cutie, the scent hit him again along with a cold drink against his pants. Before he saw Keilah's face, he saw her eyes.

"I am so sorry. It is so crowded in here. I just got some club soda to get a stain off my canvas."

André didn't hear a word Keilah said. He was caught in her eyes. Her long lashes surrounded dark slanted eyes that revealed a deepness André wanted to explore.

By the time André broke from the trance, Keilah had run across the street to another building. Tapping Chris, André decided to follow behind her.

Once inside, André found that an art show was going on. He looked around and didn't see her. Just as André was about to go, Keilah walked out from a backroom. Noticing him, Keilah smiled and put an extra twist in her walk. André smiled as he watched her. She was a piece of art herself. Keilah's hair was twisted in puffy corkscrew braids with an orange head wrap tied around it. Her copper jewelry glowed against her reddish brown skin. As he was about to approach her, a woman came up and snatched her away.

André followed behind, overhearing that someone wanted to buy a painting of hers.

"Look Keilah, this guy is fine and wants to buy your picture. I asked him what he thought about it but he just wanted to see you. I told him you had gone across the street but he waited. So you open that blouse up and work it."

Keilah smiled and playfully shoved Norelle. "I am not trying to get a date! I am trying to sell my art."

Fixing Keilah's blouse, Norelle whispered. "Whatever, girl, get both"

After twenty minutes, it was obvious the guy was not interested in buying anything. When she mentioned the price, he tells her he'll pay her twenty dollars for it if she'd give him her number. Insulted, Keilah walked away, as André approached.

"Excuse me. What's the story of this painting?"

Keilah recognized him from the club across the street. Cutting her eyes, she decided she was not wasting time with anyone else that night. "Look, it's been a long night. The painting is what ever it says to you. If you are interested in the painting, make me an offer. If not then I have to pack up."

Examining the picture more closely, André saw that some of the deepness he noticed in her eyes had found its way on the canvas. "I am not an art expert but I can tell that the people's faces aren't that important in regard to what you are trying to say."

Keilah smiled and nodded for him to go on.

"They are just painted black, no clothes or anything but everything else around them has color. You have a red tree and green apples. Then over here," he said, pointing at the painting, "you have what looks like a storm cloud but then you have the blue sky and a yellow sun. How does $75 dollars sound?"

Keilah was elated. As she left to get a receipt book, Chris walked up.

"You get the number yet?"

André shook his head. "You are going to have to pay for parking when we leave. I just bought this painting."

Chris laughed and head back to the club.

Keilah returned and knelt down to wrap the painting while André admired her long back that lead to perfectly rounded curves that flirted mischievously underneath her skirt.

When André handed her the money, she looked up at him. He knew those eyes were going to get him in trouble but he didn't care.

"My name is André Davidson, by the way. What is your name?"

When Keilah smiled and stood up, André caught that sweet scent again. "My name is Keilah. Keilah Fort."

Taking the painting from Keilah, André smiled. "Kay–lah. That is pretty, what does it mean?"

Pulling out a notepad and pen from her purse, Keilah jotted down a note. "It's from the bible. It was the name of a city in Judah that King David freed." When she passed the paper to André, he is happy to see her phone number on it.

"Hmm, that's interesting. So I guess I can call you so you can tell me what this picture really means."

Noticing that the building was starting to empty out, Keilah walked André toward the door. "Yeah, you can call me. Just make sure your girlfriend doesn't find my number."

André smiled at her. "What makes you think I have a girlfriend?"

Opening the door for André, Keilah replied, "I know you have a girl some where wondering where you are. It's cool."

Placing the photo on the corner of his desk, André loosened his tie before going through a file. Keilah always knew everything... even the first day she met him. He was living with Tanya when he met Keilah. André and Tanya had problems even before he met Keilah. By the time Tanya moved out, André and Keilah had been spending just about everyday together. Keilah never made demands on André; she filtered into his life as if she was supposed to be there. André always thought of her as his familiar stranger. André knew so much yet so little about Keilah at the same time.

Deciding to call it a day, André packed a few files away in his attaché case and left his office, not leaving the photo behind.

Looking at the photo again, André's mood slid slowly to disappointment.

By the time they broke up, André and Keilah were pretty much on the same fast track but going in two different directions. André was pushing for junior partner and Keilah was promoted to supervisor. While Keilah upgraded her Corolla for a Camry, André got a Lexus. As André delved deeper into his cases, Keilah seemed less interested. André knew that Keilah had become a little insecure after he started practicing law but she should have known her innate intellect was invaluable to him. When Keilah started neglecting her art, things started falling apart. When she traded in her bohemian chic for designer suits and high heels, André took notice for a while then retreated deeper into his career. André knew something was broken, so did Keilah but neither one of them wanted to take time to find it and fix it.

Reaching the parking lot, André entered his car and slid the photo inside the glove compartment. Turning onto K Street, André looked at the sea of cars and prepared to sit in traffic. They stopped talking, that was what it was—after the baby.

Chapter 7

What in the hell have I been looking at?
— Norelle

As Norelle watched Raymond sleep, she knew she had to end it with Tariq. She knew she not only loved Raymond but also she was in love with him. Raymond was one of the good men and she was blessed enough to get him. Norelle also knew Raymond wasn't stupid and it would only be a matter of time before he caught on. Tariq wasn't worth it.

When Norelle leaned down to kiss Raymond, he jumped up suddenly and grabbed her. "What are you doing up before me? I usually have to wake you up in the morning."

Norelle doesn't say word. She squeezed him as tight as she could and buried her face deep in his chest. "I love you so much, Ray. You are the best thing that has ever happened to me. You remind me so much of my father."

Raymond lifted Norelle's face to his and gently kissed her on the lips. "Nori, I want us to try for a baby again. I know we went through the doctors and everything but I want to try again. I found a new doctor that I want us to start seeing. Let's see what happens."

Norelle kissed Raymond softly; knowing a child of his own was what he really wanted. They had tried for over a year with no results. It caused a lot of stress on their marriage but Norelle was willing to try again.

"Sure, baby I know that's your heart's desire." Climbing on top of Raymond, Norelle leaned forward and whispered in his ear. "Let's start right now, Papa Bear."

As Keilah walked to the shuttle bus, she couldn't shake what went down the night before, at Keith's house.

Everything was going fine. Keilah prepared a nice dinner; she and Keith watched television. Nice and comfy. As Keilah got up to get a drink, she caught it...the look. Keith looked at her blankly, as if he was searching for something in her face.

"What?"

Keith at first acted as if he didn't even hear Keilah until she said it again.

"Keith, what is it?"

Keith smiled, leaned in, kissed her and replied, "Nothing."

Keilah poured them both a drink. As she returned to the sofa, she saw it again...the look.

"Keilah, why do you love me? What is this sudden change in you?"

Keilah sipped her soda, and smiled. "What do you mean why?"

Keith stood up and lit a cigarette. Slowly dragging on the cigarette, he looked at Keilah again. "Why can't you answer me, Keilah? Tell me why you are so in love. I need to know."

Nervousness shot through Keilah. How was she going to answer him? Buying time, Keilah took one of Keith's cigarettes and walked to the stove to light it. Taking a drag, Keilah chose her words carefully. "Why do you need to ask me that, Keith? Can't you tell by now? I call you everyday; I try to come out here every chance I get. We get down just about every night, so why are you asking me this? Why wouldn't I love a hardworking, sweet black man like you?"

Keith joined Keilah in the kitchen. "You tell me, Keilah."

Before Keilah could respond, the phone rung and Keith's answering machine picked up.

Beep!

Hey, Keith, I was just calling to see if you made it in. I made some shrimp and linguini; you know you can come eat some if you want. Call me.

Beep!

Keilah flashed a look of anger toward Keith and walked back to the living room. "Next time, remember to turn your phone and your answering machine off."

Keith scratched his head and followed on Keilah's heels. "You still didn't answer my question? Don't try to change the subject."

Keilah looked for her shoes. "Don't try to change the subject! Constance is the subject. No one keeps calling someone that doesn't want to see him or her anymore. You are still involved with her, more pointedly you are still sleeping with her; that's why you had guilty dick last weekend."

Keith shook his head in disbelief.

Putting on her shoes, Keilah gathered her things. She could have sworn Keith was smiling. "We went to Atlantic City, I bought brand new lingerie and you could barely touch me. I must be as stupid as you think I am. I asked you if you were still seeing her. You said no, you were handling it. I was the one you wanted. So, I said 'Okay, let me put myself out more, show him how I feel.' Damn, I am hitting an all time low with your ass."

Keith grabbed Keilah by the shoulder. "Keilah, I do want you. I just need some time. I was in love with Constance and I will always love her, we just can't work as a couple. I figured you'd understand considering how long you were with André. You didn't just get over him in a day or a month. It took time didn't it? Hell, you probably talk to his ass when you get mad at me."

Keilah couldn't believe Keith was bringing André into this. She broke away from him and grabbed her car keys. "Give me a break, Keith. How are you going to get over someone who is constantly in your face? And, since you dragged André all up into this, I'll have you know that I do not talk to him, when I am mad with your ass or otherwise. If you must know he is getting married."

Keith released a chuckle, followed by a wide grin. "Oh, so this is where all this came from. Since you can't have André, you may as well take me. I am runner up, second choice. I knew something was up."

Opening the front door, Keilah realized she left her cell phone. As she turned back into the house, her cell phone rung.

Grabbing the cell phone, Keith looked at the caller ID. "Yeah, it's a 202 number, probably old boy calling you now."

Keilah snatched the phone from Keith and looked at the number "I don't know who it is. Unlike you, Keith, when it's over, it's over. When André told me he was getting married, I heard him out and that was that; end of communication."

As Keilah walked toward the front door Keith followed her. "When André told you? What type of shit is that? Why would he need to tell you? He is full of it and so are you. You aren't going to use me Keilah."

Stepping out the door, Keilah responded, "No Keith, you aren't going to use *me*."

If you can't be with the person you love, love the person your with had become the rule rather than the exception and Keith was as guilty as Keilah. The exception for Keith was that he hadn't given up Constance and nothing was going to change. Why should he when Keilah and Constance made it so easy for him? What man wouldn't like the idea of two women competing for him? Keilah couldn't judge her mother anymore. She was doing the exact same thing, if not worse; at least her mother loved her father.

By the time the shuttle bus reached Keilah's office building, she concluded that she should have let it go when she slammed Keith's door and left. Keilah knew what Keith had said was true. It became more about André and less about Keith. She couldn't take not being chosen again. Keilah chose to fight for a love she didn't even believe in for the sake of winning.

Stepping off the elevator, Keilah looked at the clock and realized she had a meeting in less than ten minutes. By the time she dropped her things off at her desk, she noticed people entering the conference room. When she reached the conference room, she was glad there was only one seat left in the back of the room. Smiling at people as she took a seat, she thought on what went down at Keith's, the night before, shaking her head in disbelief. Why did she go back?

After calling Keith back that same night, Keilah apologized. Even though she felt she wasn't totally at fault, Keith was all she had and she was determined to win him over.

By eleven o'clock, Keilah was exiting the shower and decided to show how apologetic she was. As Keilah jumped into her car, she tried to call Keith but got no answer. Figuring he was asleep, Keilah drove a little faster and sprayed on a little extra perfume. When she pulled up, Keith's house was dark.

It took Keith awhile to answer the door. When he did answer, Keilah noticed he had on a robe and the phone in his hand; Keilah also noticed that Keith wasn't exactly happy to see her. Keilah decided to ignore the cool reception and kissed him. Reaching underneath his robe, she allowed her hands to roam, ending at his belly as she jiggled it playfully. Keith jerked away from her and pulled his robe tighter.

"Keilah what are you doing here?"

Keilah moved in closer to him and kissed him again. "Come on Buddha, what better way to make up."

Keith pulled away again and looked nervously at the door. "Keilah, why do you think that sex solves everything? Do you think my nose is so open that you can say a few sweet words to me, throw some loving at me and I will forget that you really don't want me?"

"Is this still about André? I want you! What more do I have to do? If I wanted André, I'd be with André. I am here right now. What are you talking about?"

Keith walked to his window and peeked out, lighting a cigarette. As he exhales, he checked the lock on the door. "Keilah, the only reason why you are with me is because André is getting married and you are mad at his ass. If he called you right now and told you he wasn't getting married and wanted you back, you'd break your neck getting out of here."

Keilah sat down on the sofa, knowing he is right.

"Look Keilah, I will come down your place tomorrow and we can talk. Ring my phone and let me know you got home ok."

Keilah jumped to her feet. She couldn't believe Keith was putting her out. "Why can't I spend the night? Oh, I know what the deal is. Constance must be ..."

Before Keilah could finish her sentence, there was a knock at the door. She beat Keith to the door and swung it open to a pudgy sable-skinned woman; with eyes full of fire glaring at back at her...it was Constance.

Constance swung on Keilah, ducking and moving back.

Keilah couldn't believe what she was seeing. Constance looked insane. She swung with a vengeance. Constance's long fingernails looked like claws scrapping at the air looking for flesh to devour. All Keilah heard was slut this ...whore that.

Keith didn't move, Constance's insanity had frightened him too. Eyeing an opportunity to sneak Keith, Constance jumped on his back and dug her nails deep into his face.

Bleeding, Keith flung Constance off his back, dropped to the floor and cried, laying his face at Constance's feet.

For a moment, Constance looked at Keith sympathetically, with gentleness of a woman who loved her man too deeply for her own good. Then bam, the heart strings changed from keys of love to keys of pain and Constance kicked Keith square in the face, jumping to her feet as if she wanted a round with Keilah.

Keilah tucked her purse tightly underneath her arm and prepared herself. Before Keilah could speak, Constance stopped in her tracks and breathed in slowly. Looking down at Keith, Constance brushed her hair back and spoke ...strangely calm...frightfully calm. The kind of calm that scared you because you knew the person was trying desperately to hold onto to their last ounce of sanity.

Kenda Bell

Constance's inflections were squeaky and strained, horse yet still audible. As Constance slowly walked toward Keilah, Keilah secured her stance and prepared to swing back. As Constance got closer, Keilah began to see the pain etched along her face.

"I know all about you, Keilah, and you know all about me...don't you? You really didn't think I'd let Keith go just because you showed up on the scene. I love Keith and Keith loves me. We have been together for three years and you really think four months of screwing with you would change that? I figured you to be smarter than that. We have our problems but he knows I love him. I am not going anywhere and Keith doesn't want me to. You already knew that too but you felt like your being younger would change that. Don't look surprised, he told me. It hurt but I can't give him certain *things* he may think he wants. But whatever...he loves me regardless. If you wanted to be stupid enough to get knocked up why protest. Nobody marries their baby momma's anymore, not unless they love her and Keith doesn't love you; why should I worry?"

Keilah could hardly catch her breath. Without laying one blow on Keilah, Constance had managed to knock the wind out of her. Humiliation laced with anger boiled over inside of Keilah. Quickly walking past Constance, she walked up to Keith and looked down at him. Did he hate her? How could Keith have done this to her? She thought if nothing else, they had been friends, but he had treated her like some faceless woman he met at the club.

As Keilah reached down to touch Keith's face, he jerked away thinking Keilah was about to slap him. She looked at him, unable to disregard the ugliness of what she had done to herself. Keith wasn't to blame. As her mother said, "A man will only do what a woman allows him to do." *Forget that,* Keilah thought, his rolly polly ass had played her. Turning her ring toward the inside of her hand, Keilah swung forward and slapped Keith across the face. Before he could respond, Keilah rushed toward the door, looking to give Constance a piece.

Constance looked on with a smile and opened the door for Keilah.

"You big fat nasty bastard, you should have been grateful I wanted to give your funny looking ass the time of day let alone anything else.. And you Constance, you change of life bitch, I hope when I am as old as you I am not half as desperate as you are. You can have him. The only muscle he has is that sorry little piece of meat buried somewhere under his stomach!"

Sitting in the empty conference room, Keilah couldn't help but see how desperate she had been, far worse than Constance.

When Keilah returned to her desk, she decided to make an appointment with her doctor. Keilah couldn't believe how reckless she had been to sleep with Keith unprotected, knowing he was still sleeping with Constance. Just because Keith had trust in Constance didn't mean she had to trust her.

As Norelle finished the last of her paperwork, she checked to see if her manager had put any more appointments for her in Outlook. Relieved to see there was none, Norelle decided to send a text message to Tariq making sure he met her later that day. She knew this thing between the two of them had to be broken off. Raymond was not only everything she needed but also all that she wanted; she knew that now more than ever.

Norelle couldn't figure out any logical reason why she was even sneaking around with Tariq. Glancing at the picture of her, Raymond and LT, she couldn't help but think of her dad. Her mother's deceit had robbed them both of the love of their lives. Raymond was the only man who made her feel like the princess that her dad knew she was. Norelle wasn't going to do the same thing her mother did. It was going to end once and for all.

Norelle rose out of her seat to see that the waiting area was virtually empty. Deciding she would take an early lunch, she dialed Keilah then hung up the phone, changing her mind. Norelle knew

Keilah was probably still reeling over what happened with Keith and needed some space. Keilah didn't want to listen to her so she stepped back and did nothing. Knowing Keilah was too stubborn for her own good, Norelle decided now was the time to take matters into her own hands. She was going to do something.

Logging on to the web, Norelle decided to look up the DC office of Rosenberg Klein & Rouse law firm. After confirming André was in the office, Norelle printed the directions off Map Quest and left early for the day. This madness between Keilah and André was going to end too. Keilah would probably kill her but she'd thank her later, Norelle hoped.

Norelle made it to DC in record time. It was almost three-thirty so hopefully André hadn't left yet. Even if André had, Norelle had already Googgled him and was prepared to go to his house, if needed.

As Norelle pulled onto K Street she looked at the street signs and saw she was headed Northeast and should be going Northwest on K Street. André's office couldn't be anymore than about six or seven blocks away. As Norelle stopped at the light, she spots Linc. Norelle hadn't seen him since Keilah and André broke up. The way it looked, Linc hadn't changed. As usual, he was up in some woman's face. Before she could honk her horn, Linc turned away and pulled the woman closer in to him. *Yeah, some things never change*, Norelle laughed, as she drove threw the light.

Norelle waited in the receptionist area, not knowing what André's reaction. They had been cool, but that was years ago and she was getting into his business and men didn't like that, but it was too late now. Phew, her stomach started to bubble over. If this didn't work, she might lose her friend forever. If it worked, she'd gain a brother-in-law.

When André came out to greet her, Norelle was relieved to see him smiling. He looked happy to see her. *Good sign*, Norelle thought. Upon entering André's office, the first thing Norelle noticed was

Keilah's painting hanging on the wall. *Excellent sign*, Norelle thought.
"Nice painting, Dré."

André smiled and nodded in agreement.

"Come here girl and give me a hug. How have you been? How is LT? He's a big boy now, isn't he? More importantly, what brings you here? I don't do criminal cases anymore." André laughed to assure Norelle he was joking.

Norelle looked at his hand to see he hadn't done it yet, cool.

"Whatever, Dré, you will never let me live down that melee I had with Tariq. LT is twelve years old now. I have chilled out, motherhood and marriage will do that."

André looked surprised.

"You and Tariq got married?"

Norelle shot André a funny look.

"André please, you know better. Tariq is not the marrying type. However, I hear you are. When is the big day?"

André leaned back in his chair. He knew Norelle wasn't just stopping through.

"December thirty-first."

It was already mid–October, which meant the wedding was less than two months away, Norelle thought. How would she segue to what she really wanted to say? It was no way around it. Norelle and André both knew why she was there.

"So soon, what's the rush?"

André never knew Keilah to send her friends to talk for her.

"Norelle, what are you doing? Come out with it."

Norelle closed the office door. Taking a deep breath, she walked over to André's desk and plopped down in front of him.

"You know you're still in love with Keilah why are you doing this? You don't have to marry this new chick, you know."

Loosening his tie, André rose from his chair, turning to look out of the window. He couldn't believe that Norelle was trying to have this type of conversation with him.

"Norelle you and I are cool. I always liked you but I think you need to change the subject before I say something I really don't want to say to you. You are so beyond your boundaries that it isn't even funny."

Jumping off André's desk, Norelle joined him at the window. She knew she hit a nerve; André couldn't even look at her.

"I really don't care if you get mad at me. Cuss me out for all I care but you know, if nothing else, that you and Keilah have unresolved issues. Before you walk down that aisle Dré, you two need to talk. I know what I am talking about."

Norelle backed up when André turned toward her, revealing icy gray eyes flaming full of emotion, which emotion she wasn't sure of.

"Since Keilah tells you everything, I am sure you know that I tried that. I have called her and she won't call me back. I even went to her house and she wouldn't answer the door. So what are you saying, Norelle?"

Norelle could see it wasn't anger, as she thought at first; it was hurt.

"What I am saying is the same thing I have been telling her, y'all need to talk."

André looked at his watch. "Look Norelle, I am expecting someone so I have to catch you later."

Walking toward the door, Norelle felt like she hadn't said enough. Before she could speak, André cut her off.

"Why couldn't Keilah talk to me herself? Why did she have to send you?"

Opening the door, Norelle looked at André smugly. "The same reason you sent that text message."

Before André could respond, Alisha walked up and planted a long wet kiss on his lips.

Norelle couldn't believe it. *This must be her.*

"Well, Dré, I suppose by the kiss this lady just laid on you and that gorgeous rock this must be your fiancée, Alisha."

After rushing Norelle out, André explained to Alisha that Norelle was just an old friend and nothing more. Luckily, Alisha didn't press the issue. As they went over the wedding plans, André's thoughts were somewhere else. All he kept trying to figure out was what text message Norelle was talking about. Wait, how did Norelle know that he was marrying Alisha? The way Norelle was, André would have known if the two of them had already met. Keilah couldn't have told Norelle because he never had a chance to tell Keilah himself.

"Alisha, you never found my phone, did you?"

Even though Norelle's little visit to André didn't turn out the way she planned, she was happy. It turned out better than she anticipated. As Norelle tried to remember Linc's full name, she knew she had to track him down fast. Linc had now become a big piece to an even larger puzzle.

Norelle knew Linc was a player, but she never had him down for something like this . No mistake about it, when Norelle saw Alisha slob down André, she knew she was the same girl she had seen Linc with an hour ago. Norelle also knew, by the way they were up on each other, something was up between them.

Merging onto Route 50, it came to Norelle. Lincoln Taylor was Linc's real name. She'd Google him tomorrow. André and Keilah will thank her for this later. Now back to the business at hand, Tariq.

It was almost six o'clock when Norelle reached Baltimore. Raymond had already called and told her he could pick up LT. Everything was in order.

As Norelle pulled up to Tariq's mother's house, she was greeted by a host of little grandkids with uncut hair and sticky faces. She was so glad LT didn't go down there often. Before Norelle could honk the horn, Tariq's mother came outside, sneered at her and yelled for Tariq. Norelle was surprised to see Tariq's mother sliding down the front steps in her house shoes, headed straight for her car. Norelle tips down her shades and speaks. "Hi, Miss Towanda."

Kenda Bell

With a cigarette hanging out of her mouth, Towanda takes her hand and gently glides it across Norelle's car. "This sure is a nice Lexus, Norelle; you sure done real good for yourself since you married that rich husband of yours. Why you still sniffing around my boy, Tariq?"

Norelle fanned the smoke away from her face and shook her head at Towanda. "My husband is not rich. He and I both work and pool our money together. You can get a lot of nice things when you go to work everyday and save some money."

Towanda released a huff. "You always thought you were better than us, you and your snotty mother. That's why you don't bring my grandson down here to see me. He ain't no better than any of my other grandkids. I'm tired of seeing you, when am I going to see my grandson."

Looking past Towanda, Norelle was happy to see Tariq walking down the steps.

Hearing Tariq walking behind her, Towanda leaned inside the car. "You ain't that much if you still sniffing behind him. You ain't no better."

Norelle rolled up the window and unlocked the door for Tariq.

When Tariq slid into the passenger seat, she noticed he was carrying a large greasy bag of food along with a huge brown paper bag full of liquor and two plastic champagne glasses.

Tariq leaned over and gave her a sloppy kiss, saturating half of her face, a third of her hair and missed her whole mouth.

Tariq still kissed like a fourteen-year-old, Norelle thought as she pulled off. What made it worse was his saliva smelled like stale cigarettes and alcohol.

Looking over at Tariq, Norelle realized he wasn't that cute anymore. Back in the day his rich black skin looked like velvet, now it was ashy and rough. What used to be soft jet-black waves were replaced by an uncut matted mess.

What in the hell have I been looking at?

When Tariq grabbed Norelle's hand and placed it in his crotch, to show her his erection, she quickly snatched it back.

"What's wrong baby? I know you been missing it. We're going to our usual spot by the reservoir?"

Norelle smiled nervously and blew him a kiss. "Yeah, T, but we need to talk."

Puzzled, Tariq pulled out a cigarette, "Talk! Norelle when we get together ain't too much talking going on. What you talking about?"

Norelle snatched the cigarette out of Tariq's mouth and tossed it out the window. "I told you no smoking in the car. Damn, T, you act like such a child sometime. You don't respect anything. If you had some shit of your own, you'd understand."

Tariq turned around in the seat and stared at her. "Damn, girl, what's up with you? Why are you bugging? Once we eat some of this Egg Foo Young, and hit that Hypnotic, you'll be all right. Once I hit that right there," he said, nodding down toward her crotch, "you'll be even better."

Norelle rolled her eyes and pulled into the park area near the reservoir.

Daylight was fading, so Norelle knew she had to make it quick. As they sat on the bench, Tariq tried to feed Norelle. She reluctantly took a forkful and stood up. "T, we have to end this thing. It's not right and I can't keep doing this to Raymond. I will always care about you but I don't know what else to say."

Tariq shoved the plastic fork in the Egg Foo Young and reached down for the bottle of Hypnotic.

Norelle looked over at him, waiting for a response.

Instead of speaking, Tariq twisted off the cap, took a swig and passed it to Norelle.

Norelle refused the drink and sat back down on the bench.

"Norelle, that's a bunch of bullshit! You love me; you told me you'd always love me no matter what. Girl, you better drink this drink and give me some." As Tariq clumsily leaned over to kiss her, she jumped up again and walked a few steps away from him.

"Tariq, I was a teenager. I didn't know what I was saying. We are grown now. You may be stuck in the eighties but I'm not, its 2005. I have grown up and you should too."

Taking another swig, Tariq walked over to Norelle and took hold of her. Pressing his pelvis firmly against her, he whispered coolly, "Nori, I was born a grown ass man. You feel that right there? He was full-grown from way back too. Now stop playing and give me what you know I want."

Breaking away, fear pulsated through Norelle as her heartbeat quickened. It seemed like Tariq wasn't hearing anything she was saying. "Tariq, your dick doesn't make you a man. It's more to being a man than screwing. Since you have been back in town, I can count on one hand the number of times you have seen LT. The times you did see him, it was after I gave you some. That is sick. I shouldn't have to sleep with you to encourage you to see your son. This is over. I mean it! Pack those bags up. I'm heading back to the car. If you want a ride I suggest you come on."

As Norelle turned to walk away, Tariq grabbed her from behind. Before she could turn around, he roughly stroked her hair, twining it between his fingers. Having secured a good grip, he callously pulled her back toward the bench, causing her to stumble backwards, almost falling.

"Who do you think you are, Norelle? My mother was always right; you do think you are better than I am. You can't just talk to me like that and walk away. You know how you and me is, Nori. You don't break up with me. I break up with you."

Trembling, Norelle couldn't believe what was going on. "Tariq, please, that was when we were kids. You should have never drunk that Hypnotic; you already had been drinking when I picked you up. Baby, let my hair go, please."

Tariq loosened his grip and touched her face. He smiles then grabbed her by the neck. "Okay, we can break up, but you remember how things use to go back in the day don't you?

"T, come on," she cried. "Please, I don't want to do this. Can we just go?"

Tariq looked around as he unbuckled his pants and shoved her onto the bench.

When Norelle squirmed around, Tariq placed his forearm on her chest. "Nori, you know you gotta give me some before you step. That has always been the rule."

Norelle struggled as Tariq reached in between her legs. "You a little dry. That's new." Tariq rammed his fingers inside her, as Norelle put up a fight. "Nori, you don't need to do that. You don't want to go home bruised up do you? How would you explain that to your husband?"

Chapter 8

"No, it's just the vibe she was giving off. I don't know."
— André

Keilah was relieved when the doctor's office called to say the results of her lab work were fine. Checking her email, Keilah was surprised to see that Norelle hadn't emailed her. Even if Norelle were busy, she would shoot Keilah an email. Besides, she wanted to know how things went with Tariq; she hoped Norelle went through with it. Keilah decided to call Norelle before her phone rung.

"Hey, girl, I was just about to call you. What went down last night with Tariq? You did it, didn't you? Please tell me you did." Keilah was surprised to hear silence on Norelle's end of the line. "Nori, you still there?"

Norelle took a long breath, told Keilah she was picking her up for lunch and hung up.

By noon, Keilah walked out and was surprised to see Norelle already waiting in her car. When Keilah got in the car, she couldn't help but notice something was wrong with Norelle. They drove silently to the restaurant, Keilah decided not to ask anything. By the time they were seated, Keilah couldn't hold back. "Nori, did things go bad with Tariq last night? He didn't trip, did he?"

Norelle looked up from her menu and cried.

Keilah scooted her chair beside Norelle and wrapped her arms around her to console her.

Norelle shook Keilah off and wiped her face. She called the server over and ordered only Iced Tea.

Keilah tilted and gave a fixed stare. She knew something was up; Norelle always ate. "What's going on, Nori?"

After Norelle told her what happened, Keilah couldn't finish her sandwich. "That is rape, Nori! Did you call the police?"

Norelle's face turned to stone. "Yes, I know it is rape but what was I going to say? I would look guilty as sin, Tariq in a park, with Chinese food, Hypnotic and me. Give me a break, K."

Keilah leaned in closer. "But Nori, no matter what, if a man forces a woman to have sex, it's rape."

Norelle sipped the last of her Iced Tea, and looked back at Keilah. "How would you suggest I explain to Raymond why his wife was in the park with her son's father? Plus, Towanda would have no problem telling the police how I had been creeping through there for months."

Keilah handed Norelle a tissue

"And before you ask," she smirked. "No he didn't use a rubber, and yes he came in me. I called my doctor and I am picking up a Plan B on the way home. I think I have seventy-two hours."

Keilah could understand Norelle's logic but then she thought about Raymond. "Nori, I thought you and Raymond were trying for a baby again what if…"

Norelle abruptly cut her off. "What if what? I can't chance that. Are you crazy? Raymond and I can start fresh next month."

Seeing there was no longer a discussion to be had, Keilah called the server and paid the check. "Whatever you decide, Nori, I am here for you."

Norelle pulled out her compact and freshened up her make up. "I have already decided. I am fine."

André was glad to have the day off; it gave him time to catch up on work without distractions. As he sent off his last email, his mind went back to Norelle's visit. What was that all about? Keilah wasn't the type to send her friends to do her dirty work; so why now? He refused to get caught up with that; he and Alisha had their first doctor's appointment.

When André picked Alisha up, he noticed a slight bump and smiled. Kissing her, he touched her stomach. . "Dag, girl, you're gaining wait already."

83

Playfully, Alisha pushed his hand away. "Whatever, I might be having twins. They run in my family you know."

André kissed her again. "I'm just playing; you look cute, baby. You can barely see it."

Waiting in the reception area, André looked at all the pregnant women and wondered what Alisha would look like, as she got bigger. Alisha seemed to look pregnant as soon as she told him, not like Keilah. Keilah's body changed slowly; a little more booty there, a little more...*Damn*, André thought, *why does she keep coming up in my mind*? When the nurse called him back to the examining room, he was thankful for the interruption of his thoughts

When André walked in, he noticed that Alisha had a perplexed look on her face. "What's wrong baby?"

The doctor interjects. "Oh, nothing, Dad. I just told Alisha that based on her last period she is about eight weeks. She should be due around the first week of May. I will need to do a sonogram to get a more accurate date. When I examined Alisha, I told her that she looked f..."

Alisha interrupted. "He told me that everything was fine. No worries."

The doctor looked at Alisha, then at André and closed the chart. "Just schedule a sonogram with the nurse, around the middle of December. After that sonogram, you can better plan your leave time."

Alisha grabbed André by the hand. "Doctor Palmer, can't we wait until January. We are getting married on New Years Eve. All I want to think about is my wedding."

Dr. Palmer jotted a note in Alisha chart. "Whatever you two decide; I hope you haven't already got the dress, at the rate that baby is growing you might have to let it out by December."

When Alisha stopped at the nurses' station, André overhead Alisha making the sonogram appointment for the tenth of January.

Joining Alisha at the nurses' station, André told the nurse to change it to the twenty-sixth of December.

Realizing André was driving to her place, Alisha gently pulled at his ear. "I thought we were going back to your place?"

André pulled up to the curb and unlocked the doors. "I'm a little tired and need to do some things. I'll call you on my way to work in the morning."

Alisha exited the car, trying not to show her uneasiness. "Okay, baby. I love you."

Looking back at Alisha, André responded dryly, as he pulled off. "I love you too."

André merged onto the highway and phoned Chris to tell him he was coming through. He needed to talk to his boy.

Having pulled up to the house, Norelle paused and soaked in her emotions for a few minutes. Taking a cleansing breath, she snatched the images of the night before out of mind, balled them up, along with her lingering emotions, and tossed them in her mental garbage disposal. Once her foot hit the pavement, what happened with Tariq would be behind her. Once she took the Plan B, she would have a clean slate.

As soon as Norelle walked in the house, she was greeted by the smell of Raymond's famous lasagna. LT rushed her with a big hug, while Raymond looked on and grinned. That was what it was all about...family.

Kissing Raymond, Norelle told him she was going to shower and join them as quickly as she could. Skipping upstairs, she knew things would fall back into place. She wouldn't repeat her mother's horrible mistake; her family was going to stay together.

As Norelle ran the shower, she picked out a pair sweats to put on. Reaching for her purse, she heard Raymond say he was going out for garlic bread and wanted to know if she needed gas. Before she could answer, Norelle panicked when she noticed the Plan B prescription was not in her purse. After running downstairs, she realized Raymond had left with her car. LT came into the kitchen and hands Norelle the phone. She didn't even hear it ring. Her panic turned to anger when she heard who was on the phone.

"Nori, I am sorry about what happened last night. I was messed up and you were tripping too. Things went too far and I just want to say…"

Norelle motioned for LT to go into the other room.

"Listen, don't call here ever again. Do you understand me? I hate your trifling ass and I don't want you near my son or me. You got that?"

SLAM!

What in the hell was Tariq thinking, she wondered.

By the time Raymond returned, Norelle had smoked half a pack of cigarettes. She watched him closely, looking for any signs.

Raymond put the bread in the oven, smiled at her and started whistling.

Norelle called LT for dinner; everything was fine. She decided to go to the car later to look for the prescription.

Chris's twins were cute, André thought as he watched them play. Looking over at Chris and Carla, he reconsidered what had entered his mind earlier. He and Alisha would be fine. He was just tripping out. After Carla rounded up the twins, Chris took André to the basement.

"Dré, when you and Alisha get your house make sure she understands the basement is yours. Tell her, she can have any other room in the house but stake your claim on the basement. I'm telling you what I know. This basement has saved me from a lot of arguments."

André laughed and took a seat on the sectional.

"So, Dré, what is going on with you? You getting cold feet again, what happened at the doctor's?"

André leaned back and rubbed his chin. "Man, I can't really say. Alisha just seemed weird. It wasn't what she said so much as how she was acting."

Chris sat down in his recliner and turned on the television. "Weird. Man you haven't seen weird yet. She is pregnant. She is only going to get weirder. If it isn't the crazy times she'll want to eat, it will be the crying that will change to yelling. Get ready for it."

André leaned forward. "No, it's not that. I'm expecting that. It was how Alisha was acting when we spoke with the doctor."

Chris picked up the remote and changed to Sports Center. "Dré, you still haven't said anything. What is it? Is she worried about the baby, is she having complications, what?"

André inhaled and looked at the scores. He didn't even want to say it. "When her doctor started talking about the due date, Alisha got weird. Then the doctor started talking about how she was growing and she got even stranger."

Chris reclined in his chair and stared at André. "What are you trying to say? You not thinking the baby...."

Immediately, André got defensive. "No, it's just the vibe she was giving off. I don't know. You know how things can go down man, a brother got to at least ponder the question."

Chris shook his head. "You are right a lot of brothers get screwed for mistaken identity. But you and Alisha have been together for almost two years. It was bound to happen. You didn't trip with Keilah and you had only known her for a few months."

Still defensive, "I knew Keilah for six months and that situation doesn't have anything to do with this one. They are totally different."

Chris nodded in agreement. "You're right. My bad... I'm just saying she is a sweet girl. In a few months, when you start seeing that little bump, you'll chill out. Trust me."

André looked at Chris, shook off what he was thinking again, and picked up his keys. "I'm out."

Before André left, Chris, he remembered something. "I meant to tell you Linc is back in town. He said he tried to call you but he had your old number. We are supposed to meet sometime next week."

André gave Chris dap. "Yeah, let me know. I'd like to see how Linc is doing. He just got back?"

As Chris turned the porch light off, he shrugged. "No, he's been back for maybe four or five months."

As André drove off, he forgot to ask Chris if he had spoken to Keilah. However, he knew in the back of his mind that he hadn't.

Finishing off her ice cream, Keilah decided she was too tired to venture back out to the kitchen. As she rolled over to search for her remote, Keilah realized she was functionally depressed and had been so for quite a while. The whole break up with Keith was more devastating than she had admitted, even to herself.

She couldn't figure out if she had really loved Keith or had she convinced herself that she did. Had the idea of being alone become such an ugly reality that she had decided to co-op a relationship? Oh, it was too embarrassing for her to think about it. Deciding that nothing helped moments of deep reflection than Ben & Jerry's, Keilah got up and headed for the kitchen. Stopping midway down the hallway, she looked at a painting on the wall. That was when she was in her chalk phase. Keilah laughed to herself. Touching it, Keilah began to cry. It was the last piece of art she had completed in years.

Wiping away the tears, Keilah placed the bowl in the sink and ate the ice cream straight from the pint. Returning to her bedroom, she stumbled on her sketchbook. Reaching down to pick it up, pages fell out. Each picture was half finished. Gathering the sheets of paper, Keilah climbed in her bed and laid out each one.

The first one she looked at was one of Keith. She balked at it and balled it up, tossing it to the floor. A few were nature scenes that she chose to set aside for later. The rest of them were half finished faces. The pieces in the picture became clear... it was André.

Norelle knew Raymond was in the basement watching Sports Center and probably dozing off. Quietly walking past the den, Norelle opened the back door and went to the car. After digging around for what felt like hours, Norelle didn't find the pills. *Damn,* she said to herself as she walked back inside the house to see Raymond looking at her strangely.

"Norelle, are you looking for something in the car?"

Try to suppress her nervousness, "Why, did you find something?" Her heart was beating a mile a minute. Its pace quickened when Raymond reached into his pocket.

"Girl, you are a true diva. I found your Mac when I took the car to the gas station; here woman."

Norelle exhaled, taking the compact from Raymond and headed upstairs.

Raymond followed closely behind, slapping her on her butt. "Come on girl, its baby making time."

As Raymond climbed on top of her, she tried not to flinch. *It was not Tariq, it was Raymond* she kept whispering to herself as Raymond entered her. She tried to move but she felt numb, and she couldn't take it anymore. She released a fake moan and grabbed tightly to Raymond's back.

As Raymond kissed her face, he tasted her salty tear. "Damn, Nori, it was good for me too."

Chapter 9

"Thinking back on that night, as she tucked the covers tightly around her, Keilah knew she had fallen right into Alisha's plan."
— Keilah

André was looking forward to seeing Linc. He hadn't seen him since he moved to Atlanta to expand his cell phone business. Walking into Club Deuce brought back a lot of memories. André, Linc and Chris partied hard up in there back in the day. It was funny how Club Deuce had decided to grow up too. The bass booming speakers and college night had been replaced with a live band and poetry nights. The exposed brick was actually exposed and not covered by posters. Seeing Linc and Chris already at the table, André couldn't help but notice how they were all getting older.

Linc jumped up and slapped André on the stomach. "Hey man. What happen to that six-pack? You're getting fat with your baby momma."

André gave Linc a hug and sat down. Over a pitcher of beer, they reminisced about old times.

"So Linc, you're talking about my six-pack, it looks like you've lost that keg in Atlanta. I thought southern women cooked."

Chris laughed and agreed. "Yeah man, you really took off that weight."

Linc nodded. "Yeah man I let go of meat…all kinds. I gotta stay healthy. You know."

Chris pointed to his hair. "What're you dating, some artsy chick? Get a load of this dude's hair, Dré. This use to be Pretty Boy Floyd; never would be seen without a fresh shape up. What's going on, who is it this time?"

Linc ordered another round of beers and checked his phone. "It ain't nobody in particular, you know how I do. But, Dré, on the other hand, he is the Man with the plan. Getting married and got a kid on the way. Is it that chick Keelie you were practically living with before I left? You was so deep in that, I thought that broad had put voodoo on your ass."

Chris took a sip from his beer and looked around.

André took a gulp. "Naw, man, Keilah and I are old news. It's someone else. It's all good though."

Linc, again, looked at his phone and typed a text a message. "Yeah, I guess it is all good. She got your ass on lock. That thang must be good. I don't trust women, well no one except my grandmother. I am not getting married and damn sure don't want no kids. That's out for me. I'm going to get my business to jump off back up here, maybe chill with a cute honey, or two, but that's it. Women got game man. This chick that just text messaged me, she been off the radar for almost a month. Now she need's to see me. I guess the next dude is busy. I ain't crazy, the honey got skills. Like my pops used to say, 'don't turn nothing down, but your collar.'"

André called the server over to bring the check. "Yeah man, I know how you do. I used to think like that too, but we are grown now. I want something for me at home."

Chris agreed. "Yeah, ain't nothing like knowing you got somebody at home."

Linc was looking for his wallet. "Both of you punks are whipped. Hey, one of you got me. I left my wallet in the car."

Chris pulled out some bills. "Sure. Linc, get the next one."

Watching Linc leave out the restaurant, André and Chris looked at each other. Picking up the bones left on the table from the Buffalo wings, Chris looked at André. "So much for that vegetarian kick, Linc acted like he hadn't eaten in days."

André checked his messages. "Yeah I agree. When have you known Linc to go out, anywhere, with his hair uncut?" They both knew Linc wasn't quite right.

"Let's have one more round, Alisha called and said she was going to spend the night at her mom's."

Motioning for another pitcher of beer, Chris moves on to the next topic of discussion. "Now, Dré, tell me again how Norelle came down to your job."

Keilah couldn't believe it. She had her easel out and was about to paint. What better place to work out her issues than on the canvas. Whether she liked it or not, pain was her muse. When she left the art store, she decided she would not try to paint anything in particular. Whatever came to her, she would just paint. It was Friday night and she didn't have to get up for work the next morning. She was committed to paint until she got tired. With a paintbrush in one hand and a glass of merlot in the other, Keilah was ready to go. Then there was a knock at the door. When she opened the door, she was surprised to see her sister Carlita. *When did she get back home?*

Linc was glad his little honey had called him back. It had been a while since he saw her last. He knew she couldn't cut him off. He knew if he kept calling her enough she'd breakdown.

As Linc parked in front of her place, he checked himself in the mirror. Pulling his brush out, he had to agree that he was in need of a haircut. Before Linc could get out of the car, he saw his honey walking toward the car. As she entered the car, he tried to give her a kiss, but she pushed his face away.

"Look, Lincoln, you have to stop calling me. It is over. And please stop driving past my place. I am serious. We had our fun and its over."

Linc smiled and popped a Tic Tac in his mouth. "Alisha, come on now. You know we vibed, that thing was good. I knew you had a man when I picked you up at Rumors. By the time you got in my bed, you forgot you had a man. Just gimme a little something,

something, you know you want some too. That's why you kept coming back. You know I can keep this thing going for hours."

Looking disgusted, Alisha rolled her eyes. "I don't know what I was looking at. You are a broke ass nigga that has some nice clothes. And your longevity is due to that glass pipe I found in your bathroom. Leave me alone. I'm serious."

Trying to push off Lincoln's kisses, Alisha scratched his face with her ring.

After touching the scar on his face, Lincoln grabbed her hand, looked at the ring and broke out into laughter. "See this is the very shit I was just telling my boy about…women ain't shit. You are barely a month off my Johnson and you got poor dude's ring on your damn finger. Man, forget it. Just get out of my car."

Alisha was insulted but didn't care; she hoped she pissed him off enough to leave her alone.

As Alisha slammed the car door, she froze in her tracks when the car window rolled down.

"If I ever see you two together, I am gonna tell him what you about. I hate seeing my brothers going out like that."

Alisha turned around and watched Linc drive off. She decided she would try to move in with André as soon as possible. She couldn't be sure of what Linc was capable of. Looking down at her stomach, Alisha was glad he hadn't noticed her bump.

Carlita had finally fallen asleep. Keilah couldn't believe her sister had been going through all that in Richmond. After Carlita left Atlanta, Keilah hoped she would get back on track with college and leave that dancing shit alone. But like Keilah, Carlita had seen enough of their parents and took her spin at how to utilize the lessons she had learned.

However, unlike Keilah, who wore her heart on her sleeve, Carlita tied her heartstrings around the fattest wallet. Carlita's theory was that men don't love a good woman, they love a bad one…the bitchier the better. They don't stay around, but if you pick them right they'll leave you with nice gifts. Though Keilah thought Carlita's theory was warped, it made sense in a twisted way. How could she argue with her? Daddy never stayed around, but he left nice gifts and sadly what other example could she give to her sister. It wasn't like she had any great love stories to share.

Norelle was able to get another prescription. As she closed the bathroom door behind her, she exhaled; her period was due in a few days so it shouldn't look strange to Raymond. As she opened the bottle, LT ran in the bathroom bumping into Norelle's arm. She cursed as she watched the pills spill down the toilet.

"LT! I told you about busting in the bathroom on me, damn!"

LT looked up at her, with apologetic eyes. "I'm sorry, mommy, I have to really go."

Putting the now empty envelope in her robe pocket, Norelle couldn't believe all the pills went down the toilet. It was Friday night and the doctor's office was closed on Saturday. The doctor's office gave her a hard time when she asked for a second refill. Ripping the envelope up, Norelle could only pray that her period came on time. At that moment, Norelle felt something that was familiar. *Thank God,* she whispered to herself. She had started spotting.

André knew Chris was on point. Norelle wouldn't just stop through. As André thought more on it, he knew Keilah probably didn't know Norelle came through. He just didn't feel like any games, especially with Keilah, which wasn't how they rolled. If Keilah wanted to talk, she'd call him. When Keilah didn't want to talk, she didn't. Of course, there was the question of whether or not Keilah knew about Alisha. She must know; how else would Norelle know. André was thinking the unthinkable.

Alisha knew how he was and if she called Keilah, she would know how pissed he would be. *No,* André thought to himself, *Alisha wouldn't do anything like that; she knew better.* Alisha set a lot of things in motion when she broke the single man's cardinal rule that night two years ago; don't touch a man's phone.

Back then, André had started with Rosenberg, Klein & Rouse in their Baltimore office and he was still in a financial deficit so most nights he ate at Keilah's. That night André had other plans.

As usual, André stopped past Keilah's but knew he had to make a good excuse to leave early. Leaving his laptop in the car, André decided to run in, sit for a minute and then say he had a lot of paperwork to do.

As soon as André walked in, he felt Keilah's eyes reading him. For some uncanny reason, Keilah always had her third eye at work, never saying anything.

Kissing André, Keilah took his suit jacket off and laid it on the chair. "Dré, I fixed some spaghetti tonight. I put some Italian sausage in it. Here take a taste."

André took a taste and patted Keilah on the back. "Uhmm, taste good but I'm not that hungry tonight. I had a late lunch."

Keilah looked over the stove and stared at André. "Well, ok. I'll just put some up for you later. I know you'll get up in the middle of the night hungry. Go ahead and change, I think you have some shorts in the back."

André wondered why Keilah was pushing him to answer a question she didn't ask. "Look, K, I came through to see you. I have a lot of work to do tonight so I am going to go home. Plus I have to run back to the office, I left my laptop on my desk."

Keilah stirred the pot as the sauce began to boil.

"Okay."

André looked over at her and recognized the silent inquisition she was conducting with her eyes.

"Come on, K, don't do this. I am over here every night. I can't go home one night out the week. Why are you tripping on me?"

Keilah turned down the flame under the sauce, placing the top over it. "I'm not tripping, I said ok. Just call me later."

André knew it wasn't that easy. Why was Keilah trying to make him feel guilty? What if he did just want to go home, what was the problem?

Grabbing his suit jacket, André walked toward the front door. "You know what K, you are a trip. Why are you trying to make me feel guilty? I can't deal with you if you are going to get an attitude when I need some time to myself. You know this new job is a lot of pressure for me especially since your mother hooked me up with the position. Don't start getting selfish."

The sauce boiled over and splattered onto her arm. Keilah flinched, quickly immersing her arm under the cold running water.

"Dré, if you feel guilty that's on you. I haven't said anything to you. I said Okay, what more do you want. You don't have to defend your case. Go home. Do what you do."

"Do what I do? I knew you had an attitude. I am out of here. Maybe tomorrow you'll be back to your old self." André stormed out, slamming the door behind.

As André pulled up to his condo, he knew now, like he knew back then, that Keilah knew what was going on. Even though Keilah had never spent a day in law school, she was able to make circumstantial evidence work to her advantage.

Making sure Carlita was asleep; Keilah slipped off the sofa and crept into her bedroom.

Damn, André and Alisha are having a baby.

It kept ringing repeatedly in her head. She really shouldn't be surprised; it wasn't the first time André felt the need to lie to her. She knew it when André picked that argument and left. As she replayed that night over in her head, she couldn't help but wonder how things would have turned out had that night never happened.

Keilah went about her normal evening, minus André, surfed on the web and fell asleep. At about two in the morning, Keilah woke up with a weird feeling. She felt a woman was at André's house. She wasn't going to do a drive by; she didn't have a reason at two o'clock in the morning. She decided to call instead.

As the phone rang, Keilah went over in her head what she could possibly have to say at two in the morning. When she decided to let it go and hang up, the phone finally stopped ringing and Keilah realized that a soft, and all too relaxed, voice of a woman was saying hello. It stunned Keilah so bad she hung up. Resolving that she had dialed the wrong number, Keilah redialed; knowing that there was no way in hell she had dialed the wrong number.

The woman answered again. Keilah couldn't believe she was asking some chick if she could speak to her man.

"Can I speak to André?"

The woman hesitated.

"He's busy...can I take a message?"

Keilah was barely able to catch her breath.

"Sure, tell him that Keilah called. Wait, who is this?"

The woman paused. "Alisha. Why do you want to know?"

Before Keilah could respond, Alisha hung up.

Keilah was wide-awake and furious, heart beating fast. The wave of nausea quickly turned into a wave of rage. She started talking out load.

"Wait just a minute.... I know damn well I did not hear my Kindred CD playing in the background. Oh, hell no!"

Norelle, at the time was Keilah's roommate, jumped out of bed. "Keilah what is going on? Who are you talking to?"

Keilah didn't speak; she continued to tie her scarf around her head.

"K, what in the hell is going on?"

Keilah climbed over her bed and threw on her sweatshirt. "Nori, pass me those jeans hanging behind the door."

Norelle grabbed the jeans and tossed them to Keilah. "K, what is going on dag?"

Keilah brushed by Norelle, almost knocking her to the floor.

"Didn't you buy some trash bags today? You know what, I am not wasting my Hefty bags; I'll use one of those big Value City bags."

Norelle stood outside Keilah's bedroom and listened as Keilah tore up the kitchen up. When Keilah returned, she tried to block her path. Keilah glared at her with a look that could kill, and Norelle graciously moved out of her way. Witnessing André's boxers being stuffed into the Value City bag, Norelle knew the deal.

"You're about to do some waiting to exhale shit? What happened?"

Keilah turned around and revealed tears streaming down her face. "I just called that nigger's house and some heifer answered his phone. I don't even answer his phone, what type of shit is that? This chick is bold, Norelle. I ain't got time for it. I'm taking his shit to his ass *tonight.*"

Norelle disappeared to her room, told Tariq to listen out for LT and rejoined Keilah, wearing a sweat suit and sneakers. Helping Keilah pack the bag, Norelle reevaluated the situation.

"K, you think you need to take this drama to his place this time of the morning? Why don't you chill out and deal with his ass in the morning? Plus you know he skips out here and there. She is probably just a piece of tail."

As Keilah tied a knot in the bag, Norelle backed up allowing Keilah passage toward the living room.

"Hell no I will not! The difference with this right here is that not only did he pick one of the most stupid arguments but also he lied. This chick means a little something to him. And the chick knows it, that's why she was all cute on the phone. No, hell no!"

Keilah went through CDs and stuffed them inside the bag, which by that time, was bursting at the seams.

"Okay, Keilah you know what you're doing. But I am going with you. You don't need to catch a charge."

Noticing a CD in the bag, Norelle reached down and pulled it out.

"No K, this Mary J's *My Life*. That's a classic, wait take that Maxwell out! I listen to that one myself. André is going to have to write those off as a loss."

Keilah reached Catonsville in record time. Norelle stopped Keilah, pulled out her makeup bag and had her to put on lip-gloss. "If André is going to see you insane, which by the way you are right now, you should look good. Oh, please take off that scarf. You look like a runaway slave."

Keilah placed André's bag of belongings on the hood of his car.

Norelle rolled the window down and whispered, "If you're going to do it, do it right. Throw his funky drawers over his car or something."

Taking Norelle's suggestion, Keilah tossed his clothes from the front to the rear. In her excitement, she triggered his alarm.

By the time Keilah got back into the car, André's lights were on and she could see a woman's silhouette following him as he opened the door. As Keilah pulled off, she wished she had at least seen what she looked like.

Thinking back on that night as she tucked the covers tightly around her, Keilah knew she had fallen right into Alisha's plan.

Chapter 10

"Baby is it true, does this mean what I think it means?"
— Raymond

André couldn't believe how quickly Alisha was able to pack. When André agreed it was a good idea for her to move into the condo, he expected her to do it in a month rather than a week.

Seeing Alisha trying to carry a box, André quickly grabbed it from her. "What is wrong with you? You know better."

Alisha smiled and kissed him. "Okay, Daddy. Can you go in the bedroom closet and make sure I got everything? I think I have one box that isn't fully packed."

As Alisha packed the last of her figurines, Linc walked through the door. Running over toward Lincoln, trying to push him out of the door, she looked over her shoulder and whispered, "Lincoln, I told you not come over here anymore. Get out of my place."

Brushing pass Alisha, Linc looked around the almost empty apartment.

"Looks like you're moving. I guess that's why you haven't been able to return my calls."

Grabbing on Lincoln's arm, Alisha attempted a futile effort to pull Lincoln out.

"Wait a minute, Alisha you gained some weight."

Alisha stepped back as Lincoln poked at her belly.

"That's not what I think it is, is it? You're looking a little pregnant."

Alisha looked nervously over her shoulder, hearing André walking from the back of the apartment. Lincoln smiled.

"Oh, your man is here. I'll leave after I holler at him."

Alisha paced back and forth, stopping when she saw André stop dead in his tracks.

"Damn, Linc what are you doing here?"

Lincoln, also known as Linc, smiled, walked up to André and patted him on the back.

"No, I was driving through the neighborhood and saw somebody was moving. I'm looking for a new place so I decided to check it out. Small world isn't."

Alisha felt sick.

André walked over to Alisha and kissed her. "Alisha this is my boy Linc from my Maryland State days. He just came back home; and Linc this is my baby Alisha."

Linc walked over to Alisha and kissed her hand.

"Nice to meet you, Alisha. You can call me Lincoln. Linc is my back in the day name. "What a coincidence. Let me get your number Dré, I forgot to get it last week. We got a lot to talk about."

Alisha ran to the bathroom and vomited.

While André programmed his number into Lincoln's phone, Lincoln looked around the apartment.

"She definitely is pregnant, how far is she?"

André handed the phone back to Lincoln, "I guess by now, a little over two months."

Lincoln turned his back to André, hiding his smirk. "She's only two months, most women don't start showing until like what, three or four months. That must be a big baby."

André looked toward the back of the apartment and then back at Lincoln.

"It was good seeing you man. I'll check you in a few days or so. You know you gotta come to the bachelor party."

Lincoln walked toward the door and stopped.

"You think I could get this crib. Do they already have a renter?"

André rubbed his chin. "She actually has about two months left on the lease. We were going to eat the cost."

Lincoln walked through the doorway. "Ask your girl if she

would sublet it to me. I'm good for it. Call me and tell me what she said. Later."

André checked on Alisha in the bathroom, where she sat on the floor in a daze.

"Baby, are you ok. Is the baby making you sick?"

Alisha wiped her face and laid her head in his chest. What are the chances? Of all the men between Maryland and Northern Virginia, how did she manage to sleep with André's college buddy?

Lifting Alisha's face up, André brushed her hair back. "I got some news for you that may make you feel better. Linc, I meant Lincoln, is willing to sublet the place. That way, you don't have to break your lease."

Alisha couldn't say a word.

Walking through CVS, Keilah thought how happy she was to hear that Norelle had gotten her period. Maybe now she and Raymond can have a fresh start.

Checking her basket, Keilah saw she had everything on her list. Then she smiled to herself, as she rushed to the back of the store... batteries had become as necessary as bread and milk. *A single woman has to do, what a single woman has to do*, Keilah laughed to herself. As she returned to the check out stand, her cell phone rung.

"Hey, Nori what's good?"

Norelle spoke quickly. "Where are you? Can I meet you at your place?"

Recognizing the urgency in Nori's voice, Keilah said, "I'm at CVS. I can be back to my place in about 20 minutes. What's up?"

Norelle inhaled deeply. "Can you pick me up an EPT and make it ten minutes?"

Before Keilah paid, she pointed to an EPT behind the counter. "Sure I can get you one but I don't understand. Didn't you get your period last week? It's too soon to take a test isn't it? "

Norelle let out a tired sound of exasperation. "It started then is stopped, began again then changed colors and stopped. Now my breasts are swollen and I have an ongoing headache that I can't shake. I'm scared Keilah."

Keilah paid for her things, hopped in the car and dashed home. As Keilah turned the corner, her cell phone rings and it's her sister Carlita.

"Hey baby sis. How are you? Is everything ok?"

Carlita had an upbeat tone in her voice. "Yes everything is fine. I made it back to Richmond just fine. I might need to get rid of this car and move further north."

Keilah sighed; she was not going to deal with Carlita's drama, no way.

"K, I hear you getting all quiet, I am not going to try to stay with you. I'll go to Momma's. I want to get a regular thing going, I am serious this time."

Keilah reached her house and parked the car. "Whatever. Just stay out of trouble. I thought you were into that dude you were with down in the ATL? You still never told me why you left."

Carlita laughed. "That negro had some serious issues; issues I'd rather not discuss. I was like hell no. Look, let me call you back; I am about to go get my nails done. I love you."

If it wasn't one thing, it was another, Keilah thought as she saw Norelle pulling up behind her. Can somebody not have drama?

As soon as they entered the apartment, Norelle pulled the test out of the bag and ran into the bathroom.

While Keilah put her things away, she tried to listen to any sound that might let her know what was going on in the bathroom. Not being able to wait any longer, Keilah approached the bathroom. Before her fist hit the door, Norelle opened the door.

Norelle handed the test to Keilah and pulled her pack of cigarettes from her pocket. Taking one cigarette out of the pack,

Norelle slowly placed it to her lips and crushed the pack, tossing it in the trashcan. "It's positive Keilah, I'm pregnant."

Keilah followed Norelle back into the living room and sat with her on the sofa. Norelle sat in a daze, letting the cigarette burn to the filter.

"Nori, everything is going to be alright. You have to believe that. That is Raymond's baby; I feel it in my gut. It's too soon to be Tariq's, plus you said, you and Tariq used condoms every other time, so don't worry."

Norelle smashed the cigarette butt into the ashtray.

"Condoms are not a hundred percent, Keilah. It's just that Raymond and I had been trying for so long. Why when I start messing with Tariq, I all of a sudden turn up pregnant?"

Keilah hugged Norelle and wiped her tears away. "What you are going to do is take this test home to your husband and make his day. You have to have faith."

Norelle gathered her composure. "Yeah…but for me faith is expensive. Okay, you are right, this is our new beginning." After touching up her make up, Norelle grabbed the test, puts it in her purse and left.

While Norelle drove home, she noticed that her police friend had sent her a text message. After Norelle returned the phone call, she pulled over and jotted the information down in her day planner. Yes, today is about fresh starts for everyone, Norelle declared. "K, I am about to get your old man back." Norelle would do a coincidental drive through Mr. Lincoln Taylor's neighborhood tomorrow. She was going to get to the truth about Lincoln and Alisha.

Alisha was glad André had brought her back to the condo to lie down. She truly felt sick to the bottom of her stomach. What was Lincoln going to tell André? How was she going to do damage control with this situation? As Alisha rolled over to try and nap, she heard her cell phone ring. *Damn, it was him.*

"What do you want Lincoln?"

Alisha could hear blowing and coughing from the other side of the phone.

"Alisha, you need to be nice to me, I could have blown you wide open to André. Actually, you owe me. And you know how you're going to pay me back. You are going to tell André that I can sublet your place and you'll even let me keep some of your furniture."

Alisha sat up in the bed. "What, are you crazy? You'll probably sell all my stuff. No."

Lincoln laughed. "You really don't have a leg to stand on. You are engaged to my homeboy and you are pregnant. Now I didn't want to tell you, but you look a little big for what...two months? Now I know you don't even want to go there. So you are going to do exactly what I said. And to let me know you're really grateful, you are going to pay the rent."

Anxiety began to slowly rumble and bubble inside of Alisha. "We are planning a wedding, how I am going to explain why that amount of money is still being spent."

Lincoln spoke lowly. "You are crafty, you'll figure out something. I'm sure it will be easier than explaining you have been cheating on your fiancée with his buddy and you know what question would come next; I know you don't want deal with either situation."

"Fuck you!"

"Haven't you seen Maury? The right dude is always the wrong dude."

Norelle was nervous, yet excited. She walked in the house and ran upstairs to the bathroom. She couldn't let Raymond know she took the test at Keilah's. After Norelle flushed the toilet, she called Raymond upstairs. As soon as Raymond reached the top of the stairs, she handed him the test result. Raymond wrapped his arms around Norelle tightly and started crying.

"Baby is it true, does this mean what I think it means?"

Norelle nodded and started crying to, she was so happy. She could finally give Raymond what he wanted.

Picking Norelle up, Raymond lets out a yell and kissed Norelle. "I knew that doctor was wrong. I haven't ever been much of a praying man but I did it anyway. My mother told me to pray everyday and I did. We're going to church Sunday."

Norelle is confused. "What do you mean, you knew the doctor was wrong?"

Raymond placed her back on her feet, taking her hands in his. "I didn't want to tell you, but I had been seeing a doctor. He told me some bull about my sperm count being low, but he was wrong."

Norelle couldn't say a word.

Raymond pulled her down to kneel with him. As Raymond prayed, Norelle was saying a prayer of her own.

Chapter 11

"Did you ask him if he forgave you for killing him?"
— *Norelle*

Finally, Norelle thought as she saw Lincoln emerge from the address her friend, the police officer, had given her. Adjusting her rearview mirror, she spotted him dragging a trash bag to a black Benz parked in the driveway. *Must be on the move,* she thought, as she touched up her makeup. No sooner than she was about to get out of her car and perform her damsel in distress bit, a white sports coupe pulled up. It was Alisha.

With Lincoln and Alisha quickly going in the house, Norelle raised the hood of her car and got her phone ready. She could finally use her camera phone. Plan A was now Plan B.

After almost twenty minutes, Lincoln and Alisha emerged from the house and stood in front of his car.

Snap, went Norelle's camera phone.

Alisha handed him something in his hand.

Snap!

Lincoln grabbed Alisha by the waist. Alisha shrugged him off and got in her car. As Alisha drove past, Norelle was able to snap a picture of her license plate. Now it's back to Plan A—Damsel in Distress. She knew Lincoln couldn't resist a bent over apple bottom. Lincoln was headed her way.

"Excuse me, Miss, you need some help?"

Norelle smiled as she revealed herself.

"Actually I do, wait...Linc? Get out of here, how have you been?"

Lincoln stepped back and grinned.

"Yeah, it is. I go by the name my momma gave me now, Lincoln. Damn Norelle, you still look good. What are you doing over here? Do you live nearby?"

Norelle leaned back on the passenger side door and returned

the smile, as she slyly adjusted her top. "No, I just finished visiting a friend of mine and my car started making a funny noise."

Lincoln scratched his head and walked over to the lifted hood. "I'm not a mechanic but I'll look at it for you. I see how you're driving so you must not be doing too bad."

Norelle lightly pressed against Lincoln's back and placed her arm on his shoulder. "I'm doing okay for myself, but what's up with you? Last I heard, you were headed to Atlanta to expand your cell phone business. What brings you back to Maryland; family, girlfriend... hmm?"

Lincoln lifted his head from under the hood and looked at Norelle strangely.

"Naw, I just wanted to comeback home, regroup and do some things. Why you want to know?"

Norelle sensed tension and backed up. Hoping to distract him, she bent over the hood and glanced back at him. "Linc, I mean Lincoln, I wasn't trying to get in your business. I was just curious. Chris is married and André just got engaged so I figured you were next in line."

Lincoln gave Norelle a confused look. "Oh, really? No not me."

"Oh, okay. Well have you seen André and his fiancée Alisha? She's really a cutie, about my complexion, my height, real leggy?"

Norelle paused to check for a response from Linc.

Putting on a poker face, Lincoln closed the hood, wondering what was really going on.

"Yeah, as a matter of fact I met her the other day with André. Why? Are you fishing for your girlfriend?"

Norelle tried to hide the puzzled look that flashed across her face. "No, I am not fishing for Keilah. I was just wondering since you haven't been back that long; have you? When did you come back two or three months ago?"

I'll be damn; I think Norelle knows.

"Yeah, I guess. Why don't you try starting up your car?"
Dag, I messed up. He is shutting down. "Lincoln did I say something wrong?"

Lincoln wiped away small beads of sweat collecting along his brow, and opened the driver side door. "Naw, course not. Start your car up."

Norelle realized Lincoln was not going to give up any information. She knew Alisha was the girl she saw Lincoln with, why was he lying.

"Wow, look at that! I don't hear a thing now! What did you do Lincoln?"

Lincoln knew Norelle had just run game on him. "I didn't do anything but close the hood."

Norelle knew she needed another opportunity to get to the truth about Lincoln and Alisha; she had to find out what he was hiding.

"Hey Lincoln, give me your number, maybe we can have lunch one day soon."

Lincoln walks over to the driver's side. "You're really going for it. Okay, give me your number and let me program it in mine."

Lincoln walked slowly, turning around every five seconds until Norelle's car was no longer in sight, before heading for his car.

Jumping into his Benz, Lincoln was glad Norelle hadn't seen him when he got in it. *Hell, it may be jacked up but it's still a Mercedes*, Lincoln thought.

Turning the corner, Lincoln cringed as the CV axle grinded. Looking out on the neighborhood, he got angry. He had made it out and now here he was back at thirty, a failure.

The cell phone industry had saturated too quickly. By the time the big boys went prepaid, nobody wanted Lincoln's Brother2Brother cell phones. As the wholesaling of phone lines became more expensive, Lincoln realized he couldn't keep up financially due in part to the woman that captured his heart, before breaking it. The first time Lincoln decided to fall in love, cupid kicked him square up the ass.

His sweet Caramel, as he liked to call her, was the finest woman Lincoln had ever snatched up. Caramel had a perfect brick house body that would put Buffie the Body to shame, with a pretty face to match. She did all the right things, at all the right times. Hot catfish and collard greens, with baked macaroni and cheese, in the middle of the week was never an issue for Caramel. Sexy lingerie and lots of tricks were always waiting for Lincoln, no matter what time of day or night. In the back of his player mind, Lincoln knew his Carmel was too damn sweet to be real but like most players, Lincoln couldn't conceive getting played. Plus, who falls in love with a stripper anyway? By the time Lincoln realized what was going on, his checking account was overdrawn, inventory was missing and ladylove was entertaining every baller that came through Atlanta. Lincoln still couldn't believe he trusted her with his house, and his money, considering the way his mother flipped dudes when he was a kid. He knew he should have known better but by the time he realized she wasn't as young and inexperienced as he thought, he had been tied and whipped by sweet Caramel, it was too late. Love made the smartest man dumb.

As Lincoln pulled to the corner and dug in his pocket, he was starting to accept how even dumber he had become. By the time he pulled in the nearby back alley, Lincoln pulled out his lighter and lit his little homey up. As he took his first pull, he could swear he saw his mother. Laughing to his self, Lincoln knew she was still in the Looney bin. Once she got too old and fat to flip dudes, she got some doctor to say she was crazy. She wasn't crazy as Lincoln remembered; she was on dope. As Lincoln puffed again, his mind dredged up a not so easily forgotten moment when he was back at Maryland State. He and André cruised down Baltimore Street late one Saturday night and drove up on his past.

Lincoln and André liked to pull up on prostitutes and strippers walking the strip and mess with them, as if they were going to pick them up. André liked to pick the ugliest and torn up one; well that night he did.

"Look at her ass Linc, she leaning over and slobbering... damn!"

As the woman got closer to the car, Lincoln tried to pull off but those familiar eyes some how paralyzed him.

"Lincoln baby what you doing down here?"

As Lincoln pulled off, all he heard was André's laughter.

By the time they returned to the dorm, Chris and the rest of the floor knew the story of Linc having had a Baltimore street trick. Chris just kept asking him why he was creeping down to Baltimore Street when there were free freaks on campus.

As Lincoln realized his little homey was empty, he got angry all over again. Why had he forgiven them for that shit back then? Sure, they didn't know, but they didn't care to know. They just assumed his grandmother was his mother, they knew she was too damn old to be his mother. Both of them were out of town-spoiled mamma's boys, as far as Lincoln could remember. Had André only kept his damn mouth shut? Lincoln was glad to see his man walking up to the car.

"Hey T-man, hit me up."

"Dré, I don't like her."

It had been a long and stressful weekend for André and his sister Tracy wasn't trying to make it any better.

"Tracy, you liked Alisha last year, what's different this year?"

Tracy peeked out the kitchen to make sure Alisha and their mother hadn't come back yet. "No, I dealt with her last year. She was just your girlfriend then. Now this fiancée stuff, I don't know about all that."

André looked at his coffee cup and then at Tracy. She never

111

liked any woman André dated. Ever since they were kids, she gave each one a hard way to go. André thought she was jealous since they had been so close. Now she was really on it.

"Tracy, Alisha is wonderful. I have no complaints about her. It was going to happen anyway; it was just a matter of time."

Tracy gave him a look that told him a little more information on what she was really thinking.

"Come on Tracy, I was already thinking about marrying her before she got pregnant. Give me more credit than that. I know what you're trying to imply and that isn't what happened."

Tracy refilled her coffee cup. "I didn't say anything, you did."

André took the pot from Tracy and filled his cup.

Tracy added sugar to André's coffee. "Look André, all I am saying is that you didn't even mention it to me. You tell me everything, and this you just sprung on me. I am your sister so I am going to say the things you may not want to hear but need to."

Taking a sip from her cup, Tracy quickly changed the combination of words that were jumbled in her mind. . "Dré, Alisha is cute and bubbly. She's nice but to be honest too nice for me. No one has a stress free relationship. Every couple has drama, and from what you tell me, she's damn near perfect. That's just not normal."

André laughed. "That's all you got Tracy. I never said Alisha was perfect, just perfect for me. Not every woman is a ball crusher like you. She has her stuff like most women but all in all she's it."

"Whatever, Dré, she just perfected her game. I can't put my finger on it but something is up with her."

André couldn't believe Tracy was coming hard like she was.

"Tracy you are really starting to piss me off. You think I am stupid or something. I am not going to be like your father and I am damn sure not going to have a situation like you and Terrence. Alisha and I are not going to have child support hearings every other year, me seeing my kid twice a month, no not me. I know all I need to know about Alisha. I love her. I am a grown ass man and I didn't come here for your permission. If momma doesn't have a problem with it, you shouldn't either."

Tracy sat her coffee cup in the sink. "Momma doesn't count, she likes everybody."

At that moment, Alisha and André's mother walked into the house. Coming into the kitchen, Alisha flashed Tracy an ingenuous grin as she hugged André.

I don't like you either.

"Mrs. Davidson, thanks for getting these baby things. Wait until you see them, André. They are so cute."

"Alisha, I told you to call me Margaret. You are a part of this family now. Y'all want some lunch before you get on the road?"

André walked over to his mother and kissed her on the cheek. "I'm ok but Alisha may be hungry. She seems to eat every ten minutes."

Margaret smacked André on the butt.

"You leave her alone. She needs to eat, that's a big baby in there, just look at her."

Tracy looked on with a smirk. "Yeah."

As André walked out of the room, Margaret grabbed the phone off the wall. "Dré, your father asked you to call him before you left. He said he wanted to talk with you one more time before you went back."

André took the phone and walked into the living room. Putting on an act for his mother, he quickly dialed the time and hung up. As far as he was concerned, he and his father had nothing to discuss. He indulged him on his visit because of his mother.

When Keilah opened her mother's door, she was disappointed to see her father sitting in the living room reading the Sunday paper. Last time she checked, he didn't live there.

"Hey baby girl. What brings you over here on a Sunday afternoon?"

Keilah gave him a weak wave and looked around the house. "I was going to ask you the same thing, Carl. Where's mommy?"

Carl folded the paper and glared over at his daughter.

"Girl, I done told you about calling me by my first name. I am not taking that from you. I am your father and you better respect me. I did a lot for you and your sister. I even help pay for that degree that you finally started using almost five years after you graduated. Don't start that mess with me."

Upon saying that, Carl returned his attention to the paper as Keilah took her purse off her shoulder and sat down.

"Okay, *Dad*. You are right; excuse me. I should respect you. You helped send me to school and you made sure mommy kept the house going. I should respect you, you are right, but I don't!"

Carl threw the paper to the floor. "Girl, have you lost your mind? Let me tell you one…."

"No, Dad! Let me tell you a few things. I am sick and tired of you acting as if you were the model father. You were anything but. Before you left, you beat on mommy. You only stopped while she was pregnant with Carlita and you were playing house with Gigi. Then after she had Carlita, you came back and forth, in and out. You treated my mother, your wife, as if she was the other woman. How in the hell can I respect a man that didn't respect my mother? You didn't even care how your behavior affected your daughters. The reason why Carlita's in the situation she's in now is because of you. She grew up thinking what you did was normal! I began to…"

Suddenly a door slammed.

"Keilah Yvonne Fort that is enough!"

Keilah's mother handed the bags to Carl and dragged Keilah to the den.

"Keilah, what is your problem? How dare you talk to your father like that!"

Keilah turned away, sucking her teeth, "Mommy, how can you defend him after all he has put you through? Was I lying? You know what...forget it. I am leaving. I just came pass to see you, but apparently you are busy."

Keilah's mother tenderly grabbed her by the shoulders. "Keilah there is so much you don't understand. No matter what you think your father did, he is still your father and this is his house."

Keilah started tearing up. "Mommy, why? He hurts you over and over again."

Yvonne wiped away her daughter's tears. "I don't have to explain a thing to you about me and my husband. You don't know what you won't do for love until you do it. Love don't happen over night and it doesn't go away any quicker either. Your father is going through a lot right now. Gigi is sick, she has cancer."

Keilah backed up from her mother. "Gigi has cancer. So what?"

Yvonne gave Keilah a scolding look. "Keilah, I know I raised you better than that. When ever you went over to Gigi's, she treated you real good."

Keilah rubbed her eyes and shook her head in disgust. "I'm supposed to care. No wait, I get it. You are going to play the martyr one last time. Yeah, after Gigi dies you can finally have your husband back and declare yourself the winner of this sick game."

Keilah had not anticipated the hard slap that had crashed and burned across her face. Grabbing her purse, Keilah tore out of the house.

Taking the long way home, Keilah couldn't believe what her mother had said. After all the crap her father and Gigi put them through, Keilah could not comprehend how her mother would remotely care. Keilah knew that in reality, Yvonne didn't care two beans about Gigi, but what ever affected her precious Carl was all that mattered, even at the expense of her children.

When Yvonne used to pack a bag for her and Carlita to visit her father, Keilah always cried and protested. Yvonne would kiss her daughters on the cheek and sent them on their way. As Keilah got older, she realized her mother and Carl were running a game on Gigi. Before long, Gigi figured it out too. Like Yvonne, Gigi bowed down to King Carl but took it out on Keilah and Carlita.

Carlita, being a toddler, didn't really understand what was going on. At twelve years old, Keilah knew the deal. How could her father let Gigi make them sleep on the floor while her kids slept in beds? Why didn't he care that anything Keilah or Carlita left at Gigi's would mysteriously be destroyed? Why when she told her mother that Carlita didn't run into Gigi's cigarette, Yvonne told her she didn't see it right? *Hmmm, because that was the only time she and her so called husband could have the house to themselves, that's why*, Keilah thought, as she unlocked her door. Looking at her message waiting light blinking, Keilah checked her messages.

As Keilah listened to the first one, she was happy to hear that Norelle was spending time with her mother. It wasn't often, so Keilah hoped it would be a good thing. The next message made Keilah angry all over again. How could her mother call her and try to rationalize what went down? How any woman could choose a man over a child, how could any self-respecting woman do that? As the words slid from her mind to her mouth, Keilah's spirit whispered the same question to her.

Norelle didn't plan to stay that long. Visiting with her mother was always strained. Lynette always asked Norelle the same questions that she already knew the answers to. However, on this day, Lynette caught her daughter by surprise.

"Norelle can you take me to see your father?"

Norelle turned from the television and answered, "Yes" before she knew it.

As they rode to the cemetery, Norelle's mother turned the car radio to Heaven 600 and hummed quietly to herself.

"Norelle when was the last time you been to church? You know that boy of yours needs some religion in his life. Plus it would be good for you and Raymond."

Norelle looked at her mother out of the corner of her eye. "Yeah, I guess you know. It did wonders for your family."

Lynette ignored Norelle and continued. "I'm just saying with the new baby and all it would be good. Raymond was so excited when I called. Why didn't you tell me?"

Norelle stopped at the traffic light and turned to look at her mother.

"Ma, we really don't talk so I was going to tell you when I felt like it. You could have cared less when I was pregnant with LT, so why go through that again? You have never been the doting grandmother so why would it be any different now?"

Lynette touched Norelle's hand. "Nori, you were eighteen years old and about to go to college. Of course, I wasn't happy then. Tariq was a bum going nowhere fast. This is different, Nori, you're older and married to a good man."

Norelle took a deep breath as they entered the cemetery.

"Ma how does that sound? So this baby is more legitimate to you because of my marital status. LT is still a part of you. We are here now and I am not going there with you."

As the doors unlocked, Norelle motioned her mother to open her door.

"Norelle you're not coming?"

Norelle shook her head. "Not right now. Go ahead. I'll be up the hill."

Watching her mother kneeling down before her father's grave brought tears to her eyes. Norelle wondered how Lynette could face her husband, even in death. She figured her mother's sanctified makeover helped. *It was funny*, Norelle thought, *when her father*

117

was alive; Lynette was practically dragged to church. As soon as the casket closed, her mother became sanctified, as far as she could gather. Norelle guessed that her mother figured if she went enough and tithed enough that some way God would pardon her for her sins.

Looking at her watch, Norelle was ready to go. Coming to her father's grave was never easy for her. Besides, observing her mother's theatrics made it worse. When she approached her mother, she could see a steady stream of tears running down Lynette's face. As she moved closer, she heard her mother mumbling, leaning lower and lower to the ground.

"Did you ask him if he forgave you for killing him?"

The words struck Lynette like hot daggers. She knew Norelle blamed her for the death of her father but she was never bold enough to say it.

"He forgave me for what I did if that's what you're getting to, Norelle. There are a lot of things you never knew, but since you're grown, I guess I'll tell you."

After Norelle took her mother home, she refused to accept what her mother had told her. As she got closer to Keilah's house, she was determined not to. How could her mother try to tarnish her father's memory so she could make herself look good? When she knocked, Norelle was glad to find Keilah home.

"K, you are not going to believe the lie my mother told me."

Keilah closed the door behind them. "I guess today was Mother's Day."

André was glad they were almost home. Tracy didn't know what she was talking about. His mother hit it on the nose; go with your heart and that was what he was determined to do.

Alisha was startled from napping to see Prince George's County Hospital.

André chuckled and drove a little faster.

"Hey, Dré, why didn't I meet your dad?"

André didn't understand why Alisha was going there, she knew why. "Because you don't need to. Harold has never been a factor in my life and now is no different."

Alisha took André's hand and rested it across her stomach. "Dré, come on now. You have to let go of that thing you have with your father. He's about to be a granddaddy."

André remained silent, turned into the gas station and pumped gas. Alisha knew the issue with his father was a touchy one. Why did she bring it up? André hoped that by the time he got back in the car, she would have moved on. He was mistaken.

"Dré, I know how him not being around hurt you, but come on. From what you told me, he did try to do even after he left. You and Tracy turned out great. Give your dad another chance. Maybe he can be a better grandfather than a father."

André parked the car in front of the condo and popped the trunk. André, still quiet, got out of the car, with Alisha on his heels, started unloading the trunk.

"Dré, come on. Why don't you at least…"

André slammed the trunk. "Alisha, I know your little Mitchellville upbringing makes things look a little rosier but Harold never was much of father and I can damn sure figure how he'd be as a grandfather. He left my mother with two kids to fend for herself. That is not a father and it is not a man. When he left, he took my mother too. She had to work double shifts to keep things going. We hardly saw her. Dropping off Payless shoes and cheap toys is not trying. I do not want to talk about him anymore."

Alisha watched nervously as Andre opened the front door. What had she started and was it too late to stop it?

Keilah decided to listen rather than speak; the subject of Norelle's father was one she treaded lightly.

"K, not only did my mother tell me that my dad called her before he came home that night and forgave her but he also told her some other off the wall mess. Can you believe that it took her all these years to think up a crazy lie like that just to try to make me feel some sympathy for her? Boy I wish I could smoke. Can I have some more cranberry juice?"

Keilah picked up Norelle's glass and walked to the kitchen. It could be true but Keilah chose to keep the idea to herself. Unlike, her dysfunctional parents, Norelle's parents did try to provide some semblance of normalcy.

"Norelle, tell me what she told you again, this time slowly."

Seeing Norelle eyeing her cigarettes, Keilah quickly snatched them up and replaced them with the glass of cranberry juice.

"Well, she told me that when she met my dad he had a girlfriend back in Mississippi and every time my mother saw him at work, she tried to get his attention but he kept brushing her off because of this woman he supposedly had back in Mississippi. Finally, he started taking my mom to lunch and they eventually hooked up. Got that?"

"Come on Nori, continue please."

Norelle took a sip of juice. "Okay, my mother goes on to say that all of a sudden daddy starts coming on real strong so they get serious, next thing she knew they was getting married. Now by the time they were almost a year into the marriage, she finds a letter from this woman saying she had run off with some other guy. My mother claims it was dated at about the same time he proposed to her. So she felt like she was second choice and confronted him about it. My dad got mad and told her to stay out of his stuff. So that was why she did what she did and Daddy forgave her before he died that night. Now can you tell me what *Young and the Restless* episode my mother got that from?"

Keilah didn't know how to respond. She knew Norelle didn't want to hear what she wanted to say so she pleaded the fifth through a clever answer. "Call your grandmother and ask her."

While André was in the shower, Alisha quickly pulled the slip of paper out of her pocket and dialed the number written on it. "Hello, listen I think tomorrow is a bad idea. No, no please you don't understand."

André entered the bedroom just as the person on the other end of the phone hung up. "Alisha, who are you talking to? What about tomorrow?"

Alisha discreetly placed the piece of paper back in her pocket. "I was going to meet my mother after work tomorrow for a fitting but I realized I have a lot of work to do."

André knew it was more to the phone call but he was too tired to deal with it.

By the time Norelle got home, she realized she hadn't talked to Keilah about André's little fiancée and Lincoln. Maybe she should talk to André again. No, she should tell Keilah first. Then, Norelle realized it was too complicated to hit head on. She needed more information, but who was going to give it to her? As she felt queasy, she knew she had enough stuff of her own to keep straight. Checking her phone again, she smiled as she looked at the picture. It was already November and New Year's Eve would be there before she knew it.

Chapter 12

What type of Jerry Springer bull was this?
— Nia

Norelle couldn't believe it when she got the call from the attorney; Tariq had signed the petition. By the time Norelle got home, LT and Raymond had already started dinner.

"Ray! Guess what? Tariq signed the petition. Can you believe it?"

Raymond dropped the spoon on the floor and grabbed Norelle. As he reached out for LT, Norelle and Raymond realize that LT was walking out of the kitchen. "You know what Nori, LT may not be cool about this. We talked about it but that was two years ago."

Norelle sat her purse down on the kitchen counter and walked upstairs to LT's room. Looking in on LT, she realized how big her little boy was. LT was almost as tall as she was and thick like his father. LT also had his father's smooth dark skin and dimples. Thankfully, that was where the similarity ended. He was a straight A student, gave Norelle and Raymond no drama.

As Norelle entered the room, LT looked away from his Xbox, took a breath and continued to play his game.

"LT, I am sorry for bursting in the house like that and not even talking to you. I keep forgetting you're not a little boy anymore. Have you changed your mind since last we spoke on it?"

Pausing the game, LT scooted to the edge of the bed. "No not really. At first when he wasn't around it didn't really matter. He still isn't really around but I know where he is. Now since I have seen him its kind of like weird. It's crazy that he can just write me off. I don't know Ma."

Norelle sat down beside her son and kissed him on the forehead.

"What do you want us to do, LT?"

"I want to talk to him, one last time."

Norelle tightly closed her eyes; the last thing she wanted was to deal with Tariq anymore. More importantly, she didn't want her son hurt anymore. Taking a breath, Norelle said, "Okay."

Keilah was painting and she loved what she saw. Taking a break, she took a sip from her wine glass and smiled at Sashay, her cat. She wasn't in the mood to cook, so she looked for the take-out menus.

"What will it be Sashay, Chinese or pizza?"

Sashay gave Keilah a bored meow and walked away. It was times like this that Keilah felt it the most. Even though the music was playing, the aloneness was so apparent. Besides Sashay, there was no one.

After Norelle moved out, Keilah filled her evenings with the gym, yoga and a book club. After those activities began to bore her, she decided to do an African dance class, followed by belly dancing. No matter how Keilah filled her evenings, she still felt the emptiness as soon as she hit the front door.

There were days when Keilah looked at Norelle's hectic schedule and gave a sigh of relief that it wasn't her but on an evening like this one, Keilah could only wonder if she would be clearing the dinner table or playing a counting game. Would she be preparing a lunch for daycare or fussing because she tripped over yet another toy?

Sitting on the floor, Keilah opened her robe and pulled her nightshirt up just above her waist. As she ran her fingers across the tiny white marks that had begun to stretch even more along the sides of her stomach, tears welled up in her eyes. Keilah would laugh awkwardly when Norelle blamed her son LT for her stretch marks. Looking at her own stretch marks, she wished she had someone to blame.

After putting the wedding dress in her mother's closet, Alisha laid back on her parents' bed. Maybe, she and André could get a house out in Mitchellville like her parents. Better yet maybe they would move to Northern Virginia. The commute might not be that bad. As Alisha amused herself with the possibilities, her sister Nia walked in the room.

"Mom wants to know if you are staying for dinner."

Alisha sat up and stood to her feet. "Hey Nia, let me show you the dress mommy and I picked out. You really have to get your measurements taken; the wedding is almost six weeks away."

As Alisha pulled the wedding dress out of the closet, she noticed Nia's frown. Alisha knew that Nia may have been a little jealous but she could at least try to hide it. Pulling the dress up to her body, Alisha danced and modeled around the room. "Isn't it gorgeous, Nia?"

Nia walked up to Alisha and touched the fabric. "Its pure white, I thought you'd go for an eggshell or beige."

Alisha poked her lips out and waved her hand at Nia, as she placed the plastic bag over the dress.

"You know what Nia, this sibling stuff is so old."

Nia sat on the bed and smirked. "That guy you met at the club that night called here looking for you."

Alisha slammed the closet door and walked over to Nia. "What! How did he get this number? Who got the phone?"

Nia sucked her teeth. "I don't know how he got this number. I got the phone; he said to tell you to call him. It was important."

What did Lincoln want? She had dropped the money order off at the leasing office. Nia sensing Alisha uneasiness, decided to poke at her sister.

"What's up Alisha? Why is he looking for you? Has he seen you yet?"

Alisha glared back at her sister. "What in the hell is that supposed to mean?"

Nia batted her eyes back at her sister. "What? I'm just asking if he saw you lately."

Alisha grabbed her purse and pulled out her cell phone. "Tell Mommy I'm not staying for dinner. Better yet I'll go down stairs and tell her myself."

As Nia watched Alisha walk out the bedroom, she let her mind click away. *No*, Nia thought, *Alisha wouldn't be that stupid*. Nia knew that when Alisha and André had that big argument that night back in the summer, Alisha had wild out in the club and picked that guy up. Nia was never sure if Alisha took him home or not. Nia figured not but maybe she did. "Hell no," Nia whispered to herself.

Alisha pulled into the first gas station she saw. Dialing Lincoln's number, Alisha had to figure out what she was going to do. When Lincoln answered, Alisha didn't hold back

"What is your damn problem calling my parents house? Don't you ever call there again. You reach me by my cell only. I paid the rent, so what's up?"

Lincoln laughed into the phone. "Alisha, I tried to call you on your cell but you didn't return my messages. I need some money, about fifty."

"You need what? I don't have it. I just paid your rent. That's enough. I'm not starting that."

"Well, I suggest you get it. You know what's up. Bring it over to *my place* in an hour. I'd hate to come to your new place and get it from you."

CLICK.

Alisha drove to the nearest ATM and made the withdrawal. How had she gotten sucked into this? There was no way Lincoln was going to stop. As Alisha drove to her old place, she knew she had to get rid of Lincoln. The question was how to accomplish it and still keep her hands clean.

After talking with Raymond, Norelle tried to prepare herself to deal with Tariq, hopefully for one last time. As she touched her belly, Norelle decided to relax and ran her bath water.

Peeking in on LT, contentment came over her face as Raymond played X-box with him. Patting her stomach again, she reassured herself that everything would be all right. Then Norelle's thought turned to Keilah. How would she deal with Norelle's growing stomach? Although there was nothing she could do about it, she knew someone who could. *Damn*, Norelle thought to herself. She knew something was up with that Alisha girl and Lincoln, but what real evidence did she have? It was apparent Alisha was just as clever as she was and would probably explain everything away. Norelle knew André would run her out of his office if she even tried to come at him with all this. Keilah would probably dismiss it and be even more pissed again. As Norelle stepped into the tub, she decided not to call Cheaters that would be too much.

It was after nine o'clock and André was beginning to worry. Alisha should have been home from her parents by now. When André heard the keys in the door, he was relieved. "Baby, where have you been? I was beginning to worry. I've been here since six o'clock."

Alisha tried to shake the frazzled look off her face. "I am ok. I just had to make a few stops. I didn't expect you home until about now."

André picked Alisha up and carried her to the bedroom. "Well, I didn't have court today and an appointment I had this afternoon cancelled so I actually left at a decent hour."

"Really, who was the appointment?"

Glancing over at Alisha, a puzzled look crossed his face. "When did you become interested in my appointments?"

Alisha was quick on her feet. "When I said I would, that's when."

Smiling, André headed for the kitchen while Alisha took a quiet sigh of relief. That would have been one more mess she'd have

126

to correct. What was she thinking? That appointment would have been a total disaster. Hopefully, it won't get rescheduled Alisha thought to herself.

Returning to the kitchen, Alisha was surprised to see André on the balcony, talking on the cell phone. As she approached him, he closed the balcony door.

"Are you sure? I need to think about this. Give me some time and I'll get back to you." André turned his cell phone off and walked back into the house. Alisha didn't utter a word and neither did he.

Standing behind Norelle, Raymond startled her. "Nori you know you wrong being in your girl's business like that. You need to leave it alone."

Norelle placed the phone on the receiver and climbed into bed. "Things are going to work out one way or another. All I want is for Keilah and André to talk, that's all. No matter what happens, those two have to talk."

Reaching over Norelle, Raymond grabbed the remote and joined her in bed. "Whatever, Mother Love."

André tried to work but couldn't. He couldn't understand why Norelle called him. He didn't need any drama. He tried to focus on his work, but couldn't. He knew Norelle was right but he didn't want to deal with all that stuff again. He spent the last two months releasing and Norelle brought it all back. How could André face those accusatory eyes?

The next morning, Alisha was surprised to receive a call from Nia.

"Nia you know I am on the way to work, what's going on? Did you call to apologize for that stank attitude you gave me last night?"

Nia snickered.

"No, I actually called for two reasons. First, I got a bone to pick with you. Why did you sublet your place to André's friend when

I asked you first? Secondly, why didn't you hook a sister up? I know all André's friends are fine."

Alisha tried not to swerve the car off the road. "Look, Nia, André put me on the spot so I agreed, okay. Secondly, you don't want to meet him, he ain't all that."

Nia sighed. "Let me be the judge of that. Don't you still have some stuff over there or some mail to be picked up? Maybe I can just stop through for you. You know what I mean?"

Alisha was glad she had just pulled off the highway. She felt a huge headache coming on. "No! Don't go anywhere near my old place, do you understand me? Leave it alone. He ain't nothing you want. Don't go over there, I am serious!"

Nia was shocked by Alisha's response. "Dag, okay. Calm down. I didn't mean to get you upset. Forget it."

Alisha tried to calm her voice. "No, I am not upset. It would just be rude. I don't know him like that."

Nia speculated all the theatrics were hormones. "Okay, I got you. I'm out"

As Nia disconnected the call, she couldn't shake her curiosity. He probably was cute and Alisha was just blocking. She was going to check this guy out for herself after work. Alisha would just have to be mad.

When Tariq's mother told him Norelle was on the phone, he was surprised. She hadn't spoken to him since the incident and he figured the signed petition would serve as some type of apology.

"How are you doing, Norelle? Did I need to sign something else?"

Norelle cleared her throat. "No, LT wants to talk to you."

Tariq couldn't believe what he was hearing. "Really? What for?"

Norelle released an exasperated breath. "What for? He is your son and he wants to talk to you. You know what, forget it! I knew it was a mistake but LT asked. I would have filed the papers the same day. I'll tell him you left town or something; I am used to making excuses for you."

Tariq held tightly to the phone. "No, Norelle it's not that. I just figured you had done your work on him and he was like whatever."

Norelle tried to lower her voice as a coworker walked by her desk. "Contrary to what you think, I never told LT how sorry you really were; your absence did all the talking. I'm not that damn selfish. So what do you want to do?"

Tariq tried to let go of his fear. "Call me back and tell me when and where."

Norelle hung the phone up. Before she could make her next call, her cell phone rung. It was a 202 area code, which excited her. It was André.

By five o'clock, Nia pulled up to Alisha's old spot. As she examined the Benz parked out front, Nia figured maybe Alisha was right. It was a Benz but it was dirty and dinged up. Even the hubcaps were missing; maybe that wasn't his car, Nia thought.

As she was about to ring the doorbell, André drove up. She was relieve Alisha wasn't with him.

"Hey, Nia what are you doing over here? You know your sister moved."

Nia laughed at André. "Yeah, I know. I was just checking to see if she had any mail."

André looked over at Nia, with a smirk as he rung the doorbell. "Yeah right, you wanted to check my boy out."

The sly grin on her face quickly faded as Lincoln opened the door.

What type of Jerry Springer bull was this?

Chapter 13

*"Closing her eyes, Keilah opened the door of her
heart and allowed love to free itself..."*
— *Keilah*

By the end of the day, André was tired and glad he only had one client to meet. The note his secretary left for him was very vague. He did not know what the appointment was about, only that the man specifically asked for him. From the clock sitting on his desk, it was quarter to five and he was ready to go. When the phone rang and his secretary alerted him that his four-thirty had arrived, André told her to send him back. When André opened the door to greet his appointment, beads of sweat erupted across his forehead. What in the hell was he doing here?

Backing away from the door, André tried to remember where he was and desperately collected himself.

The man walked through the door, quietly closed it and cautiously approached André.

André wiped his brow, and stared through the man. Even through his anger, André couldn't help but see the resemblance. "What are you doing here, Harold? I thought I said all I had to say to you when I was in Philly last month."

Taking off his hat, Harold placed it in a nearby chair and walked around the office. Placing his glasses firmly on his face, he examined the diplomas on the wall and beamed. "You've done real good, son. I am so proud of all of you. Tracy is a nurse like her momma, and my eldest is a lawyer."

André loosened his tie and stared at his father. He loathed having the same brow line as Harold. From the jaw line to the flared nose, André was the spitting image of the man he resented, the very sight of him made him sick. Twisting his watch around his wrist, André tried with all he had to unclench his fist. "You are proud! Proud of how my mother raised your two kids on her own all day and half the damn night. Please don't come in here with that proud papa shit. In fact, you need to leave. I really don't want to put you out but I will."

Harold stared back at his son and wished he could take back the years of hurt but he knew he couldn't. All he could do was deal with the here and now. "André, it's a lot of things you don't understand and I don't expect you to but I want to try to have something with you, son. Tracy let me come around her and, with you starting your family; I hoped maybe we could..."

André sliced Harold's words down in mid sentence.

"Play father and son? You are about twenty years too late with that one. Oh, wait to play granddad. No, man, that's not happening. I got this. I did fine without you and my seed will do even better. I can't believe you wasted my time with this."

Harold recognized the flash of anger in André's eyes; it reminded him so much of André's mother. "You got every right, André. You wouldn't understand. You are a better man than I was at your age. You know, when your mother got pregnant we had barely been together a year. I was going to mechanics school and she was working on her LPN license. We had this one room studio on the Southside. Heat hardly worked, water was rusty but we were all in love and it really didn't matter."

André looked at his father with contempt. "What does that have to do with anything thirty years later?"

Grabbing André's shoulders, Harold smiled.

"Everything, son. Your mom and I almost did something real stupid back then. But I couldn't let her do it. I just couldn't let my first just go like that."

André backed away from his father, twisted up his mouth and casually sat in the chair behind his desk. He refused to accept what he realized his father was saying. "What are you trying to say? I know you aren't saying what I think you are saying."

Harold picked up his hat from the chair and hung it on the doorknob. Pulling the chair closer to the desk, Harold leaned in and looked André square in the eyes. "You know what I am saying. I know now a day it's legal and women talk about the right to choose and all. Back then, women didn't have too many options, but I just couldn't take the idea of your mother laid up on some table in a doctor's back office going through that. No way; not my Margie."

The loosened tie felt tighter around André's neck as his own emotions choked him. The lines of disbelief that had etched across his face were about to crack.

"You see, son. I know I wasn't the best. I made a lot of mistakes with you kids and your mother but that one time, if nothing else, I did right by you. I gave you a chance to be. That's the one thing you and I have in common."

André wiped away the myriad of emotions that had escaped through the cracked lines of disbelief. "You and I don't have a damn thing in common. Get out of here! I mean it. Don't come down here anymore. I don't care who told you this was a good idea, they were wrong. Actually, I am going to call Momma right now, or was it Tracy?"

Harold put the chair back in its place. "I know how you feel André." He reached for his hat and adjusted on his head. "My father wasn't much either and I guess I followed in his raggedy footsteps but fortunately you won't follow in mine. Just don't go call your mother and upset her and don't pick no argument with your sister. It wasn't either of them." He walked over to the door, not looking back, and opened it, his grip firmly affixed to the doorknob. "Your fiancée got my number and arranged this. She didn't mean no harm. She figured maybe we could work things out with the baby coming and all."

Alisha couldn't believe it when André told her Nia was at her old place when he went past there to check on Lincoln. She wondered if Nia was going to mention it. It had been two weeks and Nia hadn't parted her lips. Going over the guest list for the engagement party, Alisha decided to focus. Apparently, Nia didn't recognize him from the club that night or maybe she did and wasn't going to say anything.

Alisha's mother pulled up a seat beside her, confirmed all the uncles from down south and jotted down more items on the To Do list. "Thank you, Nia, for finally getting your fitting done. Did you like the dress I picked out for you?"

Nia looked up from the list and nodded. "You know I can't stand orange but it's your day." Reaching over to hug her sister, Nia noticed a name missing from the guest list and picked it up. "Mom, I told you I was bringing a date to the engagement party. I don't see his name on the list."

Grabbing her pen, their mother took the list from Nia. "What's the guy's name again?"

Nia moved closer to her mother and peered down at Alisha. "Lincoln Taylor. He's a friend of André's so it should be cool, right Alisha."

Alisha tried to shut her mouth. "Who?"

Nia walked toward the end of the table and played with the silver wedding bells resting next to Alisha. "Lincoln. The guy who took over your place; we have been hanging out. He's cool. I'm sure André wouldn't mind since they go way back. Did you know they were roommates back in college? He told me André used to be off the hook."

Alisha grabbed Nia by the arm and dragged her out to the living room, with their mother looking on in confusion. "What type of game are you playing Nia? What in the hell are you trying to do?"

Nia broke away from Alisha's grip with a look of insolence "Ha! You need to ask yourself that same question. I'm trying to help your ass out."

Alisha grabbed her sister by the arm again. "Look I don't know what he told you but leave his ass alone. Something is wrong with him."

Nia cut her eyes to her sister's firm grip on her arm then gently removed it. "Alisha, he hasn't said a thing. That's what I am checking for. I'm trying to convince him to move or leave town or something. I told you I was trying to help you."

Alisha looked at her sister, unable to figure out if she is friend or foe. "Help me! How in the hell are you helping me by bringing his ass to my engagement party?"

Nia smirked and gave Alisha a Judas kiss on the cheek. "I got you big sis, I got you."

Keilah knew she should have told someone where she was going but she was embarrassed. How could she tell Norelle she was meeting a guy she met online? Norelle would joke her mercilessly. As Keilah sat at the bar, she checked her makeup once more. She hoped this one wouldn't be a dud like the last two.

The first one didn't even want to pay for a cocktail and the other wanted her to come over his house after fifteen minutes on the phone with her as if she was some desperate chick. *Maybe she was desperate*, Keilah thought to herself as she closed her Mac compact. She tried to tell herself otherwise, since the girl who worked in tech support said she had met her husband online. As Keilah thought more, Amber was not exactly a looker and neither was her online hubby.

What the hell, Keilah had to try something different; it wasn't like she had gotten it right on her own. She had to admit that she and her online beau, Justus Alexander Hunt, had great late night conversations for almost a month. Justus was a welcomed distraction from the humiliating flashbacks she had been having from that whole Keith fiasco. And, she hoped he would distract her thoughts away from André.

Reaching into her purse, Keilah pulled out the printed profile of her Nubian Online love match and gave a nervous smile. He looked good on his picture—nice eyes, teeth looked straight. His profile said he had a Masters degree in philosophy and taught at the University of Baltimore, was six-feet-one-inch tall, with weight proportionate to height. Liked to read, enjoyed outdoor activities, romantic dinners and talking for hours...*hmmm sounds damn near perfect* Keilah thought herself as she looked anxiously at every man that walked through the door.

Something had to be wrong with him. With all that going on, why would he need to place an ad online? Keilah had to laugh out loud at the irony...what was wrong with her then?

With the ringer off on her phone, she noticed the blue light blinking, alerting her of an incoming call. It was Justus.

"Hi Keilah, I am walking in right now. I have on a green sweater and jeans."

As Keilah turned around, she tried to hide her disappointment. The man in the green sweater entering the restaurant didn't look more than five-feet-five with a receding hairline.

Taking a deep breath, Keilah popped her eyes wide and forced a smile. The man smiled, gave her a strange look and join a woman at a nearby table. When she realized he wasn't the one, a tall grande mocha approached her, grinning.

"Keilah Fort, I presume."

"Very funny, Justus Alexander Hunt. Let's get a table."

Phew, Justus does look like his picture.

Realizing she had relaxed her stomach, Keilah sucked it in and smoothed out her sweater. After pulling out Keilah's chair, Justus handed her a yellow rose. Keilah smiled, as she smelled it.

Nice touch

"My mother told me that when ever you go to see a woman, a man should always have something for her. So, I hope you like that rose. Yellow is for friendship."

Keilah crossed her legs and admired his form.

Damn he looks good. He looks like a fine ass ginger snap.

"Uhmm, yes I do. Very nice and smooth, I am sure it has worked for you many times before."

Justus leaned back in his chair and took two menus from the server, placing one before Keilah.

Oh, he has big hand.

"You think? It must not have work that well. I am here trying it again. Maybe it will work this time."

Justus outstretched his leg and Keilah flinched.

"Oh, I'm sorry did I kick you?"

Keilah looked under the table and dusted off her pants, smirking to herself.

He's got big feet too. "I am fine. This is a nice place Justus, have you been here before?"

Justus laid the menu down and motioned for the server.

"Actually, no. I've driven past it a million times and just decided it might be nice. You want some wine?"

Keilah nodded, and was pleasantly surprised they both ordered Riesling.

"Come on Justus, you can tell me? I know you got a lot of hits. How many other ladies offline have you brought here? I know they were just as impressed with the place as I am."

Damn, there I go again. Whatever, he probably did. It's not like he'd tell me anyway.

Justus shifted in his seat, staring at Keilah.

His eyes look like two oval cups of Earl Grey. I have to put my game face on.

"True. I got a lot of hits but I wasn't that intrigued to meet anyone offline, until you."

Keilah curled up her lips and gave him a look of obvious disbelief.

"You can give me that look all you want, it's true. And I don't have to lie to you. Why do women assume a man is going to lie for the sake of lying?"

The server approached and sat the glasses of wine on the table. "I'll be back shortly to take your order."

Keilah sipped from her glass. "Well, Justus that is because most men do. Sorry but you brothers are a trip."

Smiling at Keilah, Justus noticed how her picture didn't do her any justice, especially her eyes. "Well, I will not argue with you on the fact that my brothers are a trip, but can I graciously request that you not act like most women and give me the opportunity to show you I am not like most men. Now what would you like to eat? I hear they have great crab cakes. Do you like crab cakes?"

Keilah wanted, so desperately, to let down her guard, but the risk of disappointment was too much of a gamble. Looking at Justus, Keilah decided to shake the dice.

As the evening progressed, Keilah and Justus ate and talked about everything under the sun. Keilah became more intrigued by Justus as he went into further detail about his parents.

"So you're father was working as a human rights advocate in South Africa when he met your mother?"

Taking a bite from his crab cake, Justus nodded. "Yes. He had worked for civil rights in the states and decided to brush up on international law and go to South Africa after a colleague of his told him there was actually a place where black people were more oppressed than in America."

Keilah stirred a French-fry around in her ketchup

"That is admirable. But with all due respect, didn't he think his own people still needed him here?"

Justus tried to hold back his laughter. "His own people meaning *black people?*"

"Yeah. I mean things still weren't that great in the 1970's. We still needed some strong black brothers on the frontline."

Justus let out an amused laugh.

What is so funny about what I said? I knew it! He's one of those uppity Negroes.

Kenda Bell

"Keilah, you know I'm biracial right?"

"Well, yes. What does that have to do with you laughing at me? Did I offend you or something?"

"No, not at all. Is it ok if I finish, Ms. Angela Davis? "

"Certainly."

Justus took a French-fry from her plate and popped it into his mouth.

"When he got there he was shocked. He said that the ghetto's here looked like the Waldorf-Astoria in comparison to the shantytowns he saw in Soweto. Johannesburg, where mother is from, was better but not much. So for most of his time he stayed at a dorm at the University of Pretoria. That was where he met my mother."

"Really? They let black people stay there back then?"

Justus finished off his sandwich and gave a serious look. "No. My mother was only able to be a day student."

Day student? What...no way!

"What's wrong, Keilah? You assumed that my dad was some black sell out who imported some white woman to father his children?"

All Keilah could do was stuff the rest of her crab cake in her mouth.

"It's ok. No matter where we traveled, from the US to Europe, people always had that same look on their face. Whether it was when my mom picked me up from school or the stares in the restaurants...people all seemed shocked. I think the worst was when I was maybe eight or nine years old and this plumber came to our house to do some work. The guy came in and looked at the sink. At the time, I didn't have this tan. He looked at me, smiled and said to my mother, 'Before I get started on this I need to talk to your boss.' My dad overheard it in the next room and practically threw him out. Oh, he was a *brotha* by the way."

As Keilah reached out to touch his hand, Justus grabbed

138

hers tightly and looked deeply into her eyes. "I'm fine with it now. But what really amaze me are the reactions from black women."

Trying to pull her hands away, Justus clutched them tighter. "What do you mean?"

Justus lifted her hands and kissed them lightly. "Why would it be shocking that a white man would fall in love with a black woman rather than the other way around? You are the finest creation that God ever made."

Keilah blushed and quickly took a drink.

"I didn't say all that. It's just that it's rare. Especially for the time and place they were living in."

Justus smiled and perused the dessert menu. "My parents have taught me many things. The most important thing they taught me was that love can not be dictated by time or space. It is what it is. Love is the only thing man hasn't figure out how to control."

As he continued to talk, Keilah learned that his mother was a dean at Medgar Evers College and his father worked for the United Nations. As he went on, she felt more and more ordinary.

"So enough about me, What about your family, Keilah?"

Keilah always hated this part. "Not much to tell. My mother is an office manager for a law firm. My father is a lieutenant for the fire department. My sister, well she is an entertainer."

Justus lit up. "Really, what does she do?"

Keilah took a sip from her glass and laughed. "She's a dancer."

Justus nodded. "Okay, now besides making sure that the staff you manage gives its customers the best customer service, what do you do? What is your passion? I can see it in your eyes."

Keilah blushed again. "Well, I used to paint and draw a long time ago. But that starving artist bit wasn't making it, you know. I had to get a real job and put it to the back for a minute."

"No, you can't do that. Your passion is what lets you know you are living. Without it you're just waiting to die."

139

"I have tried to pick the brushes back up again. It's coming back slowly but steadily."

Justus motioned to the server to bring the check. "I bet you're very good."

"How can you tell, you haven't even seen anything I've done?"

Justus took the bill from the server and pulled out his credit card. "I can tell by your eyes. They are dark and deep, just as I know you are. They remind me of my Mother's."

Norelle was happy to hear Raymond come in. She jumped off the sofa and hugged him tight.

"Wow, I'll make sure I bring home dinner more often." Norelle was barely able to break a grin. Noticing something was wrong; Raymond sat down and pulled Norelle onto his lap. "What wrong baby?"

Norelle rubbed her eyes. "You know LT is supposed to meet with Tariq tomorrow."

Raymond nodded.

"Well Ray, I called his mother's house to confirm it and she tells me that Tariq got picked up on some probation thing. To make matters worse, they picked him up in a hot spot. She didn't have to tell me anymore. He was probably out there slinging."

Raymond hugged Norelle tightly as she cried.

"How am I going to tell LT? Once again, Tariq has disappointed him. Sometimes I wish …"

Raymond gently kissed his wife "We'll get through this. When LT comes home from practice, we will tell him together. After that whatever LT wants us to do we will do. Don't worry. LT knows we love him no matter what."

When the phone rung, Raymond reached over Norelle and answered it. His irritated look relaxes as he hands Norelle the phone. "It's some dude on the phone named André asking for you. It better be Keilah's André."

Norelle smiled and kissed Raymond on the forehead.

"No, I haven't seen her today, Dré. I thought you wanted to wait until next week. Okay, but what's going on? Well excuse me. You calling here hunting her down, I got a right to ask. I'll try her."

As Norelle hung up the phone, Raymond looked at her and shook his head.

Norelle smiled at him. "What! I didn't do anything. He called me. He wants to see Keilah bad now. I bet old girl's little skeleton done fell out the closet with Lincoln attached to it."

Raymond sat Norelle on the sofa and headed toward the kitchen. Before Norelle could pick up the phone, he turned toward her. "Nori, who in the hell is Lincoln?"

I was almost eleven o'clock. It wasn't like André not to call Alisha, especially when she rung his phone off the hook. As she walked around the condo, it looked the same way it did when she left out that morning. Looking for Chris's number, she tried not to think the worst. Once she found the number, she assured herself if Lincoln had got a hold of André, she would know by now.

When Keilah pulled up to her apartment building, she was sad to see the evening end. It was nice of Justus to follow her home. She normally didn't do that but he seemed genuine in his concern to make sure she got home safe. Just as she looked to see where he went he was outside her car motioning her to unlock the door. Opening the car door for her, Justus took her by the hand and placed an umbrella over her head. She hadn't even noticed it had started to drizzle.

"If you don't mind, Ms. Fort, I would like to walk you to your door."

Keilah giggled and led him up the stairs. Reaching her door, she isn't' sure if she wants to give him a kiss. Before she reached a decision, Justus kissed her softly on the forehead.

"If I passed the first date, maybe we can go to the museum tomorrow and get you inspired."

Keilah beamed at him.

"That may be a plan, Mr. Hunt. I'll call you in the morning."

Closing the door behind her, Keilah savored the delicate kiss that seemed to have touched her deeper than she had expected. Plopping down on the sofa, Keilah emptied her purse. She reviewed her cell phone and saw that Norelle had called her several times, as well as André. Looking at her caller ID, she saw they both had called her several times at home. Determined to hold onto her feeling, Keilah ran to her bedroom and quickly changes into a tee shirt and grabbed her paint and brushes.

After positioning the easel just right, Keilah turned her lights off and lit candles and incense. She would finally make love to the canvas again.

As the drops fell harder against her windowpane, Keilah allowed the rhythm of the rain to guide her hand against the canvas. Every emotion appeared on the canvas. The gray areas of confusion exploded with color and she enjoyed it just as she remembered. She hadn't broken a sweat like that in a while. Collapsing to the floor, Keilah's euphoria was broken by a long and almost tired knock on her door.

The closer she got to the door, the more familiar the knock became. Without even looking through the peephole, Keilah flung the door wide and stretched her hands out.

Tired and wet, André fell into Keilah's arms.

As the downpour of the rain slowed to a gentle steady rhythm, Keilah let André lay in her arms. Cautiously tracing André's hairline, Keilah tried to fight back the contempt that was trying its best to take over her. Anger and hurt came as reinforcement, whispering bitter sentiments in Keilah's ears that caused her, for a moment, to stop and retreat her hand. Biting her top lip, Keilah eased her arm from under André's neck. Immediately, André wrapped his arms tighter around her waist and kissed her hand. Closing her eyes, Keilah opened the door of her heart and allowed love to free itself, pushing contempt by the wayside; leaving anger and hurt to their own devices for the moment.

Chapter 14

"Why did you let us do it?"
— André

In the wee hours of the morning, Keilah quietly rose from the sofa and removed André's shoes. Going through the closet, Keilah found a blanket and laid it across André. Standing over him, she wanted to wake him but decided not to. For that moment, Keilah wanted to enjoy his presence. Asking the questions of why and how come would only shorten the sweetness of this little moment in time. As Keilah debated whether to rejoin him on the couch, André opened his eyes and gave a slight grin.

"Keilah, can you put the butcher knife your hiding behind you back on the table and lay down with me, please?"

Keilah smiled back at him and sat on the edge of the couch. "Dré, what's going on?"

André touched Keilah's hands and looked into those knowing eyes that said a million words often left unspoken. Not knowing where to begin, André lifted his eyes toward the ceiling. "I saw my father today. He dropped some serious stuff on me today, K."

Keilah allowed her lips to pout rather than say a word. Realizing she was still in nothing but a T-shirt and panties, Keilah retrieved her robe. When she returned to the living room, she found André sitting up, admiring her canvas.

"K, this is beautiful. How long have you been working on it?"

Keilah walked pass André, heading for the kitchen. "Not that long. You want some tea?"

André nodded and joined Keilah in the kitchen.

Watching her fill the teapot, André couldn't help desiring to reach out to her. When he was about to place his arms around her shoulders, she turned around. He quickly withdrew.

"What did you two talk about? From what I remember, you never really had too much to say to him. Your upcoming nuptials caused a change of heart?" Keilah's eyes flashed the sarcasm that her words barely concealed.

Backing away, André returned to the couch, trying to figure out why his emotions had led him to Keilah. When he looked up at her, the thinly veiled love in her eyes reminded him.

"Keilah, he dropped some serious information on me and I really don't know how to take it."

Reaching for two coffee cups and tea boxes, Keilah looked over at André. "I have Earl Grey, Orange Spice and Green tea, which one?"

André tried to ignore Keilah's coolness. "I don't care what ever you chose. He said something that fucked me up, K."

Deciding on Green tea, Keilah reached for the sugar and pulled two spoons from the drawer. "You still take three sugars?"

André rose from the couch and walked toward Keilah. Grabbing her by the shoulders, he took a long, laboring breath. "Why did you let us do it?"

As the teapot whistled, Keilah dropped the spoons to the floor as a tear crept down André's face.

It was after one in the morning and Alisha called everyone she could think of. Chris hadn't seen him. The office was closed so she couldn't call there. Had he gotten into an accident or something? Where could André be? Alisha knew he should have noticed she called by now. It wasn't like him not to call or come home. Had Lincoln said something? Panicking, Alisha reached for her cell phone, and searched for Lincoln's number. Getting no answer, she hung up and called André again. When the house phone rang, Alisha jumped to answer it.

"What's up Alisha; you need something?"

Alisha is shocked to hear Nia on the other end.

"What do I want? What do you want? You called."

Nia cleared her throat. "Lincoln said you called. I'm returning the call."

Looking at the phone, she realized where Nia was calling from. "What are you doing over his house this time of night? I told you to stay away from him."

Nia laughed aloud. "Whatever. What do you need with Lincoln this time of night? I would think you'd be all underneath André right about now."

Alisha is more frustrated. "Did Lincoln see or talk to André today?"

Nia got quiet. "No, I don't think so. Why?"

Not sure whether she should believe Nia, Alisha calmed her voice. "No reason, I was just curious."

Nia snickered. "You think Lincoln spilled the tea on your ass. Wait, you are talking awfully loud; André must not be home. What happened?"

Hearing the glee in her voice, Alisha ended the conversation. "Nothing happened. He went out to get me some pickles and ice cream. I'm hanging up."

"Yeah right. He isn't home and you're trying to figure out why. You need to chill and give him his free pass considering..."

Hanging up the phone, Alisha reluctantly agreed with her sister as she looked at her ring.

Returning to bed, Alisha decided that when André did come home, she would put up a little fuss, not too much over the top and quietly let him off the hook. Why let some little side dish concern her when she knew she was the main course?

"Why did I let us? What in the hell are you saying to me?" Keilah's voice cut the silence like a machete knife. "I didn't get pregnant by myself and I didn't end it by myself either. You came over here to bring that old shit up! Why?"

André backed away and surveyed Keilah's living room. Eyeing her cigarettes, he took one out of the pack and returned to the kitchen to light it on the stove. "Keilah, you didn't give me a choice. You just walked into the place with a bottle of Jack Daniel and some pamphlets. You basically told me you didn't want the baby anymore than I did."

Trying to calm herself, Keilah poured the water from the teapot into the two coffee cups. After all these years, Keilah could not imagine that André had eased his conscious by placing blame on her.

Carefully taking the coffee cup from Keilah, André continued. " Keilah, tell me I'm not telling the truth. Did you or did you not want the baby? Don't act as if I was some cold, callous nigger. Come on now."

Keilah stared at him coldly, as she shook her head. "So you wait two years later to ask me if I wanted our child. Where was all this concern back then? You didn't even part your lips. As I remember, you ran out of here when I told you; just as I thought you would. Hell, I'm surprised you came back."

André smashed the cigarette into the ashtray, and drinks his tea. "Damn, K. Answer me. You never give a straight answer. Just say it!"

Keilah pierced her eyes as she drinks her tea. Picking up her pack of cigarettes, she pulled out two and walked to the kitchen. Lighting one of the cigarettes, she puffed it quickly as she pulled down two glasses and fills them with ice cubes. Taking a drag from her cigarette, Keilah opened the refrigerator and poured cranberry juice into the two glasses.

Returning to the living room, Keilah glared at André as she lit the second cigarette and placed it in his mouth. André blinked from the smoke as he watched Keilah enter and exit the kitchen quickly with half a bottle of Absolute in her hand. Placing the bottle on the coffee table, Keilah motioned for André to wait. Placing Lauryn Hill in the CD player and turning the lamp off, Keilah felt she was ready.

Joining André back on the couch, Keilah poured them each heavy amounts of vodka. "Okay, Dré. You want the truth. I am going to give it to you."

Taking a long gulp, André leaned back and waited.

Keilah looked over at André and wiped her eyes. "You know, Dré, when you called me a few months back I, like an idiot, thought you might have wanted me back. Like maybe, you had figured out that I was the one that loved you. Like maybe, we'd make up for lost time and get back together. When you dropped that marriage and baby shit on me, I was like damn. I was right. He never loved me, not like that at least. You liked me a whole bunch... no wait, you cared a great deal for me." Taking another drink, Keilah saw André leaning forward as if he was about to respond. "Don't say a damn thing. You want to hear it so I'm going to say it all." Pushing him back onto the sofa, Keilah freshened André's drink and poured more for herself. "That was when it hit me. I did it for you. Don't look at me like that. This is my shit, you don't have to agree with it, but you are going to listen."

André took a large gulp, emptying his glass. "No, K, don't pin that on me. No way, you did it because you wanted to. How do you figure you did it for me?"

Finishing her glass, Keilah jumped up from the couch. "Well, let's see. You passed the Bar, you got you a sweet job at one of the biggest law firms in the Baltimore-DC area and you moved to a better zip code. You're driving nice; it feels good to hand your key to the valet, when you go to work doesn't it?"

Walking over to André she gently brushed the lapels of his shirt, then stopping at the cufflinks. "Brooks Brother's suits and monogrammed cufflinks; you got a big return for your half of the three hundred dollars."

André pushed Keilah's hand away and covered his face.

"What's the matter, André? Does it sound fucked up when you

hear it? Well imagine how it feels. Let me tell you. You get pregnant and are scared to death. You fall in love with a man that you're not quite sure loves you and more importantly, you are unsure if he loves you enough to love that little part of you and him that is inside of you. Then you look at the fucked up shit you've grown up under and you start deducting what is right versus what is wrong. See Dré, my mother had a baby my father didn't want her to have. It tore our house apart. But guess what, my sister is here, regardless of how fucked up my father was. And he still did what he wanted to do. I use to think my mother put her love for my father over everything else and I still do but no matter what, her love for him was no more valuable than my sister's life. That one burden my mother doesn't have to carry."

After taking in Keilah's anger, André removed his hands from his face to reveal swollen red eyes. Lifting his glass from the coffee table, André slowly examined it. Grasping the glass tightly with both hands, André jumped up quickly and threw the glass against the wall.

Keilah tried to hide her shock by walking slowly toward the kitchen.

André removed his cufflinks, placing them on the coffee table. Eyeing Keilah's half-empty glass, André finished it off and walked slowly toward Keilah. Not sure what was next, Keilah braced herself when André stepped to her almost nose to nose. Grabbing Keilah's arm firmly, André dragged a now frighten Keilah to the sofa, slinging her down.

"You know women think they are the only ones that are hurt by "the choice." Well, your not. You say you did it for me but you did it for you. You weren't thinking of me, not André Terrell Davidson. You were thinking of Norelle's baby daddy, or some other dude you heard about on the damn bus or in the bar. You assumed I was another fucked up baby boy. Or did I look like your father to you. You didn't even ask me what I thought, Keilah! You want to talk about love, what is a man supposed to think when a woman who says she loves him has no problem killing his seed. You didn't think about that did you?

I'm the damn villain and you're the victim. It wasn't all about me; it was about you Keilah. I helped raise my sister. I saw how my mother had to struggle; you think I'd do you like that? You think when I see Chris with his boys I don't think? You didn't think I was man enough to take care of my responsibility, Keilah? That was what was on your damn mind. That day stays in my fucking head. I'm drove you to kill my child and I didn't do a damn thing about it. I'm sitting in a room full of people all killing pieces of themselves. Sisters sitting reading magazines, trying to act like it's just another day. Then dudes like me looking out the window trying not to look at their girls because they can't show how they really feel. It wasn't all me, I was a co-signer. You didn't trust me as a fucking man. You trusted in the man you feared I might become rather than the man I was. Oh, and don't get me started on the due date."

André walked over to Keilah, got down on his knees and lifted her face up to his. "You didn't think I knew did you? I found the slip in the damn trashcan. Why didn't you tell me? Damn, K, the baby was due on my birthday. What better present could you had given me?"

Keilah grabbed André around the neck and sobbed. As André held Keilah tight, he whispered "Why?" repeatedly in her ear.

Pressing her lips against André's ear, Keilah responded with a horse and shallow voice. "I never saw any happily ever after only sadly as ever. I was afraid. I trusted you as a man; I didn't have faith in **us** because of so many of **them**; people on the talk shows, on the bus, my parents, your parents, and who ever else I heard about." Laying her face on André's shoulder, Keilah let the tears flow.

Removing the rubber band from Keilah's ponytail, André stroked his hands through her hair, down to the roots, and then back up to the ends, remembering how it always calmed her. "Keilah, I'm sorry. If I could …"

Before André could finish, Keilah lifted her head and pressed her finger against his lips. "That's enough. What is done is done; we can't go back. I love you enough to try to forgive the past."

150

As Keilah traced André's lips, he took her hand and kissed it softly. Instinctively, Keilah stroked the back of his neck, leaned forward, planting kisses on his forehead, moving slowly down to his eyelids, and softly brushes her lips across his eyelashes. As she stroked André's lips with hers, he drew back and stood to his feet.

Feeling embarrassed, Keilah apologized and tightened her robe.

"You know what. We just had a very emotional moment, not to mention we have been drinking. You are engaged to Alisha. So maybe you should…"

André snapped back into reality. "How did you know it was Alisha?"

Pulling her hair back, Keilah looked at André blankly. "How did I know? You sent me a sorry ass text message, that's how. I really do not want to get into that we have done enough…"

André took his shirt out of his pants then exhales. "A text message! You think I'd send you a text message telling you something like that?" Suddenly, all the pieces fell into the places that André knew they would.

Turning on the the overhead lights, Keilah noticed that Lauryn Hill had stopped playing and Jill Scott had taken over. Before she knew it, André was pressing his body against hers as he turned the lights off. Not saying a word, André firmly grabbed Keilah from behind, and slowly stroked his tongue across her neck. When he turned her around and moved toward her lips, Keilah knew she had to do the right thing.

Drawing back, Keilah pressed her hand against André's face and looked deeply into those gray eyes that never failed to pull her closer. As she kissed André gently on the nose, then on the lips, she took into consideration all that once was and what was now, their present. When André tightened his grip around her waist and slipped his hand underneath her robe, Keilah pulled away and walked toward the coffee table.

Confused, André followed behind her. Using the remote, Keilah turned up the volume, and André understood. With his shirt unbuttoned, he led Keilah to the couch as Jill whispered seductively from the speakers *I am not afraid.*

Chapter 15

*"André can't figure out what was more unsettling;
the fact that she didn't seem to care or that he didn't."*

Norelle was up early, gathering laundry, and debating if it
was too early to call her Nana Louise. Contemplating the information
her mother had shared with her, she felt foolish to even attempt to
approach her grandmother with such a thing.

Nana Louise was always happy to hear from her and they
would talk for hours. Walking down to the basement, several articles
of clothing tumbled out of her arms and onto the steps. Dumping the
pile of clothes next to the washer, she backtracked to the steps, and
collected the clothes, laughing at how hard LT's socks were. How
many times had she told him not to wear his socks twice? Picking
up the boxers, she marveled at how soon she wouldn't be able to
distinguish LT's boxers from Raymond's. Her little boy was getting
bigger by the minute. Bringing the pile in her arms closer to her face,
she smelled something.

As Norelle sniffed more, she felt crazy but she inhaled a little
more deeply. Amidst the smell of corn curls and other assorted aromas,
she still caught a whiff of a scent that was foreign. Digging through
the mound of clothes, Norelle located the source. Turning up her face,
Norelle cautiously brought the boxers a little closer and took a few
light sniffs, familiar yet different. It was the soapy smell. Laying the
boxers flat on the floor, she realized they were the new boxers she had
gotten for Raymond the week before. Norelle knew Raymond was
a clean brother but he didn't normally shower at work; he made it a
point to come home and shower so he could get real clean, he always
told her. Lifting the boxers up to the light, Norelle examined for
stains. Just as she was about to flip them over, Raymond yelled down
to her that he was headed to the gym. Norelle smiled and laughed at

her guilty conscience, feeding her paranoia. As Norelle returned the boxers to the pile of dirty laundry, she shook off the negativity she was feeling. Maybe he wore them to the gym and showered there. Deciding to give it a rest, Norelle started the washer. After turning the dial to heavy wash, Norelle returned upstairs to fix a cup of coffee and call Nana Louise. Looking over her shoulder at the washer, the slight floral scent that smelled of no soap they had never used, grabbed her attention again. Pushing the thoughts aside, Norelle pondered on how she would start the conversation with her grandmother.

As the sun became even more invasive between the slightly opened blinds, Keilah kept her eyes closed, allowing the warm rays to keep her in that special place a little while longer. Lying next to André, she basked in the moment a few minutes more. She knew that once she opened her eyes, reality would be eagerly awaiting her with the harshness of an old rival looking on with delight. How had she allowed herself to make another memory that will only hurt her later? Feeling André stirring, Keilah acted as if she were asleep. When André touched her face, Keilah allowed a smile to skip across her face. Peeking out of the corner of her eye, she saw that André's eyes were closed as well. What have they done?

As her eyes began to focus, Keilah resolved they had done nothing. Just desserts for what had been done to her years back, Keilah convinced herself as guilt and shame tried to present their case in the courtroom convening in her mind.

The plaintiff argued that the women's code of conduct had been violated the night before, pointing to an empty vodka bottle and years of bitterness, as its evidence. The defendant quickly retorted that there were no clearly defined rules of engagements in the hostile world of singledom, adding that dating was a vicious chess game filled with guerilla tactics between queens who knew their power but not their worth. The plaintiff countered that Keilah did not exercise duty of care once André was in her domicile, showing evident signs of weakness and vulnerability that were exploited by the alcohol administered by Keilah, citing that Keilah would not want the shoe to be on her foot. The defense argued that if Keilah was guilty of anything it was petty larceny; having stolen one night spent amidst an emotionally charged cloud of confusion could not be viewed as direct and proximate damage, calling as its sole defacto witness, love, to the stand.

As Keilah became aware that she was both judge and jury, she opened her eyes painfully.

Jumping up quickly, Keilah looked around for her robe, shaking off the sickness that was beginning to come over her. Entering the bathroom, she tried began to figure out how she was going to quarantine this thing that was trying to make her ill. Flushing the toilet, Keilah wished it could be that simple to get rid of it as quickly. As she lathered and rinsed underneath the shower, she hoped she could some how wash away the lovesickness that was aggressively consuming her logic. Hoping to some how take the taste out of her mouth, Keilah brushed her teeth with added vigor. Looking in the mirror, she knew it was not going to be that easy.

André had gotten up and made his way to the living room. When Keilah entered the living room, reality laughed in her face as she watched him check his cell phone.

Noticing Keilah, he quickly closed his phone and smiled at her.

"Good morning, K-love."

Keilah smiled back as she cleared the glasses and coffee cups off the coffee table from the night before. Looking at the empty vodka bottle, Keilah shook her head; heavy emotions and alcohol are never a good mix. Glancing over at André, Keilah tried to ignore the guilt she saw saddling itself comfortably on his back. As empathy came into her heart, Keilah got angry all over again. Why should she feel bad for André or Alisha? Alisha was the one that broke them up. By the time Keilah finished loading the dishwasher she knew better; the situations were different.

Hearing André turn the shower on, Keilah knew that whatever love was trying to convince her of, it was neither the time nor place for it. She had to force love to resign to compartmentalizing this new memory alongside childhood recollections of hot summers spent on cool stoops eating fudgesicles and her first kiss from Jason in fifth grade; sweet moments meant to last only as quickly as they had transpired.

As André emerged from Keilah's bathroom, he experienced a surreal familiarity that he had to shake. In the middle of his confused state, André felt a comfort that he didn't realize he missed until that very moment. Reaching for his shirt and watch, André knew that nothing should have changed, but it had. Not knowing what to say, André turned to admire Keilah's painting again as he felt her searching him for clues.

"Dré, listen I know that we got a little emotional last night and the alcohol only magnified a lot of old stuff between us. When you walk out that door, you will exit knowing that the way things were between us is the same as when you entered."

André rubbed his goatee. Once again, Keilah was thinking for him. "How do you figure that, K?"

Taken aback, she offered André a glass of orange juice. "Simply. You are an attorney and the facts speak for themselves. I have no fanciful thoughts of you and me. We cleared up some serious issues between us and that was what should have happened. The other thing, well that was just something that shouldn't have happened but did. We cool."

Sipping his orange juice, André couldn't understand why women chose to complicate simple situations and oversimplify a complex situation. He knew Keilah was more astute than that, they both knew it was less carnal and much more emotional.

"Okay, Keilah. That's your last word on it?"

Keilah finished off her orange juice and walked to the kitchen. "Meaning what, Dré?"

Sitting the empty glass on the coffee table, André stepped into his shoes and fastened a few buttons on his shirt. Then, he grabbed his keys and jacket and walked toward Keilah, hugging her tightly. Not wanting to let go of her stoic appearance, Keilah cautiously rubbed the back of André's neck and waits.

Kissing Keilah lightly on her pouting lower lip, André paused and said, "Okay."

Hearing a knock on the door, Alisha ran to the door. Upon looking out the peephole, she was disgusted to see Nia. As she opened the door, she pondered on how to get rid of her sister; she didn't want her to see any drama that would certainly erupt once André walked through the door.

As Nia walked through the living room, she assessed her surroundings, pausing on Alisha. By the look on Alisha's face, Nia knew André hadn't come home the night before.

"Why aren't you dressed yet? We are supposed to go to pick out my shoes this morning. You look wrecked; you didn't get any sleep last night?"

Alisha didn't want to respond to her question. Looking at Nia's smirk, Alisha decided not to. "I'm fine. I totally forgot. Can we go one day next week? I really want to do some things at home. We can go Monday or Tuesday. Don't you have that book club meeting to go to anyway?"

Nia could feel Alisha trying to push her out the door; sitting down on the sofa Nia could see the growing irritation on Alisha's face.

"I told them I wasn't coming. What, are you trying to rush me out of here?"

Alisha knew Nia was aware of what was being unsaid but she persisted. "No. It's just that I have things to do and I want to get started on them."

Walking over to the balcony, Nia looked through the glass door and smiled. "André didn't come home last night, did he?"

Alisha watched Nia walk away from the balcony and grinds her teeth. "What concern is that of yours?"

Picking up her purse, Nia walked toward the door. "Well, I just wanted to know. You sounded a little crazy last night. Did you find out what or who kept André out all night?"

Before Alisha could answer, the turning of keys in the door caught both of their attention.

Looking at André wrinkled dress shirt and laptop; Nia's own question was answered. Waving goodbye to Alisha, Nia shot André a sly look and exited.

Tempted to stand on the other side of the door, Nia paused then continued her descent down the stairs. For a moment, Nia felt a little pity for her sister then remembered that night at the club and brushed it off her shoulder.

As she got into her car, Nia recalled another night at another club, when she saw André and toyed with the idea of sending him a drink. When Alisha laughed the idea off as corny, Nia agreed and went to the bathroom. By the time she got back from the bathroom, Nia was shocked to see André walking toward Alisha with a grin on his face and a fresh drink in his hand.

For as long as Nia could remember, Alisha always one-upped her. If Nia sat on their father's lap, Alisha protested until she was on the other knee. If Nia asked her mother for a special barrette, it would suddenly disappear and reappear in Alisha's hair when they arrived at school. The summer before, Nia followed Alisha to junior high, was when the sibling rivalry advanced to a new level.

Alisha was older than Nia by only a year so they were often confused for twins until Nia started budding slightly quicker than Alisha did. The boys never really chased either of them, taking noticed of the more developed plums of Keisha down the street. As Nia recollected now she didn't much care, while Alisha took it as a total a front since her first crush, Gerard, had no problems playing hide and go seek with her just the summer before.

Whenever Gerard would ride past the front of their house, Nia could hear Alisha taunting, "Go play with those Becky Bald and Nappy Pooh."

If nothing else, Alisha knew, her hair was the envy of all. It was the grease and water kind of hair that was jet black and already at her shoulders, like their mother's, while Nia's was just as long but kinky like their father's.

The taunting went on for weeks until Gerard came up the block with Keisha, handing her an ice cream cone he had just bought for her. Keisha stuck her chest out a little more as she approached their front yard. Nia was sitting on the swing bench combing her dolls hair, while Alisha sat on the front step waiting for them to cross her path. As Alisha taunted, Keisha smiled at Alisha while she licked her ice cream cone. Once she had passed the front step, Keisha turned around and shouted as loud as she could.

"At least my little sister don't got bigger tee tees than I do!"

Alisha jumped up from the step, stared at the little plums hiding behind Nia's Barbie doll, and ran into the house in tears.

For the weeks leading up to the first day of school, Alisha seemed to grow more and more envious of Nia, as she looked each morning in the mirror to see no change in her own little buttons. The night before the first day of school was the last straw.

Alisha's hair was washed and neatly smoothed back into a pretty ponytail earlier that day while, Nia had to endure washing and pulling with the bush comb for most of the evening. The only thing that kept her calm was the huge piece of Hubba Bubba that she chewed nervously, as her mother pulled and tugged at her head.

Alisha modeled her first day of school outfit choices to their father while Nia sat in the kitchen next to the stove. As the blue flames slowly turned the hot comb from black to red,

159

Nia braced herself as she felt her mother firmly parting her hair into four sections. Holding the white metal jar of Blue Magic hair pomade in her lap, Nia cringed as her mother dipped her hand in the jar of hair pomade and prepared to burn Nia's hair into submission.

Holding her ears from start to finish, Nia tried not to jump as she felt the heat on her scalp. By the time her mother finished, it was almost nine o'clock and the Hubba Bubba had turned into a hard rock that had fallen out of her mouth and onto her lap, as dozed off. Nia woke slightly when her mother jerked her head and started to laugh.

Calling Alisha and her father into the kitchen, Nia's mother made an announcement that caused a chain of events that still ignited anger in Nia's eyes, some twenty years later.

"Look at Nia's hair! It is longer than Alisha's. All them naps were hiding all this. I would have never known."

Nia smiled until she saw Alisha's frown. Stuffing two Hubba Bubba's in her mouth, Alisha slanted her eyes and chewed hard and long as she glared at Nia's hair that had fallen about two inches above her plums. As she blew a bubble, her mother told her to make sure she threw the gum away before she went to bed. Alisha nodded yes and headed to their bedroom, asking if Nia wanted her to roller set her hair.

When Nia woke up for her first day of junior high, she found that her headscarf had come off in the middle of the night. Getting nervous, Nia felt the edges of her hair and was happy to feel them still smooth and greasy like they were the night before and the large pink sponge rollers were still in place. As she headed for the bathroom, the scent of bubble gum took her attention away from the bacon and eggs cooking downstairs.

Having washed up and returning to the bedroom, Nia noticed Alisha sitting on her bed taking her ponytail out. As she watched her play with the waves in her hair, Nia decided to take her rollers out as well. The first three came out easy; as she began to unsnap the rest, she felt queasy as she touched something hard and slimy in her hair.

As she stared in the mirror, she could see Alisha smirking over her shoulder as she tried desperately to pull the clumps of Hubba Bubba out of her hair.

Hearing the loud ruckus upstairs, their parents ran to the girl's bedroom to see Alisha wedged between the dresser and her bed with Nia sitting on top her ; yanking at her hair. Asking no questions, their mother took her slipper off and started swinging. She finally stopped when she noticed Nia's hair.

Alisha tried to convince the whole family that she hadn't done it and Nia had snuck gum after bedtime. After their mother tried everything from ice cubes to WD-40, it was nothing left to do but cut the gum out of Nia's hair and try to re-do her hair.

Nia begged to stay home as her mother smoothed her hair back with Queen Helene gel and Blue Magic. As her mother placed the red headband in the front of her hair, Nia took her hand and rubbed the back of her head hoping that maybe some of her hair had been saved but knowing that it hadn't. By the time Christmas rolled around, Nia was getting her first Jheri curl.

When Nia entered high school, she had become known as Alisha's bald headed little sister with big boobs. That was still not enough for Alisha.

If Nia took African dance, Alisha had to take ballet. If Nia wanted to be a majorette, Alisha had to be one too. When word on the high school campus was that the senior quarterback had noticed the junior named Nia with the hot new Halle cut, Alisha was the first senior to circumvent it and secure him as her senior ring dance date.

Turning into Lincoln's parking lot, Nia felt the animosity turn to hurt. When was all this shit between the two of them going to end? When Nia reached for her key, she whispered to herself. "It ain't going to end until I win for a change."

The conversation between Norelle and Nana Louise moved at a comfortable pace. After almost an hour, Nana Louise had shared with Norelle what all the cousins in Mississippi were doing and how she was preparing to redecorate her living room. Taking a breath, Norelle didn't know how to approach Nana Louise with the question that was burning a hole in her head. Knowing there were no more bushes to beat around, Norelle hit her Nana straight with it. "Nana, did my daddy have another woman?"

Feeling like a child asking about grown folk's business, Norelle closed her eyes and held the phone tightly as she listened to the silence from the other end of the phone. When Nana Louise broke into laughter, Norelle didn't know if she should respond or wait longer.

"Nori, baby, why you asking me something like that now?"

Norelle, relieved to hear the easiness in Nana Louise's voice, coyly responded. "No real reason I was just curious."

Taking a cough, Nana Louise knew it was more to her granddaughter's question. "Do you want to ask if your daddy loved anyone else, besides your momma?"

Letting silence answer for her, Norelle hoped her Nana would get the clue.

"Well, Nori, people are going to always love. For every love, there is a reason. When a baby is born and that mother looks on her newborn's face, she knows she loves him. Make no difference if he looks like his daddy or not, she loves it because it comes from her. As that baby grows into a child and then into a teenager, onward to adulthood, that mother can get mad as hell with that child, yet still love him or her without question. Now the baby, on the other hand, don't know much of nothing other than their mama or their papa. When you get off into man-woman love, now that, right there, is the same thing only different."

Norelle looked at her empty coffee cup and refilled it, knowing she would need it.

"See we all got the five senses, Nori. Both women and men use sight, hearing, touch, smell, and taste. For a woman, the way a man swaggers can catch her eye, while for a man; it's the way she struts. When she hears his voice, she starts thinking how he might sound saying I love you…while the man wonders how she'll sound when she says his name. Then when that man takes his big old hands and lay 'em real soft across the small of her back while they dancing real close, that's when touch come in. Depending upon how that woman places her hands on that man, both of them pretty much know where its going to lead. If she rests her hands on his shoulders lightly, she ain't all the way sold on the man; now if she wraps her arms around his neck. Just when the song gets real good to her, she leans in and…sniffs…uhm uhm, uh! You listen, Nori?"

Norelle giggled and replied, "Yes."

"Okay, so where we at…oh…taste. Now that where it's at… the kiss tells it all. A woman can pretty much look at a man and tell where she want to go with him. Depending upon how that kiss taste, she not quite sure because either it feels so good or it feel like a whole bunch of nothing."

Norelle was entertained, yet still clueless. "What does this have to do with daddy?"

Nana Louise paused. "You young people don't know much about courting and slow dancing, I keep forgetting. When you was coming up I was worried, but now Lord have mercy, they practically trying to make babies on the doggone videos. I get BET down here, don't think I am that old; I keeps up with things. Anyhow, your daddy dated a few of these little back wood girls, most I didn't like , wasn't but a handle full I halfway tolerated. What you asking about is first love. First love thrives off all that other stuff I was talking about, like a baby do. A baby loves mama and papa on the count of they see them all the time, or the way mama feed them good things to eat or the way daddy hold them real tight when they cry. First love is dependant like a baby then it grows up and moves on. True love is full grown and strong and can stand on its own like a calf."

Norelle got irritated. "Nana, are you going to answer me? Come on now, I'm paying for this call."

Nana Louise chuckled. "I just did. Plus, you called me from your cell phone, I know about free nights and weekends."

Norelle giggled. "Come on Nana, please!"

Nana Louise laughed. "Okay, Nori I'll make it plain for you. You're daddy had a little girlfriend down here before he moved up there. They dated all through school and when he couldn't make a way down here, he gave her a promise ring and moved up north to get a better job and set things up for them. While your daddy was gone she would stop pass here, sometimes three to four times a week. They'd write and call, all that stuff. Then slowly she started stopping pass a little less as the months went by. Next thing I knew your daddy was trying to figure out what was going on 'cause she had slowed the letters down to none. He'd call her house and she never would be home. I tried to drop hints as gently as I could, I really didn't know but I did at the same time. Anyhow, your daddy was due to come home for Thanksgiving; he had been gone for almost 6 months by that time. Lily, that was her name, had promised to make sweet potato casserole. That was a dish she really...."

Norelle sucked her teeth. "Nana, what does sweet potato casserole got to do with this?"

Nana's tone turned to irritation. "If you shut your mouth long enough, you'll find out. Don't think you too grown. Now, like I was saying, Lily was going to make the sweet potato casserole so I offered to buy the potatoes and things but she said she was going to the market for her momma so not to worry. Well, I was going to the market any how so I goes down there and I see her at the Greyhound Station. Back then, the Greyhound station was right next to Gruener's Market. Before I could even wave hi to her, what do I see but her kissing all on some slick haired hi- yellow man getting on some Soul Singers something another bus. She must of felt the heat from my eyes burning the back of her neck. Lily turned around and caught sight of me and liked to passed out. The joker smirked at me and popped her on the tail as he jumped on the bus. Well, I just stood there, while she looked like a deer caught in headlights. Now I am burning mad, I mean about five alarms. Your daddy was sending her new dresses and spending change, and here she go with this mess in the middle of town. I walks up to her and don't say what was fired up in my heart, all I say is, "I ain't telling him; you're going to do it."

Excitement ran through Norelle. "So, Nana, what happened?"

Nana took a breath. "Nothing. Lily slid her sneaky feet under my table with her sweet potato casserole and grinned between nervous glances. I let guilt beat her up. Guilt can lay a worse whipping on you than any man. Come Christmas, your daddy came back down and she basically told him she always wanted to be a singer like Tina Turner and was fixing to leave with this other fella come that new year; even had this teeny ring on her hand. Crazy thing was, Lily couldn't sing much of nothing but this slickster had convinced her otherwise. So rather than kicking Lily to the side, your daddy starts upping the ante. More dresses, nice purses, even a bigger ring…nothing worked; Lily didn't want your daddy no more. Meanwhile, your daddy had started keeping time with your mother while still trying to keep track of Lily or Lily Rose as she was going by at that time. Well, she finally wrote your daddy a Dear John letter and left with Mr. Soul Singer. Lily sent postcards from all over and photographs, with famous people like Otis Redding and Smokey Robinson, to your daddy. It hurt your daddy but luckily, your mother was there to love him back. Your daddy finally started looking at your mother more serious. Unlike Lily, your mother was a full-grown woman. Your mother had her own job, her own mind and most importantly she loved him unconditionally."

Norelle sighed sarcastically. "Yeah, Ma, loved daddy."

Nana knew where Norelle was going. "I figured as old as you was now, you'd understood that love ain't black or white. As a matter of fact, the shades of gray got a lot of other colors splattered across it. You married with an outside child, so come on off of that you hear me?"

Norelle touched her stomach and knew Nana was more correct than she could ever imagine.

Nana continued. "So your parents got married and had you. Now your daddy had, by all appearances, put Lily behind him but every so often he'd get mail at my house from her. I suppose after your momma and daddy moved out of his place and bought that house, she didn't have no place to send them rose-scented postcards and letters. Most of the time I'd mark them return to sender but one day I got curious and opened up one. What I read like to knock my wig sideways." Taking a long pause, Nana told Norelle to wait a minute and sat the phone down.

Norelle yelled hello for close to five minutes before Nana got back to the phone. "Phew, I'm sorry, Nori, I had some greens on the stove, they almost burned. Where was I?"

Norelle cleared her voice sarcastically. "Uhm, your wig was knocked sideways Nana!"

"Yeah, Lily had gotten pregnant by Mr. Soul Singer and he dumped her in some flat in Chicago, *and* your daddy had been wiring her money for almost a year and she was in a bind again."

Norelle couldn't even speak as the blemish free portrait of her father began to change before her very eyes. "Say what Nana? Daddy was sending some other woman money. Naw, Nana you must have misunderstood. I don't believe that."

Sipping on a drink Nana continued. "No I didn't misunderstand nothing. I can read just like you. By the date of that letter, your daddy must have cut her off a few months after your parents got married 'cause she said something about your mother and you being born soon."

As Norelle silently digested the bitter morsels of truth, all the pieces came together. "So daddy really loved this Lily woman and had been cheating on my mother?"

"Nori, I never said neither. Make no mistake, your daddy and mother loved each other. I never thought otherwise and you shouldn't either. People make mistakes; your daddy wasn't no different. Your daddy knew your mother loved him because when he was wounded she wanted to love him in spite of his mess with Lily. Your mother knew your daddy loved her because he allowed her to."

Listening to Nana made Norelle think of her and Raymond. She was beginning to understand. "So did daddy cheat on mommy?" Norelle caught herself. That was the first time in years that she had referred to Lynette as mommy.

"Well, Nori, cheating is all in how you look at it. Some people cheat with their bodies, you know, having relations and sneaking off and stuff. That's kind of easier to deal with. But when it's a heart thang, that right there is a little more serious. The body is easy to wrangle but the heart, that takes work and your daddy's heartstrings were still tied in knots to Lily for a while. First love is hard to shake and your mother knew it but she worked hard to cut them. It took a while and that really hurt your mother but she dealt with it like most women do when they love a man. Make no mistake it don't always work, but if it's true love, that true love is strong enough. You understand, Nori?"

Norelle smiled to herself. She knew better than her Nana knew. "Thanks Nana. When you going to send me that peach cobbler recipe?"

Nana laughed. "I thought you young women didn't bake. I tell you what; I'll send it to you if you promise to bake some for your mother. Can you promise me that?" Nana's question was answered with silence. Twenty years of anger couldn't be quickly erased by a conversation or a peach cobbler.

"Nori, I know you and your mother ain't been right since your father died but if I can be at peace with it you can find a way too.

Your daddy was my only child. I know a little about what happened the night your father died and grant you I had a lot of feeling about it but your daddy had a bad heart since he was a baby. Trust me when I tell you that. You only get one mother and Lord knows that you are going to do some things that LT won't understand until he's older. You grown now, understand your mother as a woman."

Norelle knew where Nana was going. "Are you going to send me the recipe or what?"

Nana smiled to herself. "I guess that's a yes. What's your email address?

Norelle gasped at the question.

"Don't sound all shocked, Nana got a computer with email. I told you I wasn't as old as you think I am."

For the first five minutes, André and Alisha stared each other down, trying to anticipate what the other was about to say. Just as André was about to speak, he caught the glistening of a tear about to fall from Alisha's eyes.

"Where were you Dré? I was worried sick! Why didn't you come home last night? I called Chris and a couple people from the law firm, none of them had seen or heard from you."

For a moment, guilt was knocked off its saddle by contempt that had been waiting to have its say all night long.

"First off, you think you are going to start having the right to check up on me when we get married?"

Alisha turned away to hide her relief at his statement. "No, Dré, it's just that you never stay out all night, well not anymore, and I was worried that's all. Look I don't want to argue, I don't care where you have been, I'm just glad your home."

As Alisha reached out to hug him, André backed away and at stared at her.

Why would she change channels like that? No woman would just push off her man staying out all night.

168

Not quite sure how she should respond, Alisha stepped past him and headed for the kitchen. "You want some breakfast? I can fix some eggs and bacon real quick. I think we still have some bagels ..."

André quickly followed her to the kitchen. "No I don't want breakfast. I want to know something, Alisha."

Alisha started to shake as she reached inside the refrigerator for the orange juice. *What is he about to ask me?* Pouring out a glass of orange juice, she handed a glass to André.

"Alisha I don't want orange juice, I want to ask you something. Actually I want to ask you two things, but I got one that is really burning a hole in my heart."

Alisha was shaking uncontrollably, as orange spilled onto the floor. Running to grab the mop, André stepped in front of her. "Look at me, Alisha!"

Alisha's eyes became swollen with fear, as she tried to force tears. Afraid of what was next, her tears retreated.

"Why did you get my father to come and see me?"

Alisha closed her eyes and gave a quiet sigh of relief as she allows mocking tears to ease through her eyelashes. "I don't know Dré! He just seemed so nice and sweet when he came past your mom's. With the baby coming I figured that it would be great for him or her to have not only two grandmas but two granddads."

Moving her face closer to André's, Alisha kisses land on stale air as André retreated to the bedroom. Quickly following behind him, Alisha began to unbutton her nightshirt.

Watching Alisha's eyes glint as she slipped off her nightshirt, André got even angrier. Why did Alisha think sex was the all- purpose problem solver? Once again, André became perplexed as to how women chose to complicate simple situations and oversimplify a complex situation. Sliding the shirt back across her shoulders, André looked over at Alisha.

"You know how I feel about my father. He has never

been a part of my life and now is no different. You don't even understand what you did, do you?"

Pulling her nightshirt together, Alisha knew the usual wasn't going to work. "I made you angry with me and I am sorry."

André sadly looked into Alisha's eyes and realized that she didn't understand what she had done nor did she care. Watching her play with the ring on her finger, André became increasing aware of what she did care about. Watching Alisha pull her hair down from her ponytail was not as seductive as it once was.

Tossing her hair enticingly, Alisha wet her lips and gave a doe-eyed glance that looked less sweet against the sunlight that was creeping behind her. Tugging at his zipper, Alisha moved again to remedy the situation. Jerking away, André walked to the bathroom and closed the door behind him.

Rubbing cold water on his face, André realized that he had seen Alisha for the first time. As the aroma of bacon seductively danced its way underneath the bathroom door, he also realized that Alisha saw him for the first time and rejected what she saw like he was now attempting to do with her.

As the day went on, Alisha acted as if nothing had happened, asking no questions about the night before, to André's amazement. On the surface, André was relieved, but deep within he was disconcerted. Watching Alisha smile back at him as she went over the seating arrangements, André couldn't figure out what was more unsettling; the fact that she didn't seem to care or that he didn't.

Chapter 16

*"...we all cross paths at some point; it's not always the face you
remember but rather the experience."*
— Justus

After leaving the Smithsonian Institute, Justus kept bumping
his hand against Keilah's as they walked along the corridor. She thought
it was cute, it reminded her of the first time she and André went to the
Walter's Art Gallery. By the time they reached Donna's coffeehouse,
only a block away, André had nestled her hands inside his.

Pulling her coat together, she was assured winter was well on
its way. Noticing that Keilah was rubbing her hands together, Justus
stopped and reached out to warm them. As Justus began to warm her
hands, the warmth radiated all over her. Relaxing to Justus's firm yet
gentle touch, Keilah's mind drifted to the night before. Feeling her
eyes about to reveal too much, Keilah blushed and pushed Justus to
walk on.

"Who did I remind you of?"

Keilah stopped dead in her tracks. "What did you just say?"

Wrapping his arm around her shoulder, Justus continued. "My
touch took you to a place you've already been."

Feeling strangely naked, Keilah pulled out her compact
and powdered her face. "Why are you trying to ruin a perfect date
with psycho babble? Where is this Indian place you were bragging
about?"

Riding in Justus's car, Keilah couldn't help but wonder why or
how he picked up on her wandering thoughts. Looking over at Justus,
she felt a little guilty, but shrugged it off.

"Keilah, when was the last time you took a trip?"

Keilah looked at Justus and drew a blank. She couldn't
remember. Had she gotten so caught up in the rat race? Thinking

harder, Keilah remembered the Atlantic City trip with Keith and frowned. "Well, a few months back I went to Atlantic City."

Justus grimaced and tapped Keilah's hand lightly. "No, Keilah, I mean a real trip away to a place that is completely unlike the ordinary."

Feeling embarrassed and about as well rounded as a square, Keilah dryly replied. "I guess I haven't been anywhere by your standards, Mr. World Traveler."

Grasping Keilah's hand Justus smiled at her. "No, Keilah, I didn't mean it like that. With the type of occupations my parents had, I was afforded the opportunity to go to places most people have never gone. You seem like the type of woman that would benefit from a change of environment. You need to do something different; I guarantee you'd see your muse reappear. Let me ask you, if you had the chance to go some place out of the states, would you go?"

Keilah pulled her hand away and adjusted her coat collar. "Sure I would. I hear Jamaica is kind of cheap to go to these days."

Justus sat silent, staring at the traffic, seeming to search for a response. "No Keilah, I mean farther than that. Jamaica's nice, don't get me wrong, but I mean a different type of experience. Would you go? I mean no worries about how much it would cost or where you will stay. No worries what so ever, other than whether you're going to drink white or red wine with your dinner. Would you go?"

Keilah giggled. "Sure who wouldn't?"

Justus tapped the steering wheel. "I will remember you said that."

Pulling into the parking lot, Keilah felt a strange feeling suddenly overcome her. When Justus opened her door, she almost stumbled.

"I want you to fall for me, but not literally."

Keilah smiled at his corny yet cute remark as she allowed him to hold her hand.

The smell of the curry in the air some how became an aphrodisiac as their fingers interlocked. As they stepped through the threshold, Keilah suddenly felt like she was slowly walking in an ever-increasingly large pool of water. What was she feeling and why was she feeling what ever it was?

Noticing Justus slowly removing his hand from hers, Keilah worried he felt it too. As the server led them to a table, Keilah was relieved that his hands were now resting on her shoulders.

Looking around the restaurant, Keilah was once again impressed. Just when Keilah was about to release what ever it was tugging at her insides, a woman's glance caught hers. The tugging twisted itself into a knot as Keilah and the other woman exchanged salutations.

Handing a menu to Keilah, Justus noticed the distraction. "You know her or something?"

Keilah perused the menu and glanced at the woman across from her once more.

"No. She just looked familiar for some reason, maybe school or something I guess."

Justus watched Keilah glance at the woman again. "You know we are all familiar spirits."

"What are you, some spiritualist or is the term universalist these days?"

Touching Keilah's hand, Justus pulled her menu away from her face. "All of that and so much more. I am a philosophy professor with a Jewish father and a Roman Catholic mother. All I meant was that we all cross paths at some point, it's not always the face you remember but rather the experience."

While Keilah tried to digest his words, she felt that submerged feeling creep toward her temples as an all too familiar scent yanked her neck sharply left to see André sitting across from the woman, who is now identifiably Alisha by the swollen belly and the sparkler she was twisting around her finger.

The knot in Keilah's stomach snapped and let loose a burning flame that quickly spread. The throbbing of her heart was joining in rhythm to the heavy breathing that was trying its best to expose too much.

Once Keilah got pass Alisha's belly, she scrutinized the woman André had chosen over her more closely.

The first thing she noticed was the long black hair hanging down her back. Reluctantly conceding it wasn't a weave, Keilah tried to figure out what type of figure she had before André had knocked her up. She was tall and leggy, like Keilah, but sleeker and slimmer like a cheetah from what Keilah could gather. Looking at Alisha's eyes, she wondered if they were naturally hazel or were they contacts. Leaning slightly, Keilah saw why André grabbed her the way he did the night before , the girl barely had an ass. Keilah laughed to herself. Compared to Keilah's rich reddish brown skin, Alisha's was a sallow hue of brown, more yellow than brown, reminding Keilah of lumpy corn muffin batter.

Remembering that she had chipped toenail polish hidden underneath nylons and boots and a tired ponytail snapped in the back, Keilah felt less amused. Regardless of whether Alisha has a butt or not, Keilah painfully conceded that Alisha had André.

Standing in what looked like suspended animation; André cleared his throat not knowing what was going to happen next. Alisha looked at André and then at Keilah, knowing now assuredly who the woman at the other table must be.

Justus offered his hand to André. "Hey man, you must be a friend of Keilah's. I'm J. A. Hunt."

André grateful for the save, shook Justus's hands.

"Uhm, yeah my name is André."

Widening her eyes, Alisha gave an exaggerated waddle from her seat, making sure her ring was in full view. "And I am Alisha."

Deciding not to extend her hand, Alisha waved playfully. "Hi Keilah. We never officially met. How are you?"

Keilah nodded back and took a long sip from her water glass.

The fire inside of Keilah was dying down the longer she stared at the look of bittersweet remembrance in André's eyes. Seeing that look told Keilah so much more than the night before…she knew. When André kissed Alisha, he knew. When he made love to her, he knew. In the middle of the night after Alisha had satisfied him, André still yearned for *her*.

"I'm fine. Congratulations on your…uhm nuptials."

Watching Alisha twist her engagement ring, yet again, Keilah let smugness savor a little sweet justice as she replays the little secret of the night before.

André noticed that the server had left the bill on the table. "Nice meeting you J.A. and it was good running into you again Keilah."

Keilah replied with a smirk. "I know it was."

Watching as André and Alisha walked to the host stand, Justus noticed the bottle of wine that was left on the table, and began to pour. "So that's him?"

Keilah returned her attention to the menu.

"I feel like something with shrimp."

Riding home, Alisha couldn't help but notice the silence that was bouncing off the windows. Not knowing what to say, Alisha sifted through André's CDs.

Turning the volume up a little louder, André tries to drown out the crazy thoughts that were going through his head. How could Keilah be out with someone else, the very next night? Trying to shake off his jealousy, André started nodding his head to the CD Alisha had put into the CD player. Some foreign dude, André couldn't even tell where he was from. Laughing to himself, André figured the accent was as fake as he probably was.

As Alisha leaned over and kissed his bottom lip, André twitched a little, wondering if Keilah had kissed Justus the way she kissed him

175

the very night before. Slowly gliding her hand across André's thigh, Alisha joins in with the song that was now playing.

"I know that's right Jill sing it... I am not afraid...I am not afraid...you hear that baby...I am not afraid!"

Ejecting the CD, André quickly parked the car and exited. Almost forgetting to get Alisha's door, he turned and quickly opened it, kissing her on the cheek.

Upon entering the house, Alisha jumped in André's arms and kicked off her shoes. Lying on the bed, André began to undress Alisha slowly. With each button that was unfastened, another flash of Keilah surfaced in his mind. Each kiss André laid across Alisha seemed to take him further backward. Trotting past the night before, rewinding quickly through the last two years and pausing in freeze frame to cold nights like that one in a warm familiar bed, a few miles away in what now seemed like yesterday.

Stark naked and confused, Alisha looked up at André wondering where he was at that moment. As they seemed to be uncomfortably tangled, Alisha realized where he was and squeezed him tighter, hoping some how to bring him back to her. When André rose up abruptly and put on his lounge pants, Alisha knew she had been unsuccessful.

Having invited Justus inside for tea, Keilah looked over at him, sitting in the same spot André occupied the night before. As they sipped the tea, Keilah kept up with the conversation while every so often allowing her thoughts to drift to a place where she knew there was no room for her. Pulling her thoughts back, Keilah happened to catch something Justus said.

"I'd like to share a rainbow with you. Go away with me."

Keilah glanced over at Justus and stands up. "Excuse me?"

Justus smiled and grabbed her hands, pulling her down to the couch. "Keilah, don't get all uptight, I didn't mean it like that... unless you want to take it like that."

Keilah laughed and playfully hit his shoulder.

"What I meant was I am planning to go to South Africa in December. I would love you to see what beauty is like there. The rainbows look magnificent spread across a waterfall on the other side of the equator. All you need to do is dust off your passport; I have enough frequent flyer miles. Take an adventure."

Looking over at Justus, all fine and exotic, Keilah amused herself at how this all seemed like some chick lit plot twist. "I don't know you well enough to even go out of town with you for the weekend, let alone out of the country. How long have we been talking, two or three weeks?"

Finishing off his tea, Justus smiled. "It's been almost two months, counting our conversations over the telephone, by December it will be three and a half months. You know I won't harm you, Keilah. I am too familiar to you."

Slowly sipping her tea, Keilah had to agree but she wouldn't tell him. It was at that moment when her spirit whispered a few things that awaken a new awareness.

"Justus do you believe in soul mates, better yet do you believe that maybe people knew each other in another time or place…like in heaven before we are born?" Feeling silly, Keilah quickly grabbed his empty cup and walked to the kitchen to fill it with more water.

"Yes, Keilah, I do…you knew I did…you just wanted to make sure you believed it. People have affinity to one another most often not understanding why. I remember a few years back I got an email that broke it down simply."

Keilah returned to the couch and handed him a fresh cup of tea.

Blowing over the hot steam, Justus continued as he took Keilah's hands in his. "Yes, well I will go a step further. It can be triggered by a new yet familiar touch. Or a certain look you notice in another's eyes."

Turning her glance downward, Keilah attempted to hide her excitement.

Drawing his hand to her face, Justus seductively whispered, "Or a kiss..."

Turning back toward Justus, Keilah watched as his lips danced gently across her hand making that vacant space between like and love look less empty and full of possibilities. As he pressed his lips against hers, Keilah closed her eyes and the space widened and lengthened. Then, André came to mind.

Hugging Justus goodnight, Keilah locked the door behind him. Climbing into bed, she tucked her pillow underneath her and second-guessed sending Justus home. Why should she sleep alone when she knew André wasn't?

Tugging Alisha tightly, André kissed her good night once more and closed his eyes tightly. As he drifted off to sleep, André tried not to think about Justus holding Keilah as he had held her the night before. Rolling over on his side, André prayed to fall asleep.

Chapter 17

"Norelle couldn't help but notice something was a little different."

When Keilah heard the doorbell, she couldn't believe she had slept until noon. Stumbling toward the door, she knew who it was.

"Well, girl what happened Friday? You and André back together?"

Keilah gave Norelle a surprised look as she closed the door behind her.

How did she know I saw André?

"What? Girl you are crazy. Let me go wash my face and brush this morning breathe out of my mouth."

Norelle giggled as she walked to the kitchen, pulling out a bottle of orange juice and two breakfast platters out of a paper bag. Retrieving two champagne glasses from the cabinet, Norelle heard Keilah returning and quickly filled the glasses; handing one to Keilah.

"Girl, I need to know all the details, from start to finish. First, let's have a toast. Valentine's came at little late this year but it came!"

Keilah sipped from the champagne glass and broke into laughter. "Norelle! What are you talking about? How do you know I saw André?"

Norelle opened up her platter and nibbled at a piece of toast. "How do I know? I spoke to André when he was looking for you. I know you got my message. I figured you two were all underneath each other so you didn't have a chance to call. So I gave you a day. I know y'all did it. So what's the next move? Did he kick old girl to the curb? What's going on with that?"

Keilah was truly confused. "André called you? When, and for what? Wait, how did he even get your number?"

After biting into her bacon, Norelle realized she had said too much. Taking a mouthful of eggs, Norelle smiled weakly and shook her head.

"No, Nori. It seems like you know more than me right about now. What message did you leave me?"

Norelle stuffed another piece of toast in her mouth and pointed to Keilah's phone. As Keilah reached for the phone and dialed, Norelle took the juice bottle to her mouth and took a big gulp.

Hanging up the phone, Keilah turned toward Norelle, bit down on her bottom lip and stormed out of the room. When she returned, she was puffing on a cigarette and walking in a circle. Norelle wasn't quite sure what was coming next so she waited as she poured Keilah more orange juice.

"Don't you have enough going on in your own life? Why do you have to stick your nose in mine? His situation is a done deal. We talked and squared away some things but nothing has changed. Plus I got a new man."

Backing away from Keilah, Norelle propped her hands on her hips. "Done deal? You can't be serious. You mean that white collar done got Dré soft. He can't be still marrying that girl after she slept with Linc. Now, that right there is crazy. I never saw him going out like that."

Replaying in her mind what escaped from Norelle's lips, Keilah jumped when the cigarette fell out of her mouth and onto her leg. Picking the cigarette up from her carpet, Keilah took a few more puffs and looked at Norelle blankly. "What did you just say?"

Norelle opened up the next platter and handed it to Keilah. Seeing that Keilah pushed it aside, Norelle mixed the eggs with the grits.

"Norelle!!!"

"Okay, K. Before I say anything else, you have to promise me that you won't be mad with me. Anything that I did was out of love."

Keilah poured the remaining bit of orange juice in her glass, lights another cigarette and nods.

"Okay. After you told me you weren't going to pursue André I kind of tried to play cupid for you by going to have a talk with him. And on my way to his office I saw Linc all up on this chick, only I didn't know it was this Alisha girl until she popped up at Dré's office just as I was about to leave. So after that I…"

Keilah shut her eyes tightly, trying not to say a word…but failed. "You did what! Why in the hell did you do that? André probably thought I put you up to that schoolgirl shit. How could you make me look desperate and miserable like that?"

Norelle followed behind Keilah into the living room. "No, K. He didn't take it like that. He seemed kind of glad to see me. But check it. I got her butt in the act…look."

Taking the cell phone from Norelle, Keilah looked at the pictures in silence.

"I got Lincoln's last Maryland address from a cop I know and rode past there. And guess who I saw over there…Alisha. She handed him something in his hand in this picture. Move to the next one and you'll see them …"

Keilah wasn't sure if she wanted to laugh or cry. "So you went on some Cheater's stake out mission. What is this suppose to do? You don't know if Linc knows her already. They could be cousins for all you know. By the date on the pictures, you held this for almost three weeks. Why are you just now telling me all this?"

Norelle snuck and inhaled the smoke from Keilah's cigarette. "I held it mainly because of the way you are acting right now. I knew you would do just what you are doing right now. I spoke to him and he acted like he just met her. Why did he do that? I saw them up on each other a few blocks from André's job then I saw her at his grandmother's crib. They shady, I'm telling you what I know. That baby probably ain't even Dré's."

When her phone rang, Keilah pointed to Norelle to be quiet. "Hey Justus. What's going on? I would have loved to but a friend of mine just brought me some breakfast. Dinner…sure. Where? You are going to cook, really. I don't care, anything, seafood. Okay, I'll bring something sweet beside myself. Okay, six o'clock is perfect. Okay, until later."

"Who is Justus?"

Keilah's smile became twisted. "He is my next boyfriend and André is my ex. I don't know what mess André has boiling but I saw the two of them Saturday evening after I spent the night with him Friday. I felt all of two cents. They looked like a happy couple to me. So, I am moving on. We talked about some stuff and yes we did it…but it was about closure so that is that."

Norelle opened her cell phone again. "So you trying to tell me that you are not going to use this loaded gun I am handing to you. You are going to let bitterness rule you. Come on, you know something is up with this chick. You're not going to tell him! Apparently Dré doesn't know and you need to hip him to this game she trying to run on him."

Keilah walked to the kitchen and threw the empty containers into the trash. The whole situation did sound suspect but how would she look coming at him with all this. "I am saying nothing. And you better not either. If that is what is going down, that's what Dré gets. What goes around comes around. Now let me tell you about Justus. He is a professor and he…"

"K, I can't believe you are going to do André like that. If you love him, you'd at least tell him and let him do whatever he chooses but you can't just let him walk into a situation like that. I know you still love him."

Returning to the living room, Keilah reached for the remote and turned the television on.

"It doesn't matter if I love him or not. He is with the woman he is in love with. While we sit here debating on him, he is probably picking out a crib with her. No, call it what you want but I am moving on. Now let me give you the deal on Justus."

Alisha was like a kid in a toy store, André thought as he watched her go through the aisles in the Baby Superstore. Looking at the cribs, he began to wonder if they should get white or the dark oak. After Alisha handed him her purse, he saw she had decided on the dark oak and was asking how to put it on the registry. As he placed the purse in the cart, her phone vibrated. He normally didn't look at her phone but when the call came up as Lincoln, he had to answer.

"Hey Linc. What's going on?

Lincoln hesitated when he heard André answer the phone. "Hey Dré. What's good?"

"I was going to ask you the same thing, Linc."

"Uhm… nothing. Nia asked me to call Alisha about coming past here to bring her something. Just tell Alisha to call Nia back at my house."

When Alisha returned dragging a diaper genie, André gave a smile to erase his concern. "Linc just called you."

Alisha grabbed her phone and looked at it. "Really? What did he say? Something's wrong with the place?"

André saw uneasiness on her face but decided to ignore it. "Yeah, He said Nia asked him to call you; she needs you to bring her something."

Alisha fidgeted with her purse and looked down. "Oh, I know what she is talking about. I will get with her later. Let's finish our registry."

André parked the empty cart and removed her purse. "We can finish it online. Let's stop pass Linc's. It must be important since she had him call you."

Alisha tried to shake her irritation as she pulled out her bankcard and headed for the ATM machine. *Damn that Lincoln.*

Checking on the roast in the oven, Norelle was glad it hadn't burned. She had fallen asleep and needed to start the cabbage. By the time she finished cutting the cabbage, it was almost five o'clock and Raymond hadn't called all day. She knew he had some clients to see but he usually checked in. Then she thought about the boxers. Blaming this sudden case of paranoia on the hormones, Norelle turned her thoughts to Keilah.

She knew she had to respect Keilah and leave it alone but how could she. She knew Keilah and André still loved each other but as she added the cabbage to the pot, she pondered if maybe the two of them didn't belong together.

Realizing she hadn't seasoned the water, Norelle pulls a pack of smoked turkey necks out of the freezer and added them to the boiling pot with a few chunks of butter and spices.

Norelle knew this Justus character was just a distraction for Keilah but from what she told her, Justus was an interesting one. Maybe Justus would be the one for her. From what Keilah told her, he had all the right stuff—tall, fine, and educated, with a splash of eccentricity. The one thing Norelle didn't like was the whole Internet thing. She didn't know anybody who really met a decent person on the web. More often, they had something wrong with them. Then he was mixed and foreign, as far as Norelle could see all that added up to crazy and crazier. Then there was all this going to South Africa stuff; why did he want to take her to some foreign country? Normal guys take a woman to Atlantic City or even Jamaica. She couldn't believe Keilah was even thinking about it. He was fine from the picture Keilah showed her but he wasn't fine enough to follow to the other side of the world. It was all an escape from what was about to go down and she could understand where Keilah was coming from, but she had the option to change all that. Norelle knew the night the two of them spent together was not just some last meal booty thing…but she had to stay out of it, but Keilah didn't. No matter what, Keilah had to set aside her jealousy and tell André. He didn't need to get played like that.

As the smell of the onions took her breath, Norelle knew deep down she had little room to judge Alisha, even though in her realm of understanding the situations were different.

Reaching into the cabinet for the rice, LT startled her when he appeared out of nowhere. "Hey! You scared me creeping in here quiet like that. You have fun at Camron's?" LT nodded and went to his room, not saying a word. Norelle knew he was probably still upset about Tariq. All she could do was love him up the best way she knew how.

When Raymond's car pulled up, Norelle perked up. Running to the door, she greeted him with a big hug and kiss.

"Wow, let me go out and comeback in again. It smells good in here. You got some cabbage cooking. Now that's what a man likes coming home to."

Stepping back, Norelle couldn't help but notice something a little different. "How did your client visits go?"

Raymond grabbed a soda out of the fridge and opened up the oven. "Good. Two of them were simple jobs. The third was a little more complex; it is a rehab job. Damn, this roast smells good, when is dinner?"

Turning down the rice, Norelle checked the cabbage and turned the fire down low. "Soon. Did you stop past your mother's today?"

Taking the last sip of soda, Raymond crushed the can and tossed it into the trashcan.

"Naw, why?"

Norelle loaded the dishwasher. "No reason just curious. You need me to update your client spreadsheet for you?"

Raymond grabbed his cell phone from his hip and checked it. "No. I got it. I'm going upstairs to freshen up for dinner."

Watching Raymond leave out of the kitchen, Norelle saw him dialing and speaking low as he headed up the stairs. The smell of onions and cabbage couldn't mask that he smelled different.

Having almost forgotten, Norelle grabbed her cell phone and forwarded the pictures to Keilah; the ball was now in her court. As she heard the shower running, Norelle decided that it was time to check some things out in her own camp.

Chapter 18

*"I don't want to have sex with you.
I want to make love to you."*
— Justus

As Keilah drove through the neatly manicured cul-de-sac, she became amused by the street names. Snowflake Drive, Snow Drift Lane and finally Avalanche Terrace; Columbia had some of the most pretentious names. Ringing Justus's doorbell, she felt her purse vibrate. Checking her phone, she sighed and quickly closed it when Justus opened the door. Norelle would have to wait.

Keilah was immediately seduced by an exotic scent dancing around in the air as soon as she cleared the door. Eyeing the incense stick, Keilah knew she definitely smelled Nag Champa. Removing her coat, a curious aromatic mix of curry and garlic with something sweet joining the two together, distracted her nose; maybe cinnamon she thought to herself. Taking two steps down, Keilah stopped in her tracks as her eyes became fixated on a large picture hanging above his fireplace.

Taking her coat and bag, Justus smiled." You like it?"

Stepping closer to the picture, Keilah touched the edges and examined it more closely. "Like it! Yes. It's raw, yet refined. The women are not finished but clearly defined. Each has her own hue and her own crown. Like this woman has a mass of curled locs…cultivated rebellion, while this woman has a smooth long mane…refined intention and the third woman has this massive afro…self-expression, without compromise. This is awesome. But I am not quite sure of the faces."

Placing his hands on Keilah's shoulders, Justus leaned in close to Keilah's right ear, causing her to jump. "Why, because they only have eyes?"

Keilah stepped back slightly, mischievously grazing her body closer to his. "Well, yes. You tell me."

Backing away, Justus walked to a nearby bar and poured two glasses of wine. "Well, we know that the eyes are the mirror of the soul. So perhaps we are supposed to focus on what their eyes are saying... underneath their crowns, as you put it."

Taking the wine from Justus, Keilah nodded and sipped the wine. "Oh, this is good. What is this?"

Taking Keilah by the hand, he led her to the sofa. Sitting down, she eyed a lovely decorated dining room table in the next room.

"This is a Chenin Blanc from South African. Can you taste the hint of guava and melon?

Taking another sip, Keilah stood up and took a personal tour, looking around, noticing other art work that were reminiscent in style to the first one. Keilah leaned in closer to see the name.

"Who is V?"

Reaching for the stereo's remote, Justus turned on the CD player and allowed Dwele to serenade while they conversed.

"Vashti."

Finishing off her glass of wine, Justus awaits with the bottle ready to offer a refill.

"You must really like her. You have a lot of her work in your house."

Taking a pack of matches from a nearby shelf, Justus headed for the dining room to light the candles. "Yes, I do. She and I are very close as a matter of fact."

Following Justus to the dining room, Keilah hid a tinge of jealousy that had crept up her back. "Hmmm close. And what is close? Like sister friend close or ex girlfriend to friend girl close?"

Heading to the kitchen, Justus responded softly. "Closer than that, Vashti is my best friend."

Realizing she had finished off her second glass of wine in less than thirty minutes, Keilah asked where the bathroom was located, and quickly followed his directions upstairs.

Slowly as she walked past what appeared to be his bedroom, she peeked in to see more.

The bed was large and solid mahogany...unmistakably king-sized. Looking at the four thick bedposts, Keilah allowed her mind to go to a place she knew she shouldn't be going but wanted to. The four large pillows were in matching burgundy and gold shams that laid invitingly across a full and fluffy bedspread, just right for laying back in.

Getting herself together, she continued on to the bathroom, giggling to herself as she looked at the sunken bathtub and sandalwood incense cones.

He is a player. Vashti was probably up in here last night.

Quietly opening the medicine cabinet, she saw the normal things with no weird looking prescription bottles.

He probably keeps the weird meds in the sock drawer.

Once she descended to the bottom of the steps, she found the lights had been dimmed and the table dressed..

Pulling out her chair, Justus laid a cloth napkin in her lap and then removed the silver top off of the serving plates.

Lord, this going to be hard. Fine ass man cooking; damn this food smells good.

"I fixed for your culinary pleasure, sweet curry fish, saffron rice and fresh steamed string beans."

As Justus fixed her plate, she remembered Vashti.

"So you and Vashti, the artist, are *best friends*; tell me more."

Placing his plate on the table, Justus took his seat beside her and took her by the hand. "Let's say grace, shall we?"

Quickly nodding his head, Justus said a prayer. He watched her intensely as she ate.

Piercing a small piece of fish with her fork, Keilah couldn't resist being impressed with how the meat flaked. Dipping it in the sauce, Keilah returned to the question. "So tell me about Vashti."

Stuffing a chunk of fish and rice in his mouth, Justus quickly swallowed. "What do you want to know?"

Placing an even larger piece of fish in her mouth, Keilah could not respond right away, she was too busy enjoying the intoxicating mixtures of taste that were exciting her palate.

"What did you season this fish with? What is this sweetness I taste?"

Justus smiled and poured more wine into her glass.

"I added some dates to the curry sauce. You like it?"

Dates! Yes, that's right, dates. Don't get distracted he knows you are thinking of giving him some.

"Back to your best friend, Vashti. Does she love your curry fish too?"

Finishing off his string beans, Justus added a few more to his plate, along with more fish and rice. "As a matter of fact she does. Why don't you just ask me what you really want to ask me?"

I can't come right out and ask him. He'll think I am crazy or something.

"What do you think I want to ask you?"

Seeing that her plate was almost empty, Justus added more food. "What you really want to know, Miss Fort, is if she is someone I am involved with so you can decide how far you want to go with this thing."

Almost chocking on her food, Keilah took a gulp of wine and cut her eyes at Justus.

He thinks he is so smart. Arrogant is what it is.

"I am an above the board type of man. Whatever I tell you is what it is. You just have to trust in that."

Finishing off the last of her meal, Keilah dabbed the corners of her mouth and swirled the wine around in her glass. "I should just trust what you say and not question anything? Come on now."

Clearing the table, Justus motioned for Keilah to follow him into the kitchen. Reaching under the sink for the detergent, Justus continued. "You, like most women, know true from false. You know I am telling the truth but you don't want to believe it. You don't want to believe truth when you see it because you have spent so much time trying to convince yourself of so many lies."

Keilah watched him load the dishwasher, thinking on what he just said. Reluctantly, she had to agree but by no means was going to let him know it. "That sounds all nice Dr. Hunt but the reality is brothers run game. That is not to say that the sisters don't either but brothers have heard the statistics. Four women for every man...then of course we have to worry, about not only the other woman, but the other dude. And I am not even going to hit you with men who are underemployed or undereducated or over drugged or over institutionalized. So why should I trust what you say?"

Justus turned the knob on the dishwasher and grabbed the basket of berries Keilah brought and placed them in a bowl. "Why are you asking the question, when you already do? You want me to convince you not to trust me? It is what it is."

Not knowing what to say, Keilah finishes off her wine as Justus scoped two spoonfuls of cool whip on top of the fruit.

Seeing the expression on Keilah's face, Justus kissed her hand and led her back to the living room. "Let me ask you a question, Candace."

Keilah wrinkled her nose as she picked up a strawberry. "Candace?"

Justus ate a few blueberries. "Candace means queen, sweetness. Now, you say that all these experts have told you that there are four women for every one man. Correct?"

Trying to hide her blush, Keilah quickly nodded and ate another strawberry.

"Okay, now who are these four women and who is this one man? Say the first woman is a drug addict and the second one is underemployed, with no ambition or drive. Lady number three is sexually confused and slightly crazy. Who is woman number four?"

Keilah released a giggle and fed him a strawberry. "I don't know who she is? It all depends who the man is. Is it Hill Harper or LL? If it is, then the woman is me."

Justus reached for the remote and changed CDs.

How does he know I like Van Hunt?

"Okay, who is that woman? Who is Keilah?"

She couldn't believe she was actually dumbstruck. She really didn't know how to answer it. It wasn't as if Keilah didn't know who she was, or did she?

"Well, I am a strong black woman who is cute and smart. I have a good job. I mean what else am I suppose to say? I like long walks in the park and candlelight dinners."

Justus laughed and fed her blueberries. "My Candace, you have managed to place yourself right back with the other three. You don't think there isn't perhaps a woman doctor who has a cocaine habit. Some woman cashier at the KFC that has untapped talent buried deep behind the disappointments of life. You think there isn't some beautiful model or actress hiding her Zoloft behind a bookcase when her second date of the night shows up. I can tell you I know all three because I dated them. What sets you apart Keilah?"

Pouring the last bit of wine in her glass, Keilah tried to think of a clever response. "You tell me. You responded to my personal."

Dipping a few blackberries in the cream, Justus brushed them softly against her lips. "I already know. The question is do you know? My dear Candace, you still have that sparkle in your eyes that most women have lost...mature curiosity that is wrapped around expressiveness that desires expansion. You have the thing that kept Adam with Eve."

Finishing the last of her wine, Keilah felt that warm and fuzzy feeling that always seemed to lead to disappointment. "Wasn't that what got them kicked out of the garden?"

Breaking a sprig of peppermint in half, Justus placed one-half in Keilah's mouth and chewed on the other. "It's all in how you look at it. Regardless, Adam knew that when he saw her he saw himself. Flawed but beautiful and perfect as was he. When they left the garden, they went on a journey. That was when their relationship really began. A real man searches for that in a woman. If she has that, all the other generic ones don't even matter"

Before she knew what happened, Keilah's lips readily tasted his and her mind was thinking of a more intimate kiss underneath a South African waterfall.

As Justus laid her across the sofa, his lips played a sensual game of connect the dots between her left ear lobe, down her neck and downward to her collarbone, as his hands navigated her body like a familiar traveler. As Keilah kicked off her shoes, she led his hand to assure him he was on the right path. As he pressed his body on hers, she became aware that she probably wouldn't be disappointed. Closing her eyes, she let herself go as she fumbled for her purse.

As her hand touched the condom wrapper, her mind took her back to Friday night and she tensed up.

What the hell am I doing? I can't sleep with him. I was just with André. That is nasty and it's too soon any damn way. He'll think I am some Internet hoe.

Taking her hand in his, Justus gently pulled it away from her purse and shifted his weight. Laying his lips closely to her ear, Justus whispers, "I didn't do any of this for any other reason than to show you a little more of me and see a little more of you. I don't want to have sex with you. I want to make love with you. If we lay together tonight, we'd have sex. I want more and so do you."

When Nia turned the corner, she saw André's car turning out of the block at the top of the court. Quickly parking her car, she ran inside to see Lincoln fidgeting around.

"Was that André I just saw leaving?"

Lincoln was flipping sofa cushions. "Yeah, he and your sister just stopped past. Have you seen my keys?"

Noticing the edge in his voice, Nia slowly walked closer to him. "What were they doing here?"

Tossing a vase from a shelf and onto a nearby chair, Lincoln looked increasingly irritated.

"Hey, Lincoln, that's my sister's vase. What is wrong with you?"

Ignoring her, Lincoln headed for the kitchen. Nia jumped when she heard him moving the refrigerator. When Lincoln returned, his eyes were larger and sweat poured down his face. When he attempts to move the bookcase, Nia quickly grabbed his arm.

"What in the hell is wrong with you? You are going to tear up my sister's stuff."

Shoving her hand away, Lincoln rubbed his mouth and surveyed the room. "What the hell is wrong with me? What the hell is wrong with you? When did you start having this love for your sister? You burnt a hole in the chair last night and laughed. What do you care? Do you have my keys?"

Nia stumbled as Lincoln almost knocked her down. "What were Alisha and André doing over here?

"What's the problem, my boy and his fiancée can't blow though?"

Nia readjusted the pillows on the sofa. "No. How long are you going to play this game? This is wrong. I know an account executive at AT&T. She's a good friend of mine, I am sure she can

193

hook you up with an AE position. That way you can have a steady paycheck and maybe if you're nice to me, I can go half on this rent with you. What do you think about that?"

Lincoln paused and expelled a hearty laugh. "You're getting soft on me Nia? Where is this conscious coming from? How you put things down, Alisha hasn't been much of a sister to you. Hell, you even tried to act like it should be you walking down the aisle with Dré. You know she grimy."

Nia, for a moment agreed with him. "Yeah, but guess what, that's still my sister and this right here is crazy. What do you plan on doing? Some way it is going to come out, then what? I thought André was your boy."

Noticing Lincoln eyeing her purse, Nia quickly swung it over her shoulder.

"What's wrong with you? You think I am going to snatch your purse or something?"

Backing toward the door, Nia noticed her keys had fallen onto the floor. Before she could get them, Lincoln grabbed them and jiggled them in her face. "Listen I gotta make a run. Why don't you chill out here? I won't be long."

As soon as she saw Lincoln turn out, Nia grabbed her cell phone and called her sister.

"Alisha, this is Nia. We need to talk. Is André around?"

Muffling the phone, Alisha looked over to see André asleep and walked into the kitchen.

"Yes. What do you want?"

"Listen, I think you were right about Lincoln being on something."

"No shit, Nia. I told you I saw the damn pipe or did you just ignore that part."

"No, I just didn't see it... not at first. But he's been having these sweating fits and his runs to the store are getting more frequent and later. Then when he comes back, he is ... uhm..."

194

"Nonstop…I thought that was right up your alley."

"Whatever. You don't have to be nasty to me."

Alisha laughed. "Really? You are literally sleeping with the enemy. You thought it was a cute game. What he's stealing from you? Whipping on you …what?"

Listening to her sister, Nia wondered why she even called. "No and hell no. You the one with the most at stake, really. I am calling you to try to help you. What went down with you two … for real? I need to know."

Hearing André stirring, Alisha lowered her voice. "How I am supposed to trust you?"

"Because I am your sister and right now I am the only one you got in this. So tell me everything so I can help you."

Walking back toward the bedroom, Alisha quietly closed the bedroom door. "At this point, the only way you can help me is to kill his ass."

Knowing that Lincoln probably wouldn't be back for a few hours, Nia got comfortable.

"Just tell me everything. We may figure that out later."

Chapter 19

"Do you really know her Dré? Do you trust her?"
— Keilah

Sitting across from Norelle, Keilah couldn't help but notice she was distracted. Their lunch dates were usually filled with lots of talk but this afternoon it was silent.

"Nori, what's up? Everything okay?"

Norelle played with her salad and gave a weak smile.

"I am alright. Everything is good. Just thinking about what I am going to fix for Thanksgiving. You bringing that tired string bean casserole again?"

Keilah laughed and bit a large chunk out of her sandwich. "Everybody likes it except you. Actually, I will probably stop through but I am going to my mother's. Oh, did I tell you my sister is moving back up here? I gotta help her move some stuff from Virginia. Plus I won't be over there for Christmas."

Norelle raised her eyebrow. "Why? You're not saying what I think you're saying?" Noticing the smirk on Keilah's face, she knew what she meant. "You're really going to go to South Africa with some dude that you met on the damn Internet? Are you trying to make headline news or something? That it just crazy; you ain't in a Lifetime movie. I don't believe you; you're not going anywhere. Plus, he's suspect. You two were all hot and heavy and he took a rain check on the booty. Either he funny or he was having an outbreak. One or the other, I'm telling you."

Keilah bit into her sandwich and looked at her friend. Digging into her purse, she pulled out brochures and handed them to Norelle.

Norelle laid her fork down and thumbed through the pages. "So let me get this straight. You'd rather take a chance and go to the other side of the world with a guy you just met than tell the man you love he is being played and he can come back home?"

Keilah finished off her sandwich and took a bite out of her pickle. "Will you please leave this whole André thing alone? It is over, a done deal. If he's getting played that's on him and not my problem. I know this all sounds crazy but didn't you say I needed to do something I've never done for love...get a little crazy."

Folding the brochures, Norelle handed them back to Keilah and finished her salad. "So you're saying you're in love with Justus?"

"No, I didn't say all that. But I can see the possibility. We are just vibing so perfectly and it's beautiful. Can I have a little adventure?"

Norelle relaxed her frown. Her friend was falling in love. She still didn't like the whole South Africa thing, but apartheid was over. "Okay, girl. Do your thing. But I need to know his full name, his momma's maiden name, where you're staying ...all that! Wait, you got money for all that. You don't need to follow some dude anywhere with no dollars."

Keilah finished off her pickle and sipped her iced tea. "He said he will get my ticket with his flier miles, and I got some money saved up. I haven't told him for sure yet. I'm still a little nervous about the whole thing. I have to get a passport. Find out what shots I need. Maybe your right..."

Norelle sipped her lemonade and waved for the server to bring the check. "Don't get all scared now, Billy Bad Ass. I guess he is all right. I can run his stuff when I get back to the office; you know the IRS got a lock on everybody."

Relieved that her girl was with her, Keilah paid the check. "I guess I'll get on with it then. No, I need to think on it some more. You got me thinking now."

"What you need to do, K, is handle your business with André before you roll."

Working through lunch wasn't helping; André decided to take a break. Thanksgiving was two days away and the wedding was almost a month away. Invites were sent out, RSVPs received, deposits were made and he still hadn't gotten fitted for his tux. The night he spent with Keilah was looming more and more in his mind. He couldn't believe she hadn't called him since that night. He knew she felt something. He couldn't imagine that pretty boy was keeping her that occupied. He didn't even look like her type, André thought as he looked at his reflection in the monitor. Picking up the phone, he called Chris.

"Hey man. We need to hook up and get fitted for the tux."

Chris laughed in the phone. "I was waiting on you, Dré. It ain't no show without you. I tried to get in contact with you on Sunday. Did you see that I called?"

André leaned back in his chair. "Yeah. Alisha and I were running around all day. We went to the baby superstore. She spent at least two hours in there. Then we checked on Lincoln."

Chris released a hearty laugh. "That's right; he is leasing Alisha's old crib. Did y'all roll up on something? I know how Linc used to flip them honeys."

André loosened his tie and turned to look out the window. "Actually, he is chilling with her sister, Nia."

"Really? You mean Linc trying to settle down? What's going on? First you and now him?"

"I don't know about all that, Chris, but she has been over there a lot. Anyway, man I am going through a little something."

Chris changed his tone. "Dré, jitters are normal. You cool. Everybody gets them."

"Naw, it's not that. Hell, maybe it is. I feel like maybe I need a little more time. Are we ready to do this thing? She's been giving off this different vibe. I mean, she's acting the same but then she's not. Forget it!"

Chris chuckled. "Man, she is a bride to be, plus she pregnant! Just ride the wave. And whatever you do, don't see Keilah. That will have you all twisted up. You haven't talked to her or seen her, have you?"

Clearing his throat, André turned back to his desk and flipped through the paperwork.

"Naw, naw, course not. Well, actually I did see her with some dude last weekend. He had some fake ass accent."

"Dré, you sound a little jealous. You're not jealous are you? She gotta do her thing. You're doing yours."

"What! Come on Chris, why should I be tripping on her?

"I don't know, Dré, you tell me?"

Having taken half the day off, Nia quietly opened the door to Lincoln's place. Not knowing where he was, she hoped he had gone on that interview she set up for him. When she entered the bedroom, Nia saw several ties set out and figured he must have gone after all.

Starting with the boxes in the closet, Nia quickly began digging through papers. She couldn't believe that Lincoln not only had Alisha paying the rent but he was hitting her up for money. He was a ghetto terrorist and like all terrorist Lincoln got off on her fear but he won't be satisfied until he strikes. Had Alisha told André from the jump he would have been pissed but they could have worked it out, Nia thought. As she paused to look for Lincoln's car, Nia knew that would not have been the case. André was a black man. No red blooded black man is going to get over one of his boys sleeping with his woman. The whole pregnancy thing just made it worst. It was just a matter of time before karma was going to snatch her by the collar.

Finding nothing in the first box, she pulled the second box out and found a bunch of pictures. Looking at the pictures, she could see Lincoln wasn't lying about how he was living. His crib was like that. As she examined a crumbled picture, she figured the woman in the picture must have been *the* woman that Alisha was taking the beating for.

She wasn't all that, Nia thought but she did have a bad ass body and a tight weave. From the looks of her get up, she must have been a stripper. Putting the picture back in the box, Nia couldn't help but wonder why women like her and Alisha got all the men.

Alisha didn't wear her team jersey like sister girl in the picture but she ran much game while women like me sit on the damn bleachers watching them doing fake punts on men like Lucy did Charlie Brown wondering why?

Business contracts…bank statements…bingo…court papers. Examining the courts papers more closely, Nia became frightened the more she read. Hearing keys turn in the front door, Nia quickly grabbed a few things from the box, pushed it back in place and made it to the bathroom as Lincoln headed down the hallway toward the bedroom.

"Nia? What are you doing in the bathroom?"

Quickly flushing the toilet, Nia ran the water and collected herself.

"Using it! What else you think I am doing?"

When Nia opened the door, Lincoln was staring into the closet. Trying to tiptoe past the bedroom door, Nia was unsuccessful when Lincoln caught her shadow moving against the wall.

"Dag, you didn't even check me out Nia. How do I look?"

Standing at the door, Nia cautiously walked toward Lincoln. "You look good. Uhmm, how did it go?"

Grabbing Nia by the waist, Lincoln pulled her close. "I got the job. You hooked a brother up. They said I could start next week. You're really down for me, aren't you?"

Nia smiled up at him and nodded. "Of course I am."

Lincoln kissed her roughly on the cheek. "Look, I got to run out. I need to hit the health food store. Are you going to be here when I get back?"

Grabbing her purse, she walked out of the bedroom and down the hall. "No, I have a few things to take care of today. I think I am going to chill at my parent's tonight."

Passing through the kitchen, she stopped, eyeing a large bottle of vinegar. "Dag, that's a gallon of apple vinegar. What you plan on doing with that?"

Snatching her from behind, Lincoln playfully took a bite out of her neck. "Don't worry about that. What you need to be concerned with is this right here."

Feeling him pumping against her behind, she pulled away, trying to hide her awkwardness. "Boy, I told you I have things to do. It's already two o'clock; you should have gotten here earlier. I have an appointment."

Releasing his grip, he slapped her on the butt. "Alright. Don't be surprised if I'm ringing your phone later.

Trying not to run to her car, Nia quickly jumped in the driver's seat and grabbed her phone. "Alisha, we got a problem. I found some stuff and it ain't anything good. Meet me at the house…as soon as you get off!"

Deciding to call it a day, André was surprised when the receptionist said there was someone waiting to see him, but he was more surprised when she told him who it was.

Adjusting his tie, André checked himself in the mirror and went to open the door. "What brings you down here?"

As Keilah walked through the door, she wasn't quite sure. All she was sure of was that she wouldn't leave out the same way she came in. "Well, I wanted to talk to you. You got some time?"

Looking at Keilah in her business suit, André noticed how her hips had become more defined and womanly. As André extended a chair out to her, she sat down seductively and crossed her legs. Pulling his chair from behind his desk, André tried not to let his eyes linger too much on the long legs that used to wrap tightly around his waist. "What can I do for you Keilah?"

André's cool business tone made Keilah even more anxious. Not knowing where to begin, she looked around the room and laid eyes on her picture on the wall. "Wow, you still have that picture. I figured it was somewhere in storage."

André smiled at her. "Why would you think that? It's beautiful. What, you thought I bought it just to get your number?"

Happy to see his demeanor had changed, Keilah decided to ride the wave before she hit him with what she had come for. "Well, yes. How else did you think you'd get it?"

Leaning back in his chair, André laughed. "You were feeling me when you came in the club. You think that fake bump and spill trick fooled me. You threw the bait and I followed. I knew I'd get the number; I actually liked it. But back to the original question, what's up?"

Looking at André, she couldn't help but wonder if what she was about to tell him would do him more harm than good. What if she were wrong? What if she were right, where would that take things? Clutching her cell phone in her hand, Keilah knew either way her motive would look like nothing more than some jealous ex-girlfriend.

"Keilah, did you tune out on me? What does your boyfriend work down here or something? What was his name ... J.A something?"

Bringing herself back, she noticed André's eye color had changed to envy. He was jealous.

"Justus. No...he teaches in Baltimore."

"Oh, that's cool. What does he teach elementary, middle school...high school? He must really like education. They don't make very much, Alisha's a teacher in PG."

Smirking, Keilah shifted in her chair and let her skirt hike further above her knee. "Uhm, no ...he is a professor at University of Baltimore. He's looking to work on his doctorate next year maybe abroad."

"Oh, excuse me. I know you like educated brothers, no offense, K."

"None taken, Dré. How are your nuptial plans going?"

"Fine. Why are you asking? I thought you didn't care."

As she played with her blouse, Keilah wondered if she did care. Did she care because she felt like she should? What woman didn't feel a little burn when they hear an ex is getting married? Sure, the pregnancy was insult to injury and it being Alisha was the salt to the wound but this was what it was. "I don't care so much as I am curious. Dré, you were quite upset when you came past my place. But I guess you two smoothed it over."

Turning to look out the window, André's mind raced back to that night. He and Alisha didn't smooth it over so much as pushed it aside. "Yeah, I guess so but it really wasn't so much about her. I mean she overstepped her bounds with Harold and set some other things in motion. Alisha does a lot of things without thinking it through, then all she can say is she's sorry and she didn't know."

"You said your father dropped something heavy on you but you never said exactly what. What happened, Dré?"

Turning back around, André saw the tenderness in her eyes that always made him feel like he could tell her anything. "K, I really don't know if I need to rehash anything."

"Tell me, Dré."

"Keilah, really we don't need to go back down that road."

"Down what road, Dré? Please tell me."

Grabbing a nearby bottle of water, André swallowed a big gulp and closed his eyes. "Harold told me something that I would have rather not known, but thanks to Alisha trying to mend fences she wrapped barbed wire around it. She comes from a Cosby show house so she doesn't understand real family shit like you and I."

Leaning forward, Keilah stared André dead on.

"He told me that in spite of what he didn't do, he did the one thing that a real man would do and that was let his baby live. He and my mom thought about getting rid of me but he said he just couldn't do it and he was proud of me because I didn't do it either."

Trying to readjust her face, Keilah leaned back in her chair and closed her eyes. Recanting all that was said that night, it all made sense.

"See what I was saying, K? I didn't want to bring this up. So what brings you to DC?"

Not knowing how she was going to be able to change channels, Keilah paused and pulled out her phone, laying it on her lap. "I heard Lincoln was back in town. Have you talked to him?"

Wondering where he came up in the conversation, André paused. "Yeah, we hooked up. As a matter of fact I saw him this weekend, why?"

Am I sure I want to do this?

"I was just curious. Norelle saw him. She said he still looked good, had even took off a little weight. What brings him back to Maryland; I thought he was doing good in the ATL?"

Picking up his pen, André tapped it against the desk. "You came down here to ask about Lincoln? What, you want his number or something?"

No he didn't go there!

"What do you mean by do I want his number? Dré, please."

"Hey K, I don't know. Pretty boy may not be doing it for you. For all I know you may have been checking Linc from way back. I know how you women are."

Not you women… your woman.

Taking her cell phone from her lap, Keilah stands and straightened her suit. "You know, Dré, I really was debating whether or not I should come down here. My first thought was to leave it alone. What do I know? But you are right; you know how us women are… some of us."

Coming from behind his desk, André grabbed Keilah by the arm. "Hey K, I was just messing with you. You don't have to leave."

Staring back at André, she kissed him softly on the lips. As he pulled her closer, she breaks away. "No, I do have to leave."

As Keilah backed away, André moved in closer. "How well do you know Alisha?"

Stopping in mid stride André, paused. "What do you mean?"

Opening up her phone, Keilah cleared her throat. "You know her right."

Nodding, André felt prickly heat running run up the back of his neck. "What are you getting at Keilah?"

"Do you really know her Dré? Do you trust her?"

Trying to shake the feeling that had now taken residence in his temples, André squared his shoulders and looked intently into Keilah eyes, trying to figure out what they were saying.

"Of course I do. I'm marrying her and she's carrying my kid. What are you trying to get at, Keilah?"

The words fell from André's mouth like broken glass. Keilah's eyes glazed over as she glared back at André. Closing her phone, Keilah blinked to fight back the tears that had made a mad dash from the broken places of her heart.

"Okay, Dré"

The words sounded good coming out of his mouth but looking at Keilah, he knew he didn't feel the same conviction within himself. Reaching out to touch her, his hands were block by the coldness that now shielded her. "Keilah, I didn't mean it like that… well I did mean it but…"

Opening the door, Keilah placed her phone back in her purse and secured the strap on her shoulder. "No, don't apologize for falling in love again. I knew coming down here was a mistake." Quickly touching Keilah's cheek, André was startled when she grabbed his hand and kissed it. "Goodbye, André."

Deciding to take the stairs, Keilah dialed her phone, as she cleared the first flight. Her discomfort had eased for a moment.

"Hi Justus, its me. I'm going. I have all my stuff with me, how can I expedite this passport application?"

Alisha was relieved to see that no one was home but Nia. Stumbling as she made it up the long staircase, Alisha burst threw Nia's bedroom door, wide eyed and out of breathe. "What did you find out?"

Nia was stiff as a board as she sat on her bed. Turning around, she looked at Alisha and turned back around, lowering her eyes. Where would she begin? "Alisha he got some stuff with him, serious stuff."

"Serious stuff like what, Nia? Come on with it."

Sitting down next to her sister, Alisha tried to brace herself. Rubbing her belly, she exhales and nudges Nia.

"He has some charges in Atlanta. From the stuff I saw, he probably wasn't even suppose to leave Atlanta. He's on probation. He still has cases pending."

Digging in her purse, Alisha pulled out her cell phone. "Well we need to call the tip line and get his ass off the street. What, he has some drug charges, bad checks or something?"

Grabbing Alisha's hand, Nia takes the phone. "I'm not sure but he definitely was charged with assault and battery. He had an alias down there…Taylor Lincoln."

Snatching the phone back, Alisha sucks her teeth. "So he flipped his first and last name. Can I just call 911? They can pick him up from my old crib. As soon as they drag his ass out, it's yours."

Jumping up from the bed, Nia rolled her eyes as Alisha. "See, you don't think, you so quick on the damn trigger. We got to have them pick him up somewhere else. The place is still in your name, you might get charged with harboring a fugitive or something. You don't think; that's how you got in this mess in the first place. All this shit because you got mad because André wouldn't throw a picture away."

Alisha scooted off the bed and walked up on her sister pressing her belly against hers. "What! It wasn't anything but a colorful ass stick figure drawing with some damn chalk. He had the nerve to have it in a fancy frame...it was over with that bitch so I felt like I didn't have to see it every time I walked in his house. If you had a man, you'd understand what I'm talking about."

Nia lowered her eyes to Alisha's belly and exhaled noisily. Shaking her head, Nia backed away and sneered at Alisha. "You are so selfish. Damn you're almost thirty years old. When are you going to lay down that high school shit and grow up? Everything just has to be about you. He can't have anything that doesn't include you. You calling her a bitch and you snatched him from her; you took her man. What did she do to you?"

Smirking, Alisha walked back to the bed and sat down. "Look, if I see something that I want, I am on it. If some casualties occur, well that's all love and war baby sister. If he was so much hers, I wouldn't have gotten him. When I saw André he was dressed right, drinking right ...what was I supposed to do, think of another *sistah?* Please!"

Catching Nia's cool glare, Alisha paused. "Oh, you still salty two years later. Come on Nia, you were hemming and hawing for almost an hour that night; I had no idea André and I would be here."

Nia looked inside her purse, closed it and smiled back at her sister. "Lincoln is supposed to start this new job next week. Hold off the call until then, provided he passes his drug test."

Noticing Nia's preoccupation with her purse, Alisha tugged at it. "What're you hiding in the purse?"

Switching the purse to the other arm, Nia stood up and pulled her keys from her pocket. "Nothing you'd be interested in ... you think I'm hiding some Krispy Kreme's? You want me to go get you some?"

Kicking off her shoes and lying back on the bed, Alisha grinned.

Closing the door behind her, Nia tapped her purse and skipped down the stairs.

As tears welled in his eyes, Norelle knew Raymond was trying to be strong. She had to grip onto the little ounce of faith she had as tightly as she was holding onto his hand. The drive back home was long and quiet. Turning on the radio seemed to magnify the silence.

"Ray, it's going to be fine. I'll just go on bed rest like the doctor said; things will be tight but we can do it. Maybe, I can do some eBay stuff? "

Raymond pulled her hand to his lips and said nothing.

As the car pull up to the house, Raymond quickly jumped out, opened the door for Norelle and quickly helped her to the house.

"Ray, I am fine...please."

Ignoring her, he continued to guide her steps to the house and through the door. They are startled when they see LT and his friend Corey running upstairs from the basement.

"Hey Ma, hey Ray! Y'all bring something to eat?"

Norelle smiled and walked toward the kitchen. Raymond grabbed her arm softly. "No, your mom needs to rest...wait ... is that door open down in the basement, I feel a draft...go close that door... it's wintertime, boy!"

LT and Corey looked at each other and ran back downstairs. Walking toward the basement Raymond yelled, "When you finish, come and look for the China Garden menu... Nori baby you want some garlic shrimp?"

Norelle really wasn't hungry but she knew Raymond wouldn't agree with her not eating. "That sounds fine. I'm going to go upstairs and lay down."

Raymond tenderly lifted her up. "I've got you, 'Lil Mama."

Norelle smiled and wrapped her arms around his shoulders as they headed up the stairs.

Gently laying her down on the bed, Raymond rubbed his face and sat down next to her. "Nori, we don't have to talk about it right now but you know some changes are about to go down. We are not losing this baby. All that ripping and running you do... that is a done deal. I'm going to go out and pick the food up. You two want anything else?"

Lifting up to kiss Raymond, Norelle whispered "No" and kissed his nose. As soon as she heard the front door slam, she reached for the phone.

André was glad Alisha wasn't home when he got there; Keilah's visit had given him a headache. Tossing his keys on the coffee table, he grabbed his cell phone and started dialing. *No, don't call her. You know she is just messing with your head.*

Closing the phone, he glanced at the blank space next to his stereo. He couldn't bring himself to put anything else there. Alisha tried putting some flea market knock off in its place but it just didn't look quite right and André pulled it down to her dismay. Keilah's picture, in all its complexity, brought simplicity to whatever crazy day he had just by looking at it...so taking it to work actually made more sense...Alisha was still pissed.

Lying back on the sofa, André closed his eyes and tried to take his mind to another place. As his mind began to search the archives, every place seemed to lead to Keilah. The good outweighed the bad all in all, but the bad was still heavy. André never wanted to hurt Keilah but he always seemed to...even today. *What did she expect me to do? Indulge her inquisition and say that I didn't know every nook and cranny about Alisha, and yes I did have a nagging little something that kept tapping me on the shoulder? Then what, say, "I still love you Keilah and I think I might be making a mistake!" Naw*

André grabbed the remote and channel surfed. It seemed like every commercial had something to do with a baby or a wedding. Laughing to himself, he decided to get a drink. As he entered the kitchen, he noticed a few slips of paper had missed the trashcan. As he picked the paper up, he saw how they had been ripped into the smallest pieces possible. He started putting them together, like pieces to a puzzle. As the pieces fell into place, the likes of money orders were taking form. Knowing they weren't his, André wondered what Alisha would need with money orders in those amounts. He knew she was working on her student loan but she always got him to get the money orders for her. Just as he felt his head surge again, the sound of Alisha's keys turning in the door distracted him. Scooping the pieces up, he quickly placed them in his pocket when he heard Alisha's footsteps coming.

"Hey Baby. I brought some chicken from my mom's house. She gave you an extra helping of beans and rice. You want me to heat it up?"

"Naw, I'm not hungry at the moment. Listen I need to go out for a little bit."

"Dag, Dré, I just got home. You have to leave out right now?"

Ignoring her, André grabbed his keys and slammed the front door behind him.

Norelle was glad when Keilah answered the phone.

"Hey girl. I'm sorry I didn't answer right away. I was going over some things with Justus. I went to DC and put my paperwork in. I had to pay extra to rush it."

"DC? You had to go down there to get a passport?"

Taking a pause, Keilah put her car in park and walked toward her apartment. "I took your advice and stopped by to see André. So…anyway after that short visit I still had time to get it done. The paperwork has to go down there anyway so I figured since I was there I could speed it up."

Shifting her weight on the bed, Norelle sat up and turned the volume up. "No, No back up. You saw André and you're still going? What happened?"

211

Unlocking the front door, Keilah placed her keys on the hook and kicked off her shoes. "Nothing happened."

"What do you mean nothing happened? Something had to have happened if you decided to go away."

Pouring a glass of cranberry juice, Keilah grabbed a pack of matches along with the ashtray and headed for her sofa.

"My decision to go to South Africa with Justus has nothing to do with André. I need a change. I have never really been anywhere and it is exciting. André is such a small flutter in the heartbeat of the world. I need …"

"Cut the bull, Keilah…please. You can tell that to Justus while you two are on the plane. What did André do to excuse away the pictures when you showed him?"

Taking a long drag from her cigarette, Keilah knew Norelle was right. "No, he didn't excuse away anything. I never showed them to him."

"What! Keilah, why not! You had the gun right in your hand. All you had to do was aim and shoot."

"No Nori, it's not even about all that. André loves Alisha, bottom line; and there is nothing I can say or do about it. Me showing him those pictures would have just broken his heart. Why would I do that to someone I love just because he doesn't love me anymore. That's vengeful and mean. That's not me."

"No, Keilah, it's not you but it should be. She doesn't love him; she loves what he represents…I'm telling you. You were there during the grind, Keilah. The late nights helping him study, the early morning pop quizzes. Your mom got him the inroad to the law firm and you made the ultimate sacrifice for him…he owes you. You do all the work and let some other woman come on the scene and reap the benefits without a fight?"

Lighting another cigarette, Keilah absorbed Norelle's words. "I didn't let Alisha do anything…André did. If he was so much mine, she wouldn't have had a chance. No one has to fight for what is rightfully theirs."

"Keilah, anything worth having is worth fighting for. I can't believe you didn't show him those pictures."

"What was I suppose to do, Norelle, burst in his office and just flash him my phone? He was already guarded when I went in there. I tried to ease into it, I asked him how well he knew Alisha; if he trusted her... and he does... without question. His words were 'Of course I do. I'm marrying her and she's carrying my kid.' Now how in the hell am I supposed to come up against something like that?"

Norelle fluffed her pillow and placed it underneath her back. "You are so sensitive, K. What else was he going to say? He's a man. You expected him to say anything else without evidence. Men feel things like we do but they don't act on them until they have facts. He wasn't going to lay his insecurities out to you just like that. You should have hit him with it. He's going to call you. In the back of his mind he knows she shady... I'm telling you."

"I don't want to talk about André anymore. On to the next thing, how did the doctor's visit go?"

Trying to wrap her conflicted emotions around a few words, Norelle chose to say nothing; hoping that when Keilah asked her again, she would know what to say.

"Well, how did it go Nori?"

"My OB said I have a cyst in my uterus, Keilah, the size of a grapefruit."

Not knowing what to say, Keilah remained silent; allowing Norelle to continue. "They said the pregnancy is like feeding it. The baby and this thing are fighting for space and from the looks of things, its winning. Raymond is a nervous wreck."

"Damn, Nori, I'm sorry. How are you?"

"I'm ok. My back is hurting some. I'm on indefinite bed rest depending on if this thing goes down on its own."

"No Nori... I mean how are *you*? How are you *feeling*?

"I really don't know how I feel. It might be a blessing if... well you know."

Putting out her cigarette, Keilah tried not to jump on Norelle. "I know what? You can't be saying what I think you are saying."

"K, I am a realist. We can start fresh once I heal. You can't imagine what I am going through. It sounds messed up but maybe it's a blessing in disguise."

Before Keilah could respond, she heard Norelle put the phone down as she talked to LT.

"Listen, Raymond's back with the food. I'm all right. I'll probably feel differently in the morning. I'll be home so call me."

As soon as Keilah hung up the phone; it rung again. Looking at the caller ID, Keilah smiled. "Hello, Mr. Hunt."

"You know you left your work badge and some papers over here."

"Did I? I'm sorry; don't want your other woman to get upset. I can comeback to get it if you like?"

Giving a sigh, Justus turned the music down. "You know that is really getting old... borderline irritating."

Taken a back Keilah sat up. "What do you mean?"

"You know what I mean, Keilah. This other woman stuff you keep tossing in the mix. You know otherwise but you still safeguard yourself with this little word foreplay. Does a man seem more attractive to you when there's another woman in the picture? Does the idea of playing hot potato with another woman for a man's affection turn you on?"

Offended and not knowing how to answer, Keilah finished off her juice. "I beg your pardon? I can't joke with you. Maybe this trip is a bad idea."

"Did I offend you, Keilah? Well, you offend me every time you say little silly things like that."

No he did not call me silly.

"You know what? I'm going to get my keys and head out there to get my stuff. Forget about this South Africa thing. I don't know what I was thinking. You just called me silly and that is..."

"That is what Keilah ... disrespectful. I didn't call you silly... I said you say..."

"Save it! I used to date a lawyer and I read Double Speak. Silly people say silly things."

"I didn't call you silly like you didn't call me a liar right?"

"What? Justus don't turn this around. It's done."

"Why does it have to be over when we haven't even made it around the first lap yet?"

He is really pissing me off ... where are keys?

"Keilah, will you listen to me. Why is it so hard for you to accept that I want you? Every time you say what you think are cute comebacks, you are not only saying one man cannot be completely enamored with you but you are also calling me a liar. Do you hear yourself? It's almost as if you want to push me away. Is that what you really want to do?"

Letting the ugly truth eat away at her anger, Keilah slumped back in the sofa. "Why do you constantly try to dissect every word I say? Why does everything have to be so deep?"

Gathering up Keilah's things, Justus smiled. "Keilah, I want to know *you*. I listen to every word; search for the hidden message hoping it will lead me to the real you. Can I come to you? I left something in my office and it would be the perfect excuse to see you again... provided you aren't still angry."

Quickly heading for the kitchen, Keilah agreed and hung up the phone. Loading the dishwasher, she realized he doesn't know she smokes. She rushed toward the window, opened it and lit incense.

Chapter 21

"Love is constant but it still changes."
— Keilah

After showering, Keilah slipped into her cute, but sexy, red lounging set. Hearing the knock at the door, she glanced at the clock and was surprised that Justus made it there so fast. Taking an extra swig of mouthwash for good measure, Keilah remembered she had forgotten her body butter and quickly slapped some on her arms and neck, backtracking for an extra double scoop for her stomach and booty.

Flinging the door open, her mouth dropped. Before she could determine how to handle the situation, André barged in and dropped down on the sofa.

"We need to talk Keilah!"

Hearing the shower running, Norelle looked at the bathroom door then back at the phone. Knowing that Raymond was right, Norelle hesitantly picked up the phone and dialed.

"Nori, baby what's wrong? You hardly ever call me at this hour. You ok?"

As the tears welled, Norelle tried to quiet the little girl that had hid herself for so long.

"Norelle … answer me! Are you in trouble? Say something!"

The tears trickled, and then intensified, as the soft wailing crept up her throat. "Mommy, I need you."

Trying to hold back her own tears, Lynette couldn't remember the last time she had heard 'Mommy' come out of Norelle's mouth. "I'm here, baby girl. I've always been here …waiting. What's wrong? Is it Raymond? LT? No… not the baby."

"Yes…"

Trying to figure out how she allowed André to bogart his way into her apartment, Keilah turned on the lights and glanced at the clock. "André, I don't know what is with you tonight, but you gotta go. Come on, I am serious; we're not having another episode like we did last time. Get up!"

Loosening his tie, André stretched his arms across the back of the sofa and stared at Keilah. "Episode! You know if I would have said that, you would have called me a trifling dog. Naw…I'm not here for that. I wasn't here for that then but I guess it didn't mean anything to you. The next damn day you were out with another dude. I poured out my feelings to you. We made love and you're like…whatever. Then you come down my job, in your tight little business suit and greased up legs, looking intense and leave. Why are you playing with me, K?"

By the emergence of his long lost Philly accent, Keilah could see André had been drinking and she had to think fast to get him out. "Look, André, I don't know why I came to see you today. Just forget about it. Just take it as a fleeting moment I fell into."

Before she could reach to pull André up, Keilah found herself clumsily seated next to him. "What is wrong with you, Dré? You better chill out! When did you start putting your hands on women?"

"K, come now. I just want you to stop running around, sit down and talk to me. What did you come to talk to me about earlier?"

Looking nervously at the clock, Keilah attempted to get up but André had a firm grip on her arm. "André, this is not a good time. We can talk tomorrow, I'll call you."

Loosening his grip, André gave Keilah a disgusted look and got up from the sofa. "So it's like that! Some new dude breeze into your life for a minute and you just kick me to the curb…just like that? What we had doesn't mean anything to you now?"

"Dré, when you invited Alisha into our relationship two years ago did you ask yourself that same question? This conversation is two years too late. Now before we say some things we don't want to say, you need to leave."

As she headed toward the door, Keilah is stuck in mid stride. "Keilah…I… love you… damn!"

The words slapped the back of her head, before filtering inside her ears. Standing still, she let the words slide smoothly down to her heart. As her heart skipped a beat, her stomach was shaken when her telephone rang.

Trying not to make eye contact with André, Keilah quickly answered the phone. "Hey… yeah I am still up. Hungry… yes… I am. Get me what ever you are eating. Uhm call me when you are getting close…I might be in the back and not hear you knock. Okay…bye"

As Keilah hung up the phone, she shivered as André's breath tickled the back of her neck. Turning around, Keilah gazed into the eyes she had loved for so long. Gently stroking his face, her mind swirled into spirals of bittersweet memories and fading hopes and desires that had been carefully locked away for this moment. Leaning in, she grabbed him tightly. "I love you, too."

Bringing her face to his, André kissed her and held her tight.

Pushing him away, Keilah looked at him and kissed him gently on the nose. "You need to leave."

Hurt and shock erupted all over André's face. "What?"

"Dré, you may love me but you are in love with someone else. Love is constant but it still changes. We *were* and while you and Alisha *are*. I kept our love on life support hoping you'd see the light…come around…then you pulled the plug. I gave up on you loving me many lonely nights ago. Let me ask you, when you made love to her did you love me? In the quiet moments when you glanced at her in the middle of the night, did you think of how much you loved me then?"

The biting words gnawed mercilessly at the empty places Keilah used to fill in his heart. "Dré let me love again…please."

Pulling his coat tighter around him, André brushed by Keilah, towards the front door. Grabbing the doorknob, André looked back at Keilah, desperately trying to hide his hurt, "Remember this."

Turning the deadbolt on the door, Keilah prayed she could believe her own words as tears unwillingly flowed down her cheek.

Having fallen asleep, Norelle is shocked to see Raymond out of bed. Creeping out of bed, she peeked in LT's room and turned off the television. Making her way down the stairs, she heard Raymond on the phone. Before she could make out what he is saying, Norelle bumped against the dining room chair. Looking over his shoulder, Raymond disconnected from his call and rushed to Norelle. "Nori... what are you doing up?"

"I was going to ask you the same thing. Who are you on the phone with?"

Lifting her off her feet and cradling her in his arms, Raymond grinned. "You need to lie down. Let's go to bed."

Once they reached the bedroom, Norelle squirmed out of his arms and sat on the edge of the bed. "Ray, I am not handicap, I can walk. The doctor said to take it easy. I'm going to take off the rest of the week but I want to work. I'll do light duty at work. All I do is sit at a desk anyway."

Raymond placed his cell phone on the nightstand. "Look, Norelle, I pretty much let you do what you want to, however you want to. But you got a precious piece of me in you and until the doctor gives her okay, you ain't doing much of nothing. As of tonight, you are a stay at home mother. I make enough. That is that. I don't want to argue." Leaning over, Raymond kissed Norelle and headed for the bathroom.

Still burning mad, Norelle picked up his cell phone.

Damn, it's turned off. When did he start turning off his cell at night?

As she was about to turn the phone on, Raymond startled her, towering over her.

"When did you start checking my phone? What is wrong with you?"

219

"When did you start turning it off at night? Who were you talking to when I came downstairs?"

Taking the phone from her, Raymond quickly turned it on, hitting the send button. "My mother…I know you're stressed out right now, so I am going to let this go."

Reaching over for the remote, Raymond turned on Sports Center and nestled underneath Norelle. Lifting the sheet, Norelle cut her eyes at Raymond.

When did he start wearing pajama bottoms to bed?

Emptying his pockets, André felt the little pieces of paper and remembered why he left in the first place. When he reached the bedroom, Alisha was lying in bed with a bowl of ice cream resting on her stomach. For the first time, he really noticed her growing belly. For a moment, his hurt and anger melted away. Diving in the bed next to her, André removed the bowl and kissed her belly.

Alisha giggled and pushed his face away. "That tickles, Dré. You must be all right now; you left out of here all crazy. Was it something from work?"

Trying to hide the fresh hurt that was resurfacing, André grabbed Alisha by the hands and looked at her for a moment, searching for answers to the many questions invading his mind again.

"What? Why are you looking at me like that, Dré?"

"Alisha is there anything that you are not telling me?"

"Why are you asking me that?"

"I just need to know."

Looking back at André, Alisha tried to access his true mood. Taking her hands along with his, Alisha placed them on her stomach. "No."

"Will your love ever change for me, Alisha?"

Pressing his hands firmly on her stomach, Alisha smiled coyly. "Of course it will! It's going to getter bigger and bigger, with each day."

Kissing her belly again, André jumped up. "Call into work tomorrow. Let's get the license tomorrow. I want to move the date up."

"Dré, are you serious? What about the caterer...the guests? We have people coming from all over."

"I'll call Pastor Blake and see if we can do it Christmas Eve. We can still do the reception on New Years Eve."

Chapter 22

"A fine, yet broke man is like a pair of Payless shoes…"
— *Carlita*

After moving the last of Carlita's things into their mother's back room, Keilah was exhausted. Returning downstairs, she threw a bag at Carlita, who was seated comfortably in the easy chair.

"Dag, K! You almost hit me in the head."

"I didn't mean to miss. Did Mom come back yet?"

"No. You two are speaking again?"

Nudging her younger sister out of the chair, Keilah shrugged and checked her cell phone.

"You got a job up here yet? You know Mom is not going for that dancing stuff you've been doing."

"I told you I was doing that to make extra money while I was in school."

"Carlita, don't run that Player's Club story past me. I already saw the movie. I never told her. She knew you were into something, I just never confirmed. They have a couple of things at my job. They pay is okay."

Curling up in the sofa, Carlita looked around the house, wondering if the walls remembered all the things she did. "Is daddy still creeping between Momma and Gigi?"

Giving Carlita a silent nod, Keilah headed for the kitchen.

Following behind her sister, Carlita shook her head. *The more things change, the more things stay the same.*

When she entered the kitchen, she was amused by the giggly light voice she heard coming from her sister. Poking her sister in the side, Carlita laughed and opened the refrigerator.

Deciding to enjoy the show, Carlita popped the soda can top and took a seat at the kitchen table.

Recognizing she had an audience, Keilah hurriedly exited the kitchen and plopped down on the sofa, her legs folded beneath her. As soon as Carlita followed and plopped down next to her, Keilah hung up at once, trying to hide her smile.

"You and André made up again?"

Keilah's smile quickly slid into a frown. "No... it is not André."

"Well I know it's not the doughboy I saw you with the last time I was here. Who is it?"

"Whatever."

"Well, Keilah who is he? Tell me!!"

Letting out a laugh, Keilah scooted over some and beamed. "Okay, his name is Justus. He's from South Africa...well not really, he was born here and raised there for most of his early childhood, and then his parents traveled abroad. They finally settled here when he started high school. He's a professor at UB."

Carlita slapped Keilah on the leg. "Well I'll be damn...*there is* life for you after André."

Choosing not to respond, Keilah continued. "See? That is the type of stuff I don't want you saying tomorrow."

"What...you bringing him to Thanksgiving dinner? Uhm, it must be serious. You haven't brought anybody home since André. Ut oh, Dré is about to be replaced, sure enough. He must be blowing your socks off. Wait...what does he look like? You said he was South African...you really doing a three-sixty from André's yellow butt."

Playfully hitting Carlita on the leg, Keilah giggled. "You are so ignorant sometimes. Why does everything have to be based on André? Damn. "

"I'm sorry but you had it bad for André. I thought you were going to cut out your weave and join a convent for a minute. Then when I saw you with doughboy, I knew you had hit an emotional rock bottom. I'm glad the African connection brought you back. So is he paid and fine?"

Digging in her purse for her cigarettes, Keilah took her lighter out of the side pocket and headed for the back porch. Taking one for herself, Carlita followed on her heels.

Hearing the screen door open, Keilah smiled. Carlita is still the irritating little sister she loved.

"Carlita it's not always about all that. I want a true love experience...don't you?"

Taking the lighter from Keilah, Carlita lit her cigarette and exhaled long. "Yeah, sure I do but I am a realist. A fine yet, broke man is like a pair of Payless shoes that catch your eye at the mall. Once you look a little closer, you can't believe you were actually thinking about trying them on and hope nobody saw you. Be honest, love looks less attractive broke...and ugly and broke ain't lovely at all."

They both looked at each and broke into laughter.

"You are crazy Carlita. Justus is doing well for himself and he is fine. I told you he was a professor at UB."

"So does he have that sexy super dark smooth skin that looks like black velvet? I bet he has those big juicy motherland lips, doesn't he? He's not short is he?"

Trying to hide her laughter, Keilah continued. "No, yes and no. He's kind of butterscotch, like those little Brach candies Mommy used to get for us at Montgomery Ward when we were little. And he *is* tall..."

Carlita dropped the cigarette from her mouth. "No you didn't get you a white South African. Get out!"

Keilah sucked her teeth. "No, he is not white...well not all white. His mother is a native South African and his dad is white."

Stomping out her cigarette, Carlita smiled at her sister. "I knew it was a catch, you don't like them staying in the oven too long."

Keilah cut her eyes at Carlita. "That is not true; I have dated brown-skinned guys too."

"K, you know what I mean. You barely ventured past your own cinnamon. You've never dated a real dark brother. I know why...

because of Daddy. You really need to let that thing go with Daddy… seriously."

Not liking where the conversation was heading, Keilah tossed her cigarette over the fence and went back inside. She didn't have to let anything go as far as she was concerned. Carlita didn't have the same memories she did. Keilah saw the pain and abuse in living color, while Carlita sucked on her bottle and watched it all unfold like a live cartoon. By the time Carlita figured out what was going on, the dysfunction was presented as normal and that was all she knew.

As Keilah watched Carlita take off her sweater, she glanced at her arm and frowned. "Did you let go of that ugly ass scar on your arm?"

Looking at her arm, Carlita paused and continued to fold her sweater. "I don't remember Gigi burning me with a hot comb. I was barely two years old. How I heard it, she was trying to straighten your hair and I got in the way."

Biting her lip, Keilah shook her head. "So you can just excuse away everything. We are messed up because of him and Mommy, for that matter."

Carlita lets out a sarcastic laugh. "No…*I* am not messed up because I chose not to be. Yeah, I got stuff with me but I refuse to let it get in the way of who I want to be. Mommy and Daddy chose to live their lives the way they wanted so why shouldn't I. Why should I spend my life crying the blues over my "bad childhood," which in reality wasn't as bad as most and not much different from the billion other people walking around in the damn world?"

Squatting down on the floor, Keilah pulled off her boots and stared at her sister in disbelief. "Daddy was an unapologetic philanderer and Mommy was an emotionally battered wife, who co-opted her husband. Find the bright side of that Diva Daila."

Picking up one of Keilah's boots, Carlita playfully sniffed it and tossed it back at her. "Keilah, Mommy wasn't Clare and Daddy damn sure wasn't Cliff. Daddy was a man but all men are not Daddy, and you don't have to be Mommy unless you wanna be."

"What? Carlita, please, you forgot what you said earlier?"

Taking the last sip of her soda, Carlita sat on the floor next to Keilah. "No, of course not. It's like this woman told me when I first got to Atlanta. You want a man to love you more than you love him. I didn't understand it until I got my feelings hurt a few times. See, we always talking about being in love but we never really talk about a man being in love with us until after we get hurt. We don't look for them to do anything but let us love them. That is crazy…it should be the other way around; we are the prize. A prize is earned not given. They can call it gold digging all they want. That is the natural order. I don't know how that got flipped around."

Keilah laughed. Her little sister had gotten real grown real fast. "So we need to prostitute our love away to the highest bidder."

"So Keilah, you think it should be given away Ho-sale? I like expensive dinners, nice clothes, trips…that's my reference. For you it may be him fixing you dinner, picking up some flowers… whatever. The bottom line is he has to work for it. Man shortage my ass. Ain't but one of me, which is the real tragedy. That's how you need to be working this new dude…what his name again?"

"His name is Justus. But back to you, so you're trying to tell me that when you were stripping you didn't…"

Cutting her sister off, Carlita jumped up defensively. "I didn't what? Trick? First of all, I was an exotic dancer, an adult entertainer… part time. I did private shows and parties a few days a month for high rollers…classy events. I wouldn't turn tricks and didn't have to; it is too many girls doing that for a chicken box and a ride home in a fancy car. I dated some of the guys but they knew they had to work for it."

Noticing their mother was pulling up, Carlita smiled back at her sister. "Mommy's coming. Can I tell her about your new boyfriend?"

Amazed at how her sister was able to go from a woman, beyond her years, back to a ten-year-old girl in a split second, Keilah shoved Carlita out of the way and opened the front door. "No you can't! I got this."

Norelle had to admit that she liked having her mother there. Watching her mother prepare the turkey brought back some of better days when her father was alive. Norelle made her way to the sink, to finish washing the greens.

"No you don't. Get your butt back in that chair. I promised my son-in-law that I would make sure you would stay off your feet."

Ignoring her mother, Norelle ran the water over the greens.

Playfully tapping her butt, Norelle's mother motioned for her to sit down. "Why are you so hardheaded, Nori? You want to lose that baby? Until the doctor gives the okay, you need to settle down."

Shrugging like a little girl, Norelle grabbed a nearby banana and sat back in her seat. Slowly peeling the banana, she looked over at her mother and wondered if they have gotten that close so soon.

What the hell?

"Ma, I think something is going on with Raymond."

Shaking the water off of the greens, Lynette placed them on the counter and reached for a butcher's knife. Pausing for a moment, she gave her daughter a considerate look then started cutting the greens. "Something like what, Nori?"

"I don't know Ma; he just seems to be acting different. It's not like he has done a one-eighty but its little things that I am seeing that...oh I don't know. Maybe it's the hormones."

As the pot boiled over, Lynette placed a small handful of greens into the pot. "Never say that! A woman always knows something. Now it all depends on what you define as something. I love Raymond like my own but he is still a man. The worst thing a woman can do is put a man on a pedestal. No matter how good he is, he can fall. It all depends on how hard and how far from that pedestal he lands. Talk to me."

Biting slowly into her banana, Norelle looked over at her mother and retreated. "Forget I said anything. I'm just bugging out."

"Maybe not; I am your mother but I am a woman first. I know you ain't used to talking to me, but you can. What's going on?"

Tossing the banana peel in the nearby trashcan, Norelle peeked through the window to make sure LT see cleaning the driveway. "Well, Ma, he has been visiting clients later and later into the evening. Not all the time, but it's starting to increase. Then he has been really attached to his cell phone. And…well…I know ever since the doctor put me on bed rest, Ray has been real uhm… careful with his… uhm…"

"What you mean? He hasn't been doing his thing in the bedroom."

"Ma!"

"What? We're both grown women."

"It's not necessarily that…I mean, we have to make a few changes but it just feels like he isn't all the way here anymore…like his mind is elsewhere for a minute then he brings it back. You know what I mean?"

Stirring the greens, Lynette placed the lid on the pot and turned down the heat. "Well, Nori. First off, you don't need to stress yourself considering all that you've got going on with that baby right now. However, little things can become big things when they go unchecked. Keep on doing what you do, don't question him; just let Ray be Ray. Momma gonna have her eagle eye out. If something isn't right, it will make itself known. What goes on in the dark comes to light."

Fighting the guilt that was taunting the back of her mind, Norelle allowed herself to enjoy the hug she had missed for so long from her mother.

"Ray loves you and LT…can't nothing or no one take that from you. That baby of his, you carrying…that right there is too valuable to him. You keep that in mind."

As her mother hugged her tighter, Norelle remembered how good her mother's hugs used to feel.

Opening the door for his mother, André was happy to see that Alisha had left a note with a fresh bouquet of flowers. Handing the note to his mother, Margaret smiled and walked over to smell the flowers.

"Oh, how sweet. Alisha is such a doll. I don't understand what's wrong with your sister."

"Me either Ma. I shouldn't be surprised; she never liked anyone I brought home. At least Tracy didn't dump a can of garbage on Alisha like she did Danielle."

Laughing to herself, Margaret sat on the sofa. "You need to stop. You two were in high school. She still claims she saw that girl kissing some boy behind the bleachers, while you were playing football. She just didn't want to lose you... she did like one of your girlfriends though."

"Who?"

"Keilah."

Taking her luggage into the guest room, André wondered how Keilah seemed to pop up yet again. Grabbing two sodas from the kitchen, André returned to see his mother examining the blank space on the wall.

"What happened to the picture that used to be here?"

Placing the sodas on the coffee table, André reached for the remote. "I decided to put it in my office."

"Alisha tried to throw it out."

"Ma!"

"What did I say? Women don't like any reminders that a man loved someone else. We can't do nothing with the memories but anything else...well that's open for debate."

"Ma, I got the stuff you needed to make the pound cake."

"Don't try to shove me in the kitchen. You better listen to me. Every man needs a talk with their momma before they get married."

"Ma, what do we need to talk about? We are both grown; you and I had "the talk" years ago. Okay, okay…shoot."

"No, no. We will talk before I leave. For now I need to freshen up."

Heading for the bathroom, Margaret stopped in the kitchen and opened a few cabinets.

Hearing the noise from the kitchen, André investigated. Seeing his mother smiling with a skillet in her hand, André couldn't hold back his laughter.

"These pots look just like they did when I gave them to you; Alisha not cooking up in here? I see I will have to have a talk with her too.

Chapter 23

Did he just say he loved me?
— Keilah

After placing the last piece of china on the table, Keilah remembered she was supposed to be watching the rolls in the oven. By the time she reached the kitchen, Carlita had the pan on top of the stove.

"You're slipping. I'm the one that usually let's the rolls burn."

Smiling to herself, Keilah reached inside the refrigerator and pulled out a small casserole dish. "Carlita keep the oven on. I want to put my casserole in there."

Wrinkling up her nose, Carlita blocked the oven. "K, please tell me that is not green bean casserole! Can you please learn how to fix something else? Ain't your new man coming? Why you gonna do that to a brother?"

Shoving her sister out of the way, Keilah placed the casserole dish in the oven and reached in her back pocket "Whatever. I should leave a whole refrigerator of it for you at my place."

Eyeing a dangling key, Carlita snatched it like a little kid. "I knew you'd change your mind about letting me live with you. When can I move my stuff?"

Looking over her shoulder, Keilah snatched the key back and pushed Carlita into the pantry. "Lower your voice. I didn't say all that. I need you to watch my place while I go out of town."

"Oh… you and Justus are gonna do some little weekend rendezvous? Little Miss Tight Drawers is about to get loose."

"Will you be quiet and listen? I am going to be gone longer than that… about two weeks. Now if my place is still in one piece when I comeback, I may let you get the second room, provided you are registered for school and have a real job."

"Two weeks? What, he taking you on a safari?"

Noticing the sheepish grin on her sister's face, Carlita backed away and stared for a minute.

"No you not about to go to Africa with this dude? I know Mommy and Daddy don't know…do they?

Ignoring her sister's question, Keilah returned to the kitchen and checked her casserole.

"They don't know! How are you going to explain being gone for two weeks?"

Hearing movement upstairs, Keilah knew her mother was out of the shower and would be heading down stairs in a matter of minutes. "Carlita, will you chill? I haven't told them yet. I wanted them to meet Justus first. That way, they will see he's nice and not freak out."

"Keilah, you are about as crazy as hell. You're not going to Atlantic City or Las Vegas…you are going to A-fri-ca. Mommy is going to flip and Daddy…well he is gonna reach for his gun."

"Mommy will have to be okay. And Carl…well I really don't care."

"Okay, you talk big stuff when they not around. You go on to A-fri-ca. You get over there and be wife number five, talking about *Justus treat me like animal.*"

When they noticed their mother in the doorway, the sisters burst out in laughter.

"I know none of my food better not be burnt. It's almost four o'clock. Your father should be here any minute. Keilah , I need you to finish putting out the silverware and stemware. Hold it right there Carlita, you help me put the rest of the food in the serving dishes."

Hearing the screen door opening, Keilah stomach jumped. *That must be Justus.* Popping a mint, Keilah adjusted her hair and smoothed her hands over her dress. Just as she is about the turn the knob, she heard keys turning in the lock. When the front door opened, she could only stare. It was her father leading a fragile Gigi through the threshold.

Thanksgiving dinner at the Deveaux house was usually intimate and quiet, but this year it was overflowing with people and laughter.

Only Alisha could upstage a national holiday with an engagement party.

Sipping her third glass of wine, Nia couldn't help but wonder how she always ended up with the short end of the stick. It wasn't as if Alisha was that much prettier then her nor was she extraordinarily intelligent. Watching her work the room, Nia knew what it was, she was clever. Alisha had some how figured out how to pull it off effortless, while Nia stumbled around clumsily.

Looking at the clock, Nia wondered where Lincoln was; it was after five o'clock. As she reached for her cell phone, Alisha walked toward her with an all too familiar smirk. "Did you taste Ms. Margaret's pound cake? It is so good. She taught me how to fix it last night. She said it was André's favorite. I didn't even know that. Did you see some of André's friends from work? Two of them came without dates."

Walking past Alisha, Nia looked outside a nearby window and sighed. She turned around to Alisha on her heels.

"Nia, you can't count on a crack addict. He's not coming."

"Leave me alone and host your party."

"Damn, what was that for? No more wine for you. You are my maid of honor, so you are co-hostess. I can't have you mopping around here. Put a smile on and let's do this."

Deciding to go outside, Nia called Lincoln again. Frustrated when he didn't answer, she went back into the house and walked smack dab into Alisha, again.

Grabbing her sister by the arm, Alisha pulled her toward a quiet corner. "Nia, I told you he's not coming. He probably got caught up at his grandmother's house."

"What?"

"Hopefully the po-po is preparing to ship his ass back to Atlanta."

"You didn't! I told you to hold off...I was working on something else."

"Look, I can't risk you flaking out on me. I had to do what had to be done."

Trying to unclench the fist that was rising up from her side, Nia grit her teeth. "Alisha, how could you do that...on Thanksgiving...his grandmother's house? That woman is almost eighty years old. Damn, I got to go over there."

"No you don't! You need to stay right here with me. Hold on, you're acting like you care. No you didn't fall for some broke ass addict."

"Yes I care. There is a lot about Lincoln that you don't know. I gotta get over there. What if his grandmother has a stroke or something? Why did you have to get his grandmother involved? I told you I was going to handle it."

"Look Nia, you are right, I don't know a lot about Lincoln and frankly I don't want to know. All I know is that he was a seriously painful thorn in my side that had to be plucked. You were getting soft."

Seeing André approaching, Nia tucked her purse under her arm. "You know Alisha you are clever but you're not smart. You're all about justifying the means but you never finish connecting the dots. You think he is not going to call his lawyer friend. I am the only person who knew where he was going. He's going to think it was me. I gotta go...shit!"

As Nia slammed the front door, Alisha is startled by André's caress. "The bride and the maid of honor are not fighting at the engagement party, are they?"

Kissing him softly, Alisha smiled sweetly. "You know how Nia and I are. She's upset because Lincoln is late."

"Hhm, he said he was coming. As a matter of fact, he said he wanted to talk to me. Wait, I feel my phone...that might be him."

Moving slightly to André's left; Alisha nervously glanced at his phone.

"Hey Man. Where are you? Okay... no problem."

Watching André close the phone, Alisha doesn't know if she should ask or not.

"That was Elliot from work. He got lost."

Breathing a quiet sigh of relief, Alisha grabbed André by the arm and rejoined her party. Hopefully she had more to celebrate, she mused to herself.

Norelle was happy Nana could make it this year. Every holiday she was off on a cruise or some other adventure. Looking to her left, she was also happy she and her mother exchanged smiles rather than uncomfortable glances across the table.

"Nori, is Keilah coming over this year? I miss her string bean casserole."

"Ma, you know you ate that string bean mess to be nice. She may stop by later. She is introducing her new boyfriend to her family."

"Oh, must be serious. She's a nice girl. They getting married or something?"

"Not that I know of, but it must be serious. She's going to Africa with him."

Raymond took a bite out of his roll and waited for his own episode of "The View."

Nana jumped in first. "Africa! What she going to Africa for? He a African or something?"

Before Norelle could answer, Lynette piped in. "He's part African from what Norelle said. His mother is African and his daddy American...he white too. He probably needs citizenship. I saw something like that on Judge Mabelyn."

235

Nana cut Norelle off.

"You know they running scams all over the Internet. These people say they are from the Bank of Nigeria and want you to transfer money for them and they end up taking all your money and you can't trace it. I know there gotta be good black men right here in America. All of them can't be in jail or gay."

Grabbing her mother's hand so she could get a word in, Norelle finally interjected. "Actually he has dual citizenship. He was born in America though. And Nana, his mother is from South Africa. How things have been going, he really seems to like her. As far as the scamming thing, I don't think so. From what I can tell, he got plenty money of his own; he don't need nothing from Keilah. Shoot, she may have hit the jackpot with this one."

Chewing slowly on a piece of turkey, Lynette waited until Nana spoke.

"Hmm, they like you a lot when they trying to get something out of you. How you know what he got in his pockets? All you can go by is what Keilah tell you…and she may not know for real."

"Nana, she doesn't know but I do. You forget I work for the IRS. All I need is a name and some information to deduct from."

Once she realized what she had said, Raymond had already gotten up and was leading LT from the table.

"Come on man lets go watch the game. We don't need to hear anymore of this."

Norelle wasn't quite sure what type of look Raymond had on his face but she didn't like it.

When Justus arrived right on the heels of Carl and Gigi, Keilah barely had time to recover from the shock, so she jumped right into actress mode; smiling painfully as she tiptoed around Gigi like she wasn't even there.

Yvonne knew it was just a matter of time before Keilah would pop. Looking over at Justus, she was thankful he came. Maybe Keilah would hold her peace through dinner. Carl looked over at Justus, suspiciously between bites, while Carlita nibbled quietly waiting for the main event to start.

"So, Justus I hear you from Africa. What you doing here?

Keilah gave her father an annoyed glance. "Dad, I told you he was a professor at UB and that…"

Carlita quickly jumped in. "Yeah, that's right! Can you help me out in admissions? I was going to transfer to Maryland State but if the professors look like you, I might go to UB instead."

Justus grinned and grabbed Keilah's hand. "I'm sorry Carlita, most are gray-haired men in tweed jackets so you may as well go on to Maryland State. And Mr. Fort, to answer your question, I am here because this is where I am suppose to be. I was born in the states but spent my formative years in South Africa, as well as Zimbabwe, Kenya and parts of Europe; my parents moved here permanently when I started high school."

Taking a bite out of his roll, Carl looked over at Keilah then at Justus. "Hmm…"

As the two men glared intensely at one another across the table, a soft whimper snatched their attention away; sobbing quickly washed the silence away.

"Baby, what's wrong?" Carl quickly stood up and looked at Yvonne, as she gave him a somber   nod of approval. Grabbing Gigi in his arms, Carl lifted her face tenderly. "Are you in pain? What's wrong?"

Wiping her face, Gigi looked across the table and cried harder. "Yvonne, I don't deserve this kindness from you. I…"

Cutting Gigi off, Yvonne wiped a tear from her own eye and cleared the table. "It's alright, Gigi. Don't do this…it's not necessary."

As anger arched her back, Keilah grabbed she and Justus's plates and headed for the kitchen.

Recognizing the familiar clitter clatter, Keilah quickly turned around and glared at her mother. "How could you allow that woman to sit at our table and eat our food? It's bad enough to sit across from Daddy, but her too! Then her theatrics at the dinner table, I am so embarrassed. Justus and I are leaving!"

"You ain't going no where! This is my house and all that food on the table, your daddy and me bought it…except for that mushy string bean mess you brought up in here. You are going to grab that sweetbread stuff your little uppity boyfriend brought in here and finish dinner."

Giving a tired huff, Keilah grabbed her casserole dish and placed it on top of Justus's pan. "Ma, I am outta here."

"Little girl, you better get it together!"

Looking past her mother's shoulder, Keilah slung a heavily laden look of contempt directly at her father.

Taking a quick stride toward the kitchen door, Carl met her halfway, blocking her path. Covering her mouth with silence, Keilah took a step to the right, only to be blocked again.

"Excuse me."

"Your excused. Fix your face and go have a seat. Your mother and I will bring the desserts out."

Taking two steps back, Keilah looked at her mother with painfully etched eyes of disparagement. Grabbing the dishes firmly, Keilah examined her father. Tall and thick like an oak tree; rich chocolate skin …deep mysterious eyes that she had inherited. When she was little, he was the most handsome man in her world. By the time she was fourteen, his looks faded in her eyes. His perfect white teeth were surrounded by a crooked smile. Now as she stared at him, all she could think of was how wickedly handsome he still was…and he knew it.

"I am leaving. You, your wife, Carlita and your mistress can continue this Jerry Springer Thanksgiving. Justus and I are going to Norelle's."

238

Stepping slightly to the left, Carl gave Keilah space to slide past him. "Okay, you can go but I'm letting you know she gonna be here Christmas, too. Your momma and I already talked about it, so you need to get it set in your mind. You got it?"

Smirking, Keilah first walked over to her mother, giving her a gentle kiss, then headed to the open arms of her father. Letting the hug linger, Keilah took a deep breath before walking to the kitchen door. "Okay, that's fine but I still won't be here. I'm taking a trip."

Not waiting for a response, Keilah bolted out the kitchen door, promptly being greeted by thinly veiled faces of awkwardness. Gigi already had her coat while Carlita nervously watched the kitchen door. Asking no questions, Justus read Keilah's eyes and got up to get their coats.

A teary-eyed Yvonne emerged first, followed by an enraged Carl.

"You just wait a minute, little girl. What is this trip thang you dropping on me and your mother?"

After letting Justus slip her coat on, Keilah walked over to her sister, removing a key from her key chain. "I am going to South Africa, with Justus. We leave on the twenty-third of December. I'll be back after New Years. Carlita is going to stay at my place while I am gone."

Yvonne gasped, staring at her daughter.

Carl's eyes glazed over as he looked at his daughter. Grinding his teeth, Carl walked directly up to Justus.

Feet firmly planted, Justus stared back silently, waiting.

"You ain't taking my daughter nowhere. You got that? I don't know nothing about you, and frankly I don't want to. I never heard nothing about you until today and you think I'm just gonna be okay with it. Hell no! So don't even prepare any fancy words…it's damn nonsense I ain't even going to try to talk about it. End of discussion!"

Noticing Keilah's frustrated look, Justus gave her a quieting look and extended his hand to her. Nervously, Keilah tightened her coat around her and walked toward him.

"Mr. Fort, it was a pleasure breaking bread with you and your family. I hope we can get together again, under better circumstances. Keilah, if you are ready we can leave now. Good evening every..."

Carl quickly shoved Justus, causing him to stumble backward.

"Daddy!! Stop!!"

"Who in the hell do you think you are? You gonna just dismiss everything I just said and take my daughter outta here. Naw, son!"

As Carl took off his watch, Yvonne ran by his side, while Keilah jumped in between the two men.

"Mr. Fort. If I offended you, I apologize. You said there was no discussion to be had; I simply obliged you. Keilah is an adult and has made her decision. I am not taking her anywhere. She is joining me on her own. I didn't come here for your approval. I came to meet the people that raised such a wonderful woman and to assure you that I will take care of her. I love her."

Did he just say he loved me?

Tightly grabbing her husband's arm, Yvonne conceded with a whisper. "Don't do this. Let her go, Carl."

240

Chapter 24

"So you think it is all over now...like it will never come out."
— Nia

By the time Nia made it to Linc's grandmother's house, she was in a panic. When his grandmother answered the door, her weary, tear-stained face confirmed Nia's fears. Had she really fallen in love with him, Nia wondered as she entered the house. After a tearful two-hour stumble down memory lane, with his grandmother, Nia had more of the missing pieces that made up Linc—his drug-addicted mother, no father, topsy-turvy childhood of one foster home to the next; all the makings of a misunderstood adult. His grandmother did the best she could do. By the time she got custody, he was twelve and the damage had been done.

Returning to her car, the idea of how she had a hand in Linc's predicament bounced erratically between guilt and love. No matter where she stood emotionally, Nia knew she had to help him.

After the crazy scene with her father, Keilah was shocked that Justus still wanted to go with her to Norelle's. Making sure her car was locked; Keilah tweaked the alarm and joined Justus in his Jeep. As she directed him to Norelle's, her thoughts went back to three little words he had said to her father, "I love her."

Grabbing his hand, she smiled at him and laid her head on his shoulder. As they drove on the highway, she wondered if he really meant it. *What have I done to get him to love me? Maybe he meant he loved me as in a friend.*

"We take 795, right?"

"Yes, I'm sorry. I was thinking about what went down with my father. I am so sorry. I had no idea he would go off like that."

Letting out a huff, Justus shifted gears and looked at Keilah for a moment.

"Okay, maybe I did, but it wouldn't have ever been a good time to tell them. They wouldn't have cared if I were going to South Africa with the Peace Corps; they still wouldn't have liked it. Oh, take Exit 4 then bear right; take a left at the third light." She sighed heavily. "Okay, okay. I was scared. I'm sorry. Please forgive me…please. "

Stopping at the second traffic light, Justus grabbed Keilah's face and kissed her gently on the lips. "You have apologized enough… it is over. I love you."

He said it again!

As Keilah parted her lips, Justus kissed her again.

"You don't have to say it just because I said it. It won't change how I feel either way. When you say it, I want you to really mean it."

Not quite sure what to say, Keilah rubbed her lips together and pointed to Norelle's street. When they pulled into Norelle's driveway, it hit her. The 'I love you' that fell from André's mouth was saturated with uncertainty, while Justus said it with a steady confidence that settled peacefully inside her.

Nia was relieved to see that guests were still there when she pulled up. She could avoid questions regarding where she had been, from her parents, at least. Upon entering the house, she was immediately greeted by a scolding look from her mother, followed by a backward glance from her father. Walking past the living room, she saw André and a few men yelling at the football game.

It's a damn shame…he has no idea…none at all.

Nia thoughts were broken by the sound of a high-pitched shrill her sister called laughter. Making her way to the dining room, she saw that Alisha was in her glory, center stage, soaking up all the attention.

"Well, I hope you were out getting my present, Maid of Honor. I didn't see one gift on this table from you!"

On queue, curious eyes searched Nia for signs that confirmed or countered their thoughts.

Nia walked past the table, poured a glass of wine and joined the table. "I have a very special present for both you and André, so you will have to wait until wedding day."

Looking satisfied, Alisha excused herself and pulled Nia to the kitchen. Before they made it through the kitchen door, their mother swooped up behind them.

"Nia, I am upset with you. This was your sister's engagement party and you just left. What was so important that would cause you to miss the whole dinner and everything...you are the Maid of Honor?"

Before Nia could answer, Alisha gave her mother a doe-eyed look and hugged Nia tightly. "Mommy, it's okay. We were just going to talk about it. Really, it's okay."

"Whatever. I don't want to think you aren't happy for your sister, Nia. You should have outgrown that sibling thing. I am going to talk with André's mother; Nia make sure you introduce yourself to her properly."

As their mother turned on her heels, Alisha dragged Nia through the kitchen door. "Is he locked up? Did they get him?"

Nia dryly responded. "Yes."

"Great! Now all they have to do is extradite his ass back to Atlanta and you get my place. It is a win–win. Good work, little sis."

In the midst of her glee, she noticed tears in Nia's eyes. "Wait a minute, I know you are not about to cry. Give me a break; you caught feelings for him. Listen, André has some fine brothers from work out there. Not married, no kids, decent pay checks. Linc was a has been. He'll be fine. He probably got some girl down in Atlanta just waiting to fill his commissary. You're better than that."

Contempt quickly evaporated Nia's tears, as she stepped back and took a long hard look at her sister.

"What? Don't look at me like that. It is the truth."

"Alisha, you really don't feel bad about any of this...not even how this may have affected his grandmother? She's eighty-something years old."

"Look, it is about self-preservation. I love André and I made a mistake…one night. Linc was threatening me. What was I suppose to do? You are the one that volunteered to do the job. So don't act like I did this on my own. Nobody told you to get caught up. I thought you were mature enough to handle it."

"So you think it is all over now…like it will never come out?"

Nia looked down at Alisha's swollen stomach and smirked.

"Don't even go there. It was one time and we used condoms. So whatever he said…"

"Yeah well, I wouldn't get comfortable. He won't be locked up forever. What makes you think he won't tell André later?"

"I just need to get passed this wedding. Once the baby is born, we will be stronger than ever. I'll deal with it then."

The sisters are startled when a woman comes through the kitchen door.

"Hi Alisha, I decided to make it down. I hope I am not too late."

"No, of course not. Tracy, this is my sister Nia. Nia this is André's sister."

As the two sisters exited ahead of Tracy, she wondered what words preceded the few she had just heard outside the door.

Keilah peeked into Norelle's den and was happy to see Justus and Raymond had hit it off.

"He is fine girl."

Keilah giggled and followed Norelle into the kitchen. When she saw Nana and Ms. Lynette perched at the kitchen counter, she knew it was grilling time.

Nana sipped on her coffee and peeled back the foil from one of the dishes Keilah had brought. "What is this, some sweetbread or something?"

Keilah beamed. "It's soetkies. It is a South African dessert.

Justus made it; it is good. You want a piece?"

Upon hearing that, Nana quickly placed the foil back and reached for the peach cobbler. "No thanks, baby. I don't eat everybody's food, especially nothing I can't pronounce made by no foreigners."

Lynette quickly sliced a piece of the soetkies for herself.

"Mama!"

"What did I say wrong?"

Norelle laughed while Keilah looked back at the den.

"Girl, they are fine. How did things go with your parents? Did they like him?"

Clearing her throat, Keilah eyed a bottle of wine on the counter and grabbed a nearby wine glass. "Well, things went as I expected."

Pouring wine helped Keilah divert eye contact. When she looked up, Nana was standing next to her, reaching for the bottle.

"Hmm, that must mean they ran him out their house."

Lynette tried to hold in her laughter. "Will you please?"

Finishing her wine in one gulp, Nana preceded to pour another. "You two can sit up here and act like nothing is wrong with it. No parents in their right mind would like some foreign man they don't know nothing 'bout coming up in their house, grinning in their face, talking about taking their daughter to some damn Africa. Come on now. That's just crazy."

Keilah slowly sipped her wine as she digested what Nana had said.

Norelle slowly scooted out of her chair and hugged her friend. "Well, Nana. You may think it's crazy, I did too but you know what, this is a once in a lifetime opportunity. Love is crazy."

Lynette took another piece of soetkies and smiled. "Keilah is a smart woman, she'll be fine. Plus, Norelle done got the scoop on him so we can track him down if we have to."

Keilah cut her eye at Norelle. "You didn't! I thought I asked you not to do that."

Norelle playfully blew Keilah a kiss and sat back down. "Look, I had to make sure he was legit. And girl based upon what I saw, he doing real good... hell d-double damn good, pushing six figures. Shoot he might be a prince or something in Africa."

All of the women fell into laughter.

"So you love him?"

"What did you ask me, Ms. Lynette?"

"Girl, I know you heard me."

Nana let's out a long hmmm. "Well, Lynette I guess you got your answer. Any woman that is head over heels would light up at the mere mention of the word love. What's going on with you?"

Trying to adjust under the scrutinizing looks, Keilah blushed.

"Oh, okay she embarrassed, that's what it is?"

Norelle jumped in quickly. "Nana, she is not embarrassed. You asked the question wrong. Keilah is in love; loving someone and being in love are two different things."

Amused at her daughter's statement, Lynette grabbed the bottle of wine and poured for herself and Keilah. "Really? Do explain O' Wise Woman."

Tracing her stomach, Norelle closed her eyes and spoke. "Being in love is the act in process, like drawing up the blueprint when you build a house. For so long you've always known what you had in mind but now you can see all the possibilities, so you start working on it, tirelessly day and night. Loving a person is the end product; that concrete state of being that just is, no matter what. Some people just look at a house, like it and move in, then later notice the house needs work, never factoring in the cost for upkeep."

"Nori baby, I need to run out. I'll be back." Raymond quickly kissed Norelle and left out the house.

As the door slammed, the women sat in silence.

"You know it is getting late. Justus and I are going to break out. I am off tomorrow so maybe I will come by for a while."

Letting a tired smile ripple across her face, Norelle shakes her head. "You spend time with your architect; you need to find out what type of tools he's working with before you get on that plane. That will be a long trip."

Nana playfully spanked Norelle's knee. "Watch yourself; you ain't never gonna be that grown next to me."

As Alisha got comfortable in her old room, she couldn't help but laugh to herself. *I am getting married. I am getting married to a man that loves me. Damn!* Alisha's thoughts were broken when Nia opened the door.

"I didn't know you were spending the night?"

"I got bumped out since André's sister decided to drive back in the morning. Hey why don't you get in the bed with me like when we were little?"

Letting out a sarcastic sigh, Nia looked through the closet. "Uhm, let's not forget I had insomnia for almost a year after you cut all my hair off, that was why we got separate rooms."

"Nia please let that go. I got a whipping of a lifetime and I said I was sorry for almost a year. We were kids; I didn't know what I was doing."

Having second thoughts about what she was about to do, Nia reluctantly kept on task and found the envelope she had been looking for. Keeping her back to her sister, Nia stuffed the envelope in between a stack of clothes. "You knew what you were doing then just like you know now. Don't you know what goes around will most certainly come around?"

Scooting swiftly off the bed, Alisha walked up on her sister and stared intently into her eyes. "What, you threatening me now? You are my sister, don't you know blood is thicker than water."

"Yeah, I know…but blood burns when it gets in your eyes. Don't worry about me…when things unravel…I won't pull the string …you will." Grabbing her sister's hand, Nia led her back to the bed. "Listen you are my sister and I love you but you make it hard for me to like you. You can't keep doing stuff and think it's not going to comeback…life doesn't work like that. Just know I will be there for you, regardless."

"Why are you saying stuff like that? You sound like you want something to happen."

Hugging her sister, Nia tucked the clothes under her arm and shook her head. "No…I really don't."

Keilah wasn't sure how she was going to make it through the night without a cigarette, but she didn't care, as she lay snuggled next to Justus.

Oh, he smells so good. His arms feel so good wrapped around me. The only thing that is ruining it is that damn pillow he has wedged in between us.

As yet another seductive brush of his lips teased the back of her neck; Keilah jumped out of bed and turned the light on. "What's up Justus? You got something going on down there? I can't do this!"

Sitting up slightly on one elbow, Justus's frown turned to a smile. "Keilah, please come back to bed."

"No. You gotta explain to me why you won't have sex with me. Do you have *something*? Do you have ED?"

Justus sits upright in the bed. "ED?"

"You know… erectile…"

Justus laughed and pulled the covers tighter. "No! Why do you think I put the pillow here? I told you I wanted to wait. I want our first time to be special. Trust me when I say that I want you. Please come back to bed."

Keilah tried to shake the frustration as she turned off the light and climbed back into bed. Kissing Justus mischievously, Keilah snatched the pillow, tossed it to the other side of the room and turned her back to him. When he grabbed her tightly, Keilah wiggled closer and smiled. *Tools feel fine to me…ha, Norelle.*

248

Having stayed up for as long as she could, Norelle kissed Nana and her mother goodnight. By quarter past twelve, she heard the backdoor close quietly and soft footsteps walking toward the den. As she laid waiting for Raymond to come upstairs, she was surprised to hear the sound of a soda can opening and the television.

A tear dropped as Norelle rolled over and closed her eyes.

Seeing that her brother was fast asleep on the sofa, Tracy closed the bedroom door and nudged her mother. "Ma, wake up for minute."

"What's the matter?"

"I am glad I came after all. I heard that girl and her sister talking. She's trying to take my brother for a ride."

"Tracy, it is late. Go to sleep."

"Ma, I can't. I heard her telling her sister '*I just need to get passed this wedding. Once the baby is born, we will be stronger than ever. I'll deal with it then.*' What do you think that means? What is *it*?"

After adjusting her hair bonnet, Margaret grabbed her daughter's hand.

"*It* can be a lot of things. Leave it alone…all you gonna do is make things bad between you and your brother. You remember when you got married; you and André were at odds the whole time because he didn't like Terrence."

"Yeah, but Ma… André was right…Terrence wasn't nothing."

"Tracy, leave it alone!"

"Ma…I'm telling you… that nicey-nice stuff is all show."

"Go to sleep Tracy."

249

Chapter 25

"I am as real as you allow me to be. Are you ready?"
— Justus

Sitting in the airport, Keilah couldn't believe the next day would be Christmas Eve and she would be in a whole other continent and season.

"I am not going to pass out from the heat, am I?"

Kissing her forehead, Justus laughed. "If you can handle a month of one-hundred percent humidity in Baltimore, during August, you will be fine during the eighty-degree days of summer during December in Cape Town."

While Justus returned to his magazine, Keilah reassured herself that she had not forgotten anything. She had made sure to deliver her presents for Norelle, Raymond, and LT, the night before. Carlita had already opened hers. Her parents' presents were next to the front door with a big note on them, so Carlita wouldn't forget them. That was when it finally happened, the queasiness. She knew her nerves were going to kick in sooner or later.

Looking at Justus, she really felt like this trip was going to be definitive in so many ways…or at least she hoped. Tomorrow she would be on the other side of the world and the man she loved will be another woman's husband. As heaviness washed across her head, Keilah laid her head on Justus shoulder.

"Are you feeling okay? Sometimes those shots can make you a little sick."

Lifting her face to kiss his, Keilah nodded. "I guess I am just nervous…okay scared."

"Scared of what, the plane ride, the trip itself or being alone with me for more than a few hours?"

There he goes, over analyzing me again.

"Yes, yes and definitely no."

As they laughed, Keilah's cell phone rang, it was Norelle. "Nori, I feel like I am leaving my Siamese twin home. We haven't missed a Christmas together in what, eighteen years."

Norelle released a laborious laugh as a sharp pain shot up her back. "Yeah, K, since we were twelve years old, but don't worry about me, I am going to be fine. You have fun. I think he is the one...for real."

Stepping away for a minute, Keilah whispered. "I am scared to say it but I think I know he is the one, too."

"What do you mean you think you know?"

"I keep thinking about André."

Shifting her weight, Norelle hoped the pain would lessen. "Listen, you will always think about André...you may always love André but don't let that keep you from someone that is in love with you. When you board that plane, leave André behind you. When he walks down that aisle, trust me, he will be doing the same. I shouldn't have ever encouraged that, I am sorry."

"It's okay. I had to go through the motions one more time. Did you just grunt? Are you okay, Nori?"

As the pain gripped her stomach, Norelle tried to hide it with laughter. "Yeah, I'm fine. Take lots of picture. Call me if you can. I love you, sis."

"I love you too, Nori."

Closing the phone, the queasiness hit her again. Noticing the strange look on her face, Justus walked her back to their seats. "I am going to get you some tea and a bagel."

Watching Justus get into a long line, Keilah cautiously looked at her phone, opened it and quickly dialed. Relieved that the message picked up, she took a breath. "I am just calling to say that I wish you well and I love you, Dré. Bye." *It is finished.*

The other nagging thing in the back of her mind was quickly being erased when she saw her mother walking swiftly behind her sister. Before she could say a word, her mother pulled her close.

"You think I was going to let you get on that plane without kissing you goodbye?" When Yvonne released her daughter, she saw tears welling up in her eyes. "Don't you start that, you hear me? I love you; we all love you. You're grown and can do whatever you want to with who ever you want to do it with. Your father still mad, but he's coming around. He got these for you."

Taking the envelop from her mother, Keilah smiled when she saw the travelers checks and phone card.

"He got that phone card at the gas station, it's suppose be for Africa calls."

Noticing Justus approaching, Yvonne pulled her daughter closer. "You got plenty of condoms packed don't you? I don't want you coming back with a baby unless you married. I ain't saying you need to marry him. What I meant to say…"

Carlita giggled and interjected. "Mommy, she understands."

Hugging Keilah tightly, Justus greets Carlita and Yvonne with a big smile. "I am glad you came to see her off. I know that makes the trip easier for her. I promise you, I will take care of her. She is valuable to me too. Please assure your husband of that."

"I will try my best. He won't be convinced until she's back home."

When the overhead speakers announced the boarding of their flight, Keilah quickly hugged her mother and sister one more time. As they made their way to the terminal, Justus paused.

"Love, you need to drink your tea and take a few bites of this bagel."

Taking a large gulp, Keilah felt tea spilling down her chin. Before she could reach for a napkin, Justus kissed the few droplets away. The simple tenderness of that very moment released the last chain that was wrapped around her heart.

"Justus, I'm in love with you."
"I know."

By the time Raymond got home that evening, most of the pain had stopped. Even though the doctor told her to stay in bed, Norelle wanted to make sure the ham was thawing.

"Norelle, what are you doing out of bed?"

"I had to make sure the ham was thawed. You know how you have been forgetting things lately."

"Didn't I tell you I took it out this morning before I left? My mother said she'll come over and help your mother cook. Why are you up? I'm taking you upstairs."

When Raymond lifted Norelle, she smelled it again. "Put me down Raymond. Damn it put me down now."

Afraid her wiggling would cause him to drop her, Raymond placed her back on her feet. "Woman, what is wrong with you?"

"No, the question is what is wrong with you. I tried to wait it out but it seems to be getting worst. What's going on?"

"Look, Norelle, I know your hormones are up and down and you're worried about the baby so I am not going to go there with you. Now, I am going to take you upstairs. You need to lie down."

Shoving him back, Norelle stumbled slightly. "NO! You need to tell me what you doing. Are you seeing someone else?"

A look of exhaustion covered his face as he peered at his wife. "No, I told you I have some projects I have been working on. You know contracting jobs slow up when it gets cold. I have been doubling up on a lot of jobs so we will be straight through the winter. Plus I'm trying to finalize some snow plowing contracts."

Before she could speak, a sharp pain took the words out of her mouth. Falling into Raymond's arms, the increasing familiar scent made her nauseous.

When they reached the bedroom, Raymond gently laid her down and propped pillows under her back and feet. Taking off his shirt, Raymond climbed in bed next to her and held her. "Nori, I love you. I would never be unfaithful to you, never baby. I just got a lot of stuff going on. I love you and my baby you carrying, LT too."

As tears streamed down her face, Norelle accepts the unspoken truths...the first being the explosion of pain that had caused the gush of blood that was sliding down her thigh...the second yet to be revealed.

"So you ready to do this?"

Alisha giggled like a schoolgirl on the other side of the phone. "Of course I am. In a few hours, I will be Mrs. Alisha Davidson. You haven't changed your mind have you?"

Exhaling loudly, André looked over at his cell phone. "No baby."

"Well, okay...I just got my nails done and the lady is ready to do my makeup. I have to make sure I look perfect when we you see me coming down that aisle. I love you Dré. Bye."

The familiar snatched him for a moment. "Wait, when did you start calling me Dré'?"

"I don't know, I guess just now. Why, you don't like it?"

"Never mind, forget it. Love you, Mrs. Davidson."

Hanging up the phone, André glanced over at his tux and was glad that he didn't answer that call from Keilah. It wasn't that it would have changed things. She would have put thoughts in his mind that he knew he shouldn't have. *Damn, she did anyway.*

The knock on his door was a welcomed distraction. When he opened the door, he was glad to see Chris and his barber.

As the barber lathered his face, André couldn't believe that no one had heard from Linc.

"Chris did that knuckle head Linc ever call you? He just disappeared...ghost. You think he went back to Atlanta?"

Chris brushed off André's tux and laid his next to it. "Alisha's sister didn't tell you? I thought you'd be the first person he would call.

The cops picked him up Thanksgiving and took him back to Atlanta the next day."

Remembering there was a straight razor next to his neck, André tried not to move. "Naw, she didn't tell me. What did they get him for?"

"Bench warrant for an assault charge. The woman that pressed the charges didn't even show up. They dropped the charges for assault but got his ass for not showing up for the hearing and violating probation. He wasn't supposed to leave out the state, dude."

"How do you know all this?"

Chris took off his glasses and laughed. "He called me collect and one of the twins answered the phone. By the time I got to the phone, the call was connected so I listened."

"I wonder why he didn't call me, or Nia didn't tell me. That's my boy regardless. I know Alisha knew."

"Man, you getting married. Linc is a big boy. He'll be out by the end of January. Plus from what I heard his girl, Nia, looking out for him. He told me she was going to handle something for him here then go down there after the wedding."

As the hot towel pressed against his skin, André couldn't help but wonder why neither Nia nor Alisha said anything. It didn't make sense to him.

"Man, you're thinking too hard. Now can you get up out that chair so I can get a shape up?"

After twenty-four hours in the air, Keilah was happy to get off the plane. She was a little wobbly but was glad the sickness had passed. Just before her knees buckled, Justus lifted her up in his arms and kissed her.

"Oh… no don't kiss me yet. I know my breath is rancid."

"You are fine, K-love."

The words shook her stomach and brought the queasiness again.

"What did you call me?"

"K-love…what you don't like it?"

Climbing out of his arms, Keilah adjusted her clothing and pushed aside that familiar feeling that had tried to yank her backwards. "No…No…I just never heard you call me that before."

Even though it was night, the landscape looked like nothing she could have ever imagined. Noticing her intense gaze, Justus knew the time was right and dug in a bag and nudged her.

"This is for you."

Keilah gleefully grabbed the sketchbook and pencils. "Thank you."

By the time they reached his house, Keilah had gone through three pages of her sketchbook.

When the car came to a stop, Keilah was taken a back, yet again. When the driver opened the door, she sat there, not believing her eyes. The house was sitting on top of a mountain.

"This is not your house…this is not your house."

After tipping the driver and getting their bags, Justus grabbed her hand, leading her up to the door. "No, this is not my house… this is my parents house. But it is ours for the next two weeks. You don't like it?"

Walking toward the patio, Keilah wasn't quite sure if she is actually looking at the Atlantic Ocean. "Justus… this is absolutely beautiful…I am …I am…"

"Home… you are home."

Not noticing that Justus had left the room, Keilah sunk into the sofa and closed her eyes. *If this isn't real, I don't want to know, ever.*

A sweet smell of freshly lit candles brought her back for a moment. When she opened her eyes, Justus was hovering over her with a t-shirt and two glasses of wine.

"I am running you a bath. You want me to fix you something to eat?"

Please Lord...please let him be real...please. Taking a glass from him, she sipped slowly. "Are you for real?"

Joining her on the sofa, Justus relaxed her ponytail and kissed her with deeper intentions. "I am as real as you will allow me to be. Are you ready for me?"

Keilah was finally ready to surrender her heart to another. "Yes."

Having heard what he wanted to hear, Justus silently led her to a sunken tub filled with fresh freesia flower petals.

As she undressed, Justus stops her and meticulously removed layer after layer, gently. Having reached the last two articles of clothing, Justus stopped.

Confused, Keilah covered herself. "What's wrong?"

"Nothing. You are absolutely beautiful to me."

Unsnapping the hooks on her bra, Justus lavished her with what felt like a million sweet kisses. After sliding her panties slowly to the floor, Justus playfully wiggled her socks off and placed her in the tub. As he lathered her body, Keilah felt more of her hurts being washed away with each caress of the sponge. Taking a deep breath, she completely submerged herself in the water. Stretching her body out as far as she could, she floated, feeling like a baby about to be born all over again.

Lifting her gently by the neck, Justus slowly kissed each eyelid, moving on to her cheeks and then to her waiting mouth. As she reached for him, he quickly grabbed her hands and smoothly guided them across his body, as he joined her in the tub. Tracing her breast tenderly with his tongue, Justus carefully lifted her hips and moved downward, with the quiet intensity of a huge wave approaching an awaiting shoreline. As he lingered, she could think of nothing more than the satisfaction a mountainside must feel every time the tide rolls in; forcefully steady and passionately intense. When Justus joined with her, she finally felt what she had mistaken so many times before, , her soul mate deeply connected within her very being. It was then that tears of mourning fell for what was, quickly followed by tears of joy for what is now.

For the first time since she was twelve, Norelle didn't have Keilah to help her make sense of her pain. Raymond did the best he could do, but they both knew she needed Keilah. She couldn't believe the hospital only kept her overnight. She was better off home anyway, she thought to herself. Even though she tried to settle in her mind that maybe it was for the best, she couldn't. The grief of the possibility that she had lost the baby her husband so dearly wanted wouldn't allow it. Looking over at Raymond, how could she have feared otherwise?

"Nori, you need anything?"

"No, just that prescription. You better go pick it up before the pharmacy closes. I'm fine, Ray, go ahead. If you need to take a drive...I understand."

Kissing her feet, Raymond grabbed his keys and turned his cell phone on. "If you need anything...you call me."

"LT is here. My mom should be here soon anyway."

Norelle hadn't realized she had fallen asleep until she heard the doorbell. She thought she had given her mother a key.

"LT! Go downstairs and get the door for your grandmother."

Running to the door quickly, so he can get back to his game, LT swung the door open and was surprised to see a strange woman standing there. Not quite sure what to do, he just let's the cold air burst through the door. As the early winter breeze ran through the first floor, making its way up the stairs, Norelle instinctively sat up. She smelled it.

"Is your father around? I need to talk to him please."

As Norelle eased off the bed, she got her game face on. The other shoe had finally dropped and made its way to her doorstep.

André had always heard it was bad luck to see the bride before the wedding. He thought it was an outdated wives tale until the words he heard coming from the mouth of his bride-to-be kicked him in the chest. Leaning against the door, André's eyes burned as though blood was trying to burst past the tears that were making their way to the corners of his eyes.

Almost tearing the door of the hinges, André was seething with anger as he burst in the room. "What in the hell did you just say?"

Startled by André, Nia quickly slid a large envelope into a trashcan while Alisha stared like a deer in headlights.

"You and Linc! Naw, Alisha…not you and Linc."

Nia backed away from her sister. "André…what…what are you talking about?

Grabbing her by the arm, André tried to restrain himself as he pulled Alisha to a chair. Catching Nia trying to leave, he quickly jumped in front of the door. "No Nia… you stay too."

"André, you are scaring me. Let go of my arm."

Releasing his grip, André ripped off his tie. "Alisha I heard you…I heard you. You said you couldn't believe Nia is going to Atlanta to be with Linc after all he put you through. Then you said…" Unable to speak, all she could do was look at her sister. "Come on baby…say it again…just like you said it a few minutes ago."

As panic sets in, Alisha felt trapped and bolted for the door. Beating her to the door, André locked the door and blocked her path.

Dropping her bouquet to the ground, Alisha touched André as he jerked away. "I love you, Dré…please…I…"

At those words, the broken pieces of André's heart became inflamed. "Don't say you love me…and don't call me Dré…ever. Say it Alisha…SAY IT!"

Lowering her face, she muttered.

André lifted her face up to his. "I couldn't hear you… can you say it louder?"

Feeling her jaw lock defiantly, André let her face go and slowly walked toward Nia. "Nia, since she was talking to you…you say it."

Kenda Bell

Frozen in André's cold stare, Nia could barely speak. "No"
"SAY IT, DAMN IT!"
"She didn't know you and Linc were friends."
"What do you mean she didn't know we were friends?"
As her sobbing intensified, Alisha ran to André and wrapped her arms around him. "I love you... please ...please."
Peeling her off, André released out a lunatic laugh. "Okay... okay...I am going to say it so you can hear how it sounded to me. You ready?"
Nia cautiously moved past André and stood next to her sister.
"Alisha, you said Linc was the craziest one-night stand you ever had."
Leaving over   a nearby chair, Alisha was on the verge of collapse..
"Yeah, cry...cry for me too. I am so hurt I can't even cry."
As all the coincidences he always knew never added up came crashing in, André plucked the flower out of his lapel and tossed it next to the bouquet. Watching Alisha grab her stomach, tears formed in his eyes. "When?"
"André, I made a horrible mistake. I didn't know you were friends...I wouldn't have ever done that to you. You have to understand..."
"When Alisha?"
"I had too much to drink...I was mad at you. You still had women calling the house...and we argued over that ugly ass picture you refused to get rid of...I ..."
"WHEN!"
"In August...when you went out of town... but..."
Grabbing his tie off the floor, André stuffed it in his pants pocket and headed for the door.
"André... please...baby please. Don't leave...I love you... no..."

Not able to look at her, André kept his back to her. "I want your things out of my place by the time I get back."

Before he can make it to the church door, a firm grip tugged him. "Hey man…you going the wrong way."

Shaking Chris's grip off, André tried to pull back his tears. "Naw, I'm going the right way. The wedding is off."

"Dré…man you are kidding right? What happened?"

"Don't ask me…ask her."

Jumping in the limo, André slammed the door and locked it. The driver is stunned when he sees only André. "Just drive."

The driver adjusted his hat. "Sir, what about the bride?"

"There isn't a bride anymore…just drive."

Snuggling underneath Justus, Keilah couldn't imagine being anywhere else.

Finally…Uhmm.

"Merry Christmas."

Rolling over, Keilah kissed his chest and laughed. "It's still Christmas Eve, you are early."

Squeezing her closer, Justus sumptuously covered her with wet kisses. "No, it is Christmas. We are now six hours ahead."

"Really…are you serious?"

Nestling his face playfully in her chest, Justus nibbled at her. "Yes, K-love. This is your first summer Christmas."

Yes it is…it most certainly is.

When Justus pulled her on top of him, she playfully pushed him. "You don't have jet lag."

"What…you don't like it?"

"No…I love it…I am just tired. I lost twenty-four hours and gained six more in what feels like two days. Plus … you wiped me out."

"That is fine, go too sleep. You need your rest. You'll meet Vashti tomorrow. "

"Your mother! Oh no, I need to move into one of the other rooms. I can't share a bed with you while she is here, oh no!"

Flipping her coolly on her back, Justus slowly stroked her neck, working his way down. Closing her eyes, Keilah laid back, waiting to see another rainbow. As he nibbled on her stomach for a moment, and continued further along on his journey, Keilah realized she had forgotten something.

I am late. No, no...please no. I can't be...not now.

"What do you mean she's not here?"

Carlita saddled her hands on her hips while a smirk danced gleefully across her face. "Where are you coming from with a tuxedo on?"

Storming past Carlita, André entered the house, calling for Keilah.

"Who do you think you are just walking up in here, you not her man no more. I told you she is not here. I don't have to lie to you."

Noticing his disheveled demeanor, Carlita began to get frightened. "Honestly, she is not here but I will tell her you came through... for real."

"No, I have to see her. I'll wait. When will she be back?"

"Next year."

"What! Next year."

Moving closer to the front door, Carlita wasn't sure if she should tell him the rest.

"Look, you need to leave; you are acting strange. When she calls, I will tell her to call you."

"Where is Keilah...tell me please?"

... "South Africa"

"What! South Africa, are you serious?"

Carlita gave him an affirmative nod. "With her boyfriend."

As the remaining chambers of his heart crumbled, André

allowed that one solitary tear that had been hidden behind pride to tumble clumsily from his right eye. Mercilessly crushing love in its fury, humiliation let out a holler as the tear ran insanely down his cheek, where remorse had been waiting patiently for months.

Other Xpress Yourself Publishing Titles

P.O. Box 1615, Upper Marlboro, Maryland 20773, Attn: Book Sales

QTY	TITLE/AUTHOR	ISBN-10 ISBN-13	PRICE
	Anything Goes/Jessica Tilles	0-9722990-0-9 978-0-972990-0-8	$15.00
	In My Sisters' Corner/Jessica Tilles	0-9722990-1-7 978-0-9722990-1-5	$15.00
	Apple Tree/Jessica Tilles	0-9722990-2-5 978-0-9722990-2-2	$15.00
	Sweet Revenge/Jessica Tilles	0-9722990-3-3 978-0-9722990-3-9	$15.00
	Fatal Desire/Jessica Tilles	0-9722990-5-X 978-09722990-5-3	$15.00
	One Love/Bill Holmes	0-9722990-4-1 978-0-9722990-4-6	$15.00
	Dangerously/Makenzi	0-9722990-7-6 978-0-9722990-7-7	$15.00
	That's How I Like It/Makenzi	0-9722990-8-4 978-0-9722990-8-4	$15.00
	Love Changes/Michael J. Burt	0-9722990-6-8 978-0-9722990-6-0	$10.95
	For Every Love There Is A Reason/ Kenda Bell	0-9722990-9-2 978-0-9722990-9-1	$16.95
	Unfinished Business/Jessica Tilles	0-9792500-0-5 978-0-9792500-0-2	$15.00
	Lustful Inhibitions/Nyah Storm	0-9792500-1-3 978-0-9792500-1-9	$15.00
	Confessions of a Sex Therapist/Nyah Storm	0-978-9792500-2-6	$15.00

www.xpressyourselfpublishing.org

I am enclosing $_____ (plus $2.50 shipping for 1st book, $1.00 for each additional book). No cash or C.O.D.s please. Send check, money order or credit card payment to:

Xpress Yourself Publishing
P.O. Box 1615
Upper Marlboro, MD 20773
Attn: Book Sales.

Please allow 4 to 6 weeks for delivery. Fax credit card orders to (530) 685-5346.

Name _____

Address _____

City _____ State _____ Zip Code _____

For credit card payments, please complete the following:

_____ American Express _____ MasterCard _____ Visa

Card Holder Name: _____

Account #: _____Exp. Date: _____

Total amount to be charged: $_____

Authorized Signature: _____
Date: _____
Note: Credit Cards are the preferred form of payment.

Printed in the United States
69450LVS00002B/124-156